CW01498788

SCALLYWAGS

SCALLYWAGS

win some—lose some

MARK HOWELL

Copyright © 2011 by Mark Howell.

Cover portrait photograph: Clare Whiteley
Research: Debi Whiteley, Neil Marshall

Library of Congress Control Number: 2011913860
ISBN: Hardcover   978-1-4653-0251-9
                 Softcover   978-1-4653-0250-2
                 Ebook   978-1-4653-0249-6

All rights reserved. No part of this book may be reproduced or transmitted in any form or by any means, electronic or mechanical, including photocopying, recording, or by any information storage and retrieval system, without permission in writing from the copyright owner.

This is a work of fiction. Names, characters, places and incidents either are the product of the author's imagination or are used fictitiously, and any resemblance to any actual persons, living or dead, events, or locales is entirely coincidental.

This book was printed in the United States of America.

To order additional copies of this book, contact:
Xlibris Corporation
0-800-644-6988
www.XlibrisPublishing.co.uk
Orders@XlibrisPublishing.co.uk
301647

Contents

For my mum and my dad

PART 1

Full Moon in Amsterdam

1

Kurt Cobain once sang "I'm on a plain". I'm thinking the same thing right now except it's not a plain I'm thinking about, it's a plane. That's right, for the first time in my life I'm in flight. Cruising at thirty thousand feet above the North Sea and I'm terrified. My ears are killing me and I can't hear a fucking thing. Sadie's doing her best to talk me through the whole procedure and to put my mind at rest, but I can hardly hear a word she's saying so I'm in my own personal hell.

We're on our way to Amsterdam. We had to make a quick getaway for obvious reasons, and for Sadie Amsterdam had a certain lure. She'd been there before and enjoyed it, I hadn't, so it made the perfect choice. I was just looking forward to hitting the tarmac at Schipol.

The flight was approximately an hour according to the budget airline's website when we had double checked before setting off, so that gave me precious little time to chill out. The pilot had sounded like he was high on uppers when he briefly introduced himself and his first mate, and for some reason that seemed to multiply my fears, and now I'm in my own little bubble constantly thinking were going down. Every time I close my eyes I see Buddy Holly's face so I keep them open but I don't know which is worse.

I glance over to Sadie, she looks absolutely gorgeous. She's wearing black leggings, a tie and dyed design T-shirt with ruffled piping at the shoulders, and a pair of the sexiest sandals I've ever seen on a woman, stilettoed platforms with a delicate floral pattern. You can tell she's been pampering herself prior to the trip, she's immaculately done out, hair, fingernails, toenails, everything. Her eyebrows plucked into fine arches, a light dusting of make-up, similar to the caster sugar coating on cakes—not the colour, the amount—and a deep red lipstick that sets off the rest of her sultry features. I can see her bare arms, and as I drift off into daydream land as I imagine caressing her soft skin.

I can see her mouth moving but I'm only hearing every other, other word. So it's like "Can . . . the . . . see . . . ants." Or at least that's what it sounds like to me, and none of it makes any sense to me in my befuddled state.

I just shake my head in reply hold my arms out by my side and shrug. Sadie goes back to flipping through the complimentary magazine. And I go back to sipping my red hot black coffee.

So here I am sat breathing in everybody's burps, farts, and bad breath.

I let my thoughts drift to the events of the past two weeks. Ally's death, and the subsequent shit that followed it, culminating in the massacre during Sadie's rescue, now here I am on the would-be run with a foxy sidekick heading to the drugs and sex capital of Europe. What could possibly go wrong?

Sadie catches my eye as she leans forward, I can see her mouth moving but like before I only hear half of it,

"It's . . . flight . . . bit . . . ."

I look to my left and see the woman sat in the chair next to me nod her head and reply,

". . . , okay."

I daren't even look out the window so I resort to staring ahead or at Sadie, which is fine by me, I could stare at her for hours without disruption.

My stomach heaves as the plane starts its descent. It's only a subtle change but it has me digging my trainers into the cheap durable carpeting, and my fingers into my one and only arm rest. Sadie notices the look of sheer terror in my eyes and reaches across to squeeze my hand to reassure me, I give her a shy smile and a wink to let her know I'm okay but I'm far from it. I chance a look out the window and soon wish I hadn't, we're just breaking through cloud cover, and the plane starts to rock up and down and from side to side as it encounters turbulence. The wings are shaking with the force of the wind, and they don't look like they're fixed on properly. My grip got tighter on the arm rest and on Sadie's hand; I start to bite my bottom lip as I am prone to do under stress. But strangely enough Sadie's touch did have a calming effect on me, like heroin to an addict, like the rush from the trapper's neck to his brain, soothing, calming, bliss. I just stared at nothing and hoped for the best.

It's amazing how the mind and body copes and reacts to stress; with the necessary training you can deal with anything. Subconsciously I'm trying to create my own version of tunnelled vision, and it's working. I'm staring dead ahead and ignoring everything else, apart from Sadie that is. I just keep glancing over to her; she keeps smiling and doing all the right things, so in a way I am okay.

I watched as the trolley dollies make one last dash up and down the aisle to collect everyone's trash with their forced smiles and phony concern. I settled my gaze on one of the TDs not because she was particularly good looking, far from it, but because it was better than looking out through the window. I watched her with fascination, she had a smile for everyone, she smiled at the row of passengers on her right, she smiled at the passengers on her left, and then she sneered until she was in view of the next row. And that's how it went, smile right, smile left, sneer, smile right, smile left, sneer, and then she was at my row. In spite of my discovery I gave her a smile, even though I knew it would fall on blind eyes.

Pretty soon the TDs were all sat on their fold-up seats, everybody buckled up, and we braced ourselves for the black top at Schipol, well at least I did.

*   *   *

We sailed through customs. I even had to ask the customs officer behind the thick sheet of Perspex to stamp my passport I was so giddy with the whole flying experience.

Trains from Schipol to Amsterdam's central station run pretty frequent, every twenty minutes to be precise. So we had barely found the right platform and sat down on our cases when a train came trudging up the track.

We boarded; the train was only approximately a quarter full, so we had no problem in finding two empty seats together. The train journey from Schipol to Amsterdam's centraal took twenty minutes so we had time to take in our surroundings. Our visuals were accompanied by music thanks to the busker seated a couple of seats up from us who was tuning in his guitar and practicing a couple of numbers he was probably going to play on the streets tonight, one of which was Bob Dylan's 'Like a Rolling Stone'.

We settled back in our seats. Well, Sadie did, I was sat on the edge of my seat looking out through the window like a three year old hardly able to contain my excitement.

2

As soon as I stepped out of Amsterdam's central station a weird vibe hit me. My headache had gone, but it had been replaced by a funny feeling I couldn't comprehend at first. It was weird, hard to explain, it was as though a foreign body was making its way through my system scraping along my veins ready to burst into my brain, and stop me dead in my tracks. The feeling had come from nowhere, out of the blue and blindsiding me.

I reached out a hand to steady myself as a wave of nausea rolled over me like foam on sand. Only I misjudged how far I was away from the wall, totally missing it with my hand and went stumbling into the path of an oncoming cyclist. I dropped the hand luggage and dived out of the way, the cyclist spotted me virtually straight away and swerved to avoid a collision, but he swerved the same way I dived, meaning he had to slam on to avoid hitting me. His breaks squeaked under the pressure, I did a Starsky and Hutch type roll and ended up sprawled, winded in the gutter, and he stopped just inches away from me, his back wheel lifted about ten inches off the ground, and then slammed back down. He looked at me the way a disappointed parent looks at a wayward child. Then without a word he shot off giving me the finger as he zipped past.

I had been carrying two sets of hand luggage, both mine and Sadie's. They now lay discarded next to each other half on the pavement and half off, the casings scuffed and grazed. Sadie rushed over to me, concern on her face, but I held my hand out in front of me like a drunken traffic controller and said,

"I'm fine."

It didn't stop her, she carried on regardless. She grabbed my hand and pulled me back onto the relative safety of the pavement. She shook her head as she looked me up and down and started to brush me off and straighten my clothes while cooing in my ear. Which without a doubt made me feel instantly better.

"Come on." she said kissing my cheek. "We need to check in."

I surveyed the buildings around us while I found my Dutch legs. You could tell this city had a lot of history, everywhere I looked there were grand gabled houses, and some even had elaborate statues carved into the stone. It is a beautiful city. I stared open mouthed in astonishment as all around me the hustle and bustle of Amsterdam's natives returning home after a day's work, everybody seemed to have somewhere to go, and everybody seemed to be in a rush to get there.

We crossed the main road, which consisted of four sets of tram lines, a four lane black top split in two, and two bike lanes. Our hotel was situated on the street next to the Dam Rak, right on the corner of it, nestled inbetween a quaint little cafe called Carla's and a supermarket.

We checked in, the hotel was nice enough; it had a retro design inside. The walls in the room were whitewashed with grey and red vapour trail slashes, and all in all it had a modern look to it, even though the building itself would probably date back to the late eighteen hundreds. We dumped our clothes in our room, and then hit the red light district in search of fun.

The time was now seven pm. I had my first introduction to the real Amsterdam on the corner of Dam Rak and Centraal by the way of a street hustler draped in shadows, and wearing a scowl.

"Pssst." he hissed. "Coke, pills."

He was of African descent and looked like he hadn't washed or shaved in days; his clothes were dirty and street worn, needless to say we didn't take him up on his offer and we walked on.

"Just ignore him, he'll go away." Sadie whispered in my ear.

He didn't, he kept on following, his gait awkward, like a disabled primate.

"Pssst, coke, pills." He hissed again, obviously high on something and not wanting to take no for an answer.

I waved him off and shook my head, but he persisted, following us down the street, that is until I turned round and mouthed the words fuck off to him. He finally got the message and targeted some other unsuspecting tourist looking for a good time.

Amsterdam is a maze, especially the red light district. It goes street, canal, street, canal, street, canal and so on, it's like a real life version of a Scooby Doo cartoon, like when shaggy and Scooby are running from a monster down a corridor and everything repeats itself as though it's on a visual loop, well if you can picture that in real life that's exactly how Amsterdam is, a visual loop.

We crossed the road; to our left was an expanse of water, the water looked black in the impending gloom. It must have been some sort of dock, because there were a few boats of various designs scattered round the sides, moored up. The water was gently lapping at their sides, with its multitude of black tongues.

We crossed a small bridge over a canal; the tall gabled houses to our right were perfectly reflected on the dock's shimmering surface. The Grasshopper coffee shop, which was now directly in front of us, was perched right on the edge of the red light district. It stood three stories tall, and its neon grasshopper sign was on and shining bright to tell people that it was open for business. The neon sign appeared like a mirage on the black water, ruffled and wavering as a slight breeze caught the surface.

We breezed past the Grasshopper and into the red light district. Things changed drastically from normal tourist location to dark and sinister, all in the space of a few steps. All of a sudden without warning scantily clad girls occupied the seven by ten windows in various stages of undress, behind them a bedroom scene laid out. Soft lighting and provocative ornaments seemed to be the norm. Some were laid on their beds with their heads tilted back so they could see the passers by, some had on lingerie, and some were just barely covered up with flimsy baby doll nighties, some were combing their hair, some were rubbing themselves up against the glass beckoning would-be punters in with a crooked finger, and some (the more good looking ones I might add) were on the phone looking bored whilst examining their nails, occasionally swapping the phone from hand to hand to examine the other set of nails and then back again. With some of them it was like watching a game of pass the hot potato.

"Should we try a coffee shop?"

It was Sadie who broke the silence, I was just stood twirling around, looking at everything with child like amazement, I was like a kid in a sweetshop and a bull in a china shop all rolled into one. This was my kind of town, my kind of place; and I just knew I was going to enjoy it here.

"Yeah, I could do with a drink." I replied.

"Well, there is that as well." she said with a wink and a cluck of the tongue. "Come on." she said, linking arms.

The streets were awash with different cultures, it looked as though every continent was represented on the streets of Amsterdam that night, and probably every other night of the year, all races, all religions mixing with harmony.

I'm glad we arrived at the time we did, because it gave me a chance to see the two sides of Amsterdam. Day and night. As they change from one to the other something remarkable takes place. It was like watching the transformation of Doctor Jekyll to Mr Hyde, or a man to a werewolf. That's right Amsterdam is schizophrenic. As the light begins to fade it changes from a fluffy bunny into a snarling slavering monster.

You get the sense both good and evil have walked these streets, both a long time ago and still to this day. In every other shady alcove the potential for danger lurked, I got the feeling I had to keep my wits about me if I was going to get through the next ten days or so unscathed.

I felt in my pockets for my cigarettes, I dug them out, shook two out and handed one to Sadie, put the other in my mouth and lit it and offered Sadie my outstretched hand. She held my hand steady with her fingertips while she lit her cigarette. We perched ourselves over the railings of a bridge while we smoked. The bustle of tourists was constant as we stood on the bridge, smoking, talking and laughing, at that exact moment it seemed like the whole world was passing us by, and that suited me just fine.

"So which coffee shop do you want to try first?"—it was Sadie who broke the silence again.

"Mmm, I'm not sure, any recommendations?" I said glancing up and down the narrow street. By now it was as dark as it was going to get, the thin sliver of sky visible inbetween the buildings was the colour of charcoal, the moon had just cleared the rooftops and was slowly climbing. The time was nearly touching half past eight. I had been wandering around goggle-eyed for an hour and a half, typical tourist mindset pointing to buildings and saying such things as "look at that" or "I ain't seen nothin' like that before."

Sadie too looked up and down the street before pointing to her left.

"We could try the Bulldog?"

I looked to where she was pointing; alongside the canal was a strip of sex shops, and coffee shops, and various other businesses. But why, I started off a chain of thought, would a baker want his premises situated in the red light area is beyond me. Well I suppose the gratified are in need of food after doing the deed; thinking about it, it could well have been a master stroke pulled by the baker.

Three round neon signs stood out from the rest, intermittently spaced along the street. The sign consisted of a bulldog's head and studded collar cartoon style, with the word Bulldog scripted underneath. It looked a good a place as any, and me being British the cap fit where the bulldog was concerned, for me that word is reserved for the British public's spirit.

"Yeah okay, let's try the Bulldog." I said pushing myself off the railing, I hooked one hand round her midriff and pulled her close. I could detect the delicate fragrance of her perfume, it was a mixture of water melon and Brazilian lime, and it never failed to arouse me. I pulled her even closer so she could feel me, poking against her thigh, we kissed, to any onlookers we were just another romantic couple on a break, and that's exactly what it felt like. We pushed our way through the crowded pavements and made our way to the world famous Bulldog coffee shop.

Inside the Bulldog it was dark and dingy. Like most houses and businesses in Amsterdam, it was just a narrow slip of a room with tables and benches along the right hand side wall. It was all dark wood and mood lighting, with a few wall lights scattered here and there. All in all it gave you a sense of shady, without being too extreme. To me it had the look of dodgy without the feel or the fear, just right so the upper classes can experience the real thing, and I don't mean Coca-Cola.

To our left there was a bar that ran half way along the wall; it looked to be made from the same wood as the tables and benches. There were two assistants tending the bar, a man and a woman. The woman was in her late twenties and had on a hippy style pair of dungarees. Underneath the dungarees she wore a Bulldog T-shirt, and her auburn hair was braided and tucked under a checked flat cap. The man was in his early thirties, he had on a pair of blue denim jeans, and a Bulldog T-shirt. He also had on a white skull cap; a light brown buzz cut poked out from under it.

A couple of the tables were occupied by different sorts, most people were either chatting or sat back smoking, and the air was thick with the pungent, sickly sweet smell of cannabis. The mood was relaxed, it matched the lighting. We made for a table; I slid in next to Sadie.

"What do you want to drink?" I asked Sadie as she peered at the drinks menu.

She held a finger up for me to hold on.

While Sadie studied the menu, I studied her different facial expressions. After a pause of about twenty seconds or so she looked up at me, her whole face smiling.

"I'll have a hot chocolate please." She replied plopping the menu back down onto the table.

I got up and started to make a move for the bar, Sadie grabbed my arm as I started to walk away and said,

"Ask to have a look at the weed menu as well will you, pick what you think." she whispered. My God her voice was sexy, a voice like that could empty your scrotum in seconds, and I shivered at the thought.

I spun round on my heels and without a second thought I headed for the bar. It wasn't until I got to the bar that it had actually registered what Sadie had said—weed menu. I hadn't touched the stuff in almost ten years. It was about three months after the prank I'd stopped smoking it, due to the detrimental effect it was having on my mental health. And Sadie had borne the brunt of some of my mood swings. But on the plus side the instigator of these feelings, Ally, was dead and gone. No longer was he around for his spectre to hang over me, mocking me, haunting me. Craig was also out of the picture in a way, he was on remand and was looking at five years for cultivation and intent to supply, and with Ally gone there was just him to take the rap so he would bear the judges wrath alone. Ian too was in prison, on a separate charge to Craig's—he had took it upon himself to hold up a jeweller somewhere in Derbyshire, and got caught during the getaway; he was on remand awaiting trial. I had found out about Craig and Ian through Mik and Dim's contacts, it is easy when you know how. On the plus side the panic attacks had stopped not long after I had started shadowing Ally, all the reasons why I had stopped smoking it in the first place appeared to dead and buried, or long gone. Ah well—when in Rome, murder Christians and all that.

The woman made a move towards me, smiling.

"What can I get you?" she asked in a whining, grating, nasally voice.

"Can I have two hot chocolates please?" I said, I had my palms face down on the bar as I spoke, looking up and down for a weed menu. There didn't seem to be one, so I had to ask.

"Do you want squirty cream and chocolate sprinkles on those?" she asked me. Her voice was going right through me to the point of irritation.

"Both please thanks." I replied. "Hey do you have a weed menu that I can take a look at?" I said to her arse and back.

The woman looked to her left where the man was still leant against the work top behind the bar and gave him a look, the man gave her a half smile and a shrug and then pushed himself off the work top and made a leisurely path towards me, there wasn't a rush in him. He stopped short of crashing into the bar by a couple of inches, instead he plopped himself on it with one hand propped under his chin and reached around a dark wood box that was situated on the bar next to me. He pushed a well worn button and the front of it lit up displaying a whole array of different strains of cannabis. I stepped back so I could see the menu better.

"Cheers mate." I said and nodded, feeling like a tourist.

He let go of the button but stopped where he was, plopped on the bar. The woman was busy making the hot chocolates; she was now bent down retrieving the squirty cream from a small box fridge nestled underneath the counter. I pushed the button again and studied the now lighted box menu for the weed of my choice. I settled on one and a half grams of northern lights. The bill came to nineteen guilders, which wasn't bad if you took into account the exchange rate.

I left the change on the bar, tucked the nip bag of weed into the palm of my hand, hooked my two index fingers round the cup handles and spun round with the weed and the hot chocolates and headed back to Sadie. I slid in back next to her, giving her a peck on the cheek as I got close. And then I closed my lips around the mound of squirty cream on top of the light brown liquid and took a sip of the hot chocolate. I just melted, apart from it being red hot it was also gorgeous.

Sadie was rummaging around in her handbag for something; after a minute or so of moving around the contents of her bag back and forth, and back again (why women have to fill their bags with all that shit is beyond me,) she pulled out a large pack of Rizla, and a twenty carton of Marlboro lights. I watched her as she broke the seal and unwrapped the cigarettes. I don't know if it was intended, but every movement and every look she gave me indicated sex to me in my mind. The way she slowly unwrapped the cellophane whilst looking at me and dragging her top teeth across her bottom lip as she did it, or maybe it was just me, I don't know, I don't like to make assumptions, after all I am a newcomer to these kind of situations. I might be a newcomer but I'm a quick learner, and I was growing more confident around Sadie with each passing day, she made it easy to be around her, and I would die for her. What was I thinking of, all those years ago, I must have been mad.

"You make one; I'm going to read these." Sadie said handing me the Rizla and cigarettes before pulling out a couple of leaflets to read she had acquired during the trip. I had insisted on adding to the collection of leaflets, not because of the content of the leaflet itself, but because it could be used as a weapon. Developed in the south of England by a notorious football hooligan crew who found out that by folding a match programme a couple of times it created a rock hard edge, and when used properly will do some serious damage. Handy when searches became mandatory at certain football grounds. I had found out about the technique whilst working in London. I had spent eighteen months doing all the electrical work on a shopping centre near the Dartford tunnel. I had made friends with a local crew and they showed me how to transform any leaflet into a weapon. The work at the shopping centre dried up a couple of months before Ally, Craig, and Ian had staged the prank that was to go on and ruin ten years of my life.

Now I hadn't made or smoked a joint for going on ten years, but it's like riding a bike, once you've learnt how to do it you never forget. I pulled one large Rizla out of its pack and one small; I placed the large Rizla face down and stuck the smaller one to it at one end, overlapping it slightly less at the bottom than the top. Then I turned it back the right way and folded it at a slight diagonal angle. Then I broke off just over half of the cigarette and sprinkled it out evenly along my new concocted Rizla. I opened the nip bag and broke off a bud putting it to my nostril and inhaling its magical essence. Hello old friend, it's been far too long I thought to myself, as I started to sprinkle the bud over the tobacco. It was like meeting up with an old girlfriend after years and years apart and falling straight into bed. The coffee shop door opened, shattering my mental illusion, and old habits die hard, used to being persecuted for smoking it back home I instinctively covered up what I was doing by using my shoulders as a shield so the newcomer couldn't see anything. As I looked towards him, I felt someone grab hold of my arm. I thought here we go and was ready to spring up at a second's notice. I looked back and it was Sadie who had hold of my arm.

"They're okay with it, its legal here, remember." she said giving me her fifth reassuring wink of the day; she'd handed out three of them on the plane.

I nodded and smiled as it slowly dawned on me that I need not be paranoid about smoking here, of course I knew it was legal, I'd been told by different people that it was and that I had to try it out, but actually being here now it was a different story and like I said before old habits die hard. So reluctantly as I dropped old habits and without another word or anxious glance I carried on with my own tried and tested technique of rolling a spliff; it took me a couple of minutes of rolling and gently twisting before I was tugging on it to get it going. Once it was going properly I took a massive double hit off it and inhaled deeply, held the smoke in for about ten seconds or so before blowing it out through my nostrils—apparently you can taste the weed better that way. Straight away the effects were knocking on the door of my mind, and once I had opened the door and welcomed it in like a long lost relative it went creeping further into it like a cat burglar. Because I hadn't tasted the forbidden herb for years it took me by surprise, effect wise, I had totally forgot its medicinal qualities the way it gently soothes away all your stresses and worries and leaves you feeling happy and content. See, the way it is when you smoke cannabis is every strain is different, not only in the way it looks, and smells, but the way it affects your mind when you smoke it. Weed is different to say cannabis resin, when you smoke resin the effects are quick to hit you, admittedly they're nowhere near as strong as the effects of weed, but they do arrive twice as fast. Whereas with weed when you smoke it, you can probably get three quarters of the way through it before you feel anything at all. But because I hadn't smoked it for years, the weed was calling the shots and not the tolerance, which is why it is and always will be for that very reason every weed smoker's nemesis.

I passed the spliff on to Sadie who took it with a smile and went back to studying a map on one of the leaflets. I took the chance to scan the surroundings, apart from us there were six other people in the coffee shop. Four out of the other six people were sat together in couples, and the other two were sat alone. There was the gentle hum of people talking in the background and every now and then I had to pinch myself to make sure I wasn't dreaming all of this. Not so long ago, I was too afraid even to sleep in the dark, I had to have a light on, and it didn't have to be dark to fray my nerves. Sometimes just a quick glance at my watch or my noticing the drop in air temperature, a sure sign that dusk is on its way would be enough to do it. Yet here I am in a coffee shop in Amsterdam having the time of my life, and the time is now nine o'clock. Sadie passed the spliff back; I took it with a kiss and a smile.

"What should we do the rest of tonight?" I asked Sadie as I crushed the endo out into the multi-faceted glass ashtray.

She looked up from the leaflet she was reading and replied,

"Anything you like." Her words were accompanied by yet another smile.

"What do you recommend we do?"

"Well we could have another smoke in here and then find somewhere to have a drink, or we could go straight back to the hotel. It's up to you I don't mind honestly."

I didn't even need to think about it, it was a double no brainer.

"We can have another drink and smoke in here and then go back to the hotel." I said getting up from the bench with a grin that stretched effortlessly across my face.

"If you're sure." she whispered, sliding forwards on the bench, propping her chin in the palms of her hands, her elbows resting on the table.

Her mannerisms alone drove me wild beyond belief, she had me sweating and wanting her right here, right now. I know this city had few inhibitions and turned a blind eye to soft drug use and sex but I doubt that the proprietor of this particular establishment would take kindly to what I had in mind. So I struggled, for the moment anyway, to keep my desires in check. I got the feeling I was fighting a losing battle and I knew the gun in my pants would betray me. The only consolation was it would be betraying me for a worthwhile cause.

"Do you want to make one and I'll get us some refills." I said grabbing my cup off the table looking towards the bar, trying to catch one of the assistants' attention.

"Hang on a minute." Sadie replied raising the cup to her lips and slurping the last of her froth up.

I glanced back over to the bar and caught the woman's attention, nodding to her and sticking two fingers up meaning two more hot chocolates. She nodded back to me and went to work fixing the drinks.

3

*T*wenty-six minutes later we staggered out of the door due to the effects of the weed. We made our way through the red light district blindly, not really knowing where we were going, but hoping it was in the general direction of our hotel. There were still a lot of people out and about on the streets. I'd not noticed them before but now in my higher state of consciousness they stuck out like sore thumbs—Victorian style street-lamps were scattered along the edge of the footpath giving the place an olde worlde feel and look to it; their white cones of light splashing onto the pavement giving hope and a little guidance to the masses.

We muddled our way through the crowds, drawing the occasional dirty look from the odd person as we accidently collided into them. Our shadows overtook us numerous times on each street as we passed each streetlamp in turn. We stopped under one particular streetlamp to study a map of the city centre, trying in stoned vain to get a fix on our location, without much luck. Although we had wandered away from the red light area during our trek, we were now wandering back into it. We both stood swaying under the eerie cone of light; Sadie was looking at the map, I was trying my best to read the street sign fixed to the wall of the shop we were standing near.

"We're on who'd zis voorburgal, at least that's what I think it says." I said struggling to pronounce the street name whilst squinting up at the sign, hand over my brow like a captain out at sea.

"It's okay I've found where we are on the map." Sadie said slurring slightly and pointing her immaculately done index fingernail at an area of the map.

I glanced over her shoulder so I could see whereabouts on the map she was pointing to. It might as well have been a map of the moon's surface for what good it did me. I was struggling to focus; I was seeing double, there was a translucent mist around everything, adding a ghostly tint to an already sinister background.

"This way" Sadie said linking arms again. "I think it's this way."

I followed Sadie's lead willingly, the idea of not wanting to stop in any one place for any length of time appealed to me. Especially studying a map like we were, under a street lamp, and looking to all and sundry like targets, we might as well be walking round with bulls-eyes on our backs. So we staggered on, until we reached a tiny alleyway, I pulled Sadie into the alley and squashed her up against the wall, kissing her hard on the lips, she responded with grace. Pretending to be all flustered and that, wiping her hand across her brow and swooning.

"Oh," she whispered in my ear, her breath and voice vibrations tickling to the point where it was driving me wild. "Mr Naylor, whatever are you going to do to me?"

We kissed for a couple more minutes; she was pushing against me, I was pushing against her. Something had to give, Sadie gave first and I pushed her back up against the wall. As I moved in for another kiss my attention was grabbed by someone knocking on a window further on in the alley. I ignored it and leant in a little further, and then the knocking turned frantic, so much so it stopped me in my tracks.

"What's up?" Sadie asked curling her bottom lip down as I turned round to see where the knocking was coming from.

I couldn't see in through the window from my position because of the glare from the street lamps. So I edged further into the alley to get a better look. My curiosity got the better of me; I should've stayed where I was, with my tongue down Sadie's throat. But with me nothing is ever simple like that; I have a tendency to follow my nose, and that generally leads me into trouble. I seem to have a homing device in my head that seeks it out. Not the best quality if you want to lay low, granted, but there you go some of us have to make the best of what we've got.

Pulling Sadie along behind me by her hand, I took a few tentative steps further into the alleyway, which was all I needed to see where the knocking was coming from. About ten yards further on, on the opposite side of the wall to where we had been stood was a massive ten foot by eight window with a door by its side, it had thick velvet black-out curtains hung down limply at either side of it, like soldiers at the end of a forty eight hour stag. At the side of the door fixed to the wall was an old fashioned door bell. A press button on the top of a raised mound. There was a young woman stood in the window—she had on a turquoise basque, white suspender belt and white stockings. A white lacy garter had settled half way down her left thigh. She was knocking on the window, running her tongue across her lips and nodding to me. I pulled Sadie up level with me and put my arm round her and carried on walking. As I took a few more steps I could see window after window, on both sides of the alley, each had a woman with a beckoning finger behind it. I don't know if it was supposed to but it reminded me of a stud farm with all the fillies lined up ready for action. The further we walked in, the narrower the alley got, until it got to the point where it felt almost claustrophobic. I could feel Sadie's grip tighten, as the walls visibly closed in. The only light was the seductive ambient light coming from the windows that didn't have their curtains drawn. It was the type of place where you don't find out that you're in danger until it's too late to turn back.

We were about twenty five steps in, halfway through a particularly dark patch of the alley, when I felt the first one, a loiterer bumped into me. It's a good job I had my wits about me; I was stoned, but not out of it. I felt his arm snake around my back in a quick fluid movement, and if I wasn't so switched on to the environment and the threat of potential danger he would have had my wallet away. I felt my wallet start to slide out of my back pocket, so to counteract his play in one movement I turned sideways on so I was facing the pickpocket and grabbed hold of his wrist with a vice like grip, so much so he yelped out in pain. He immediately let go of my wallet and when I let go of his wrist after a couple of seconds of eye to eye, nose to nose contact he backed off, almost disappearing into the shadows. I pushed my wallet back down into my pocket and carried on pulling Sadie close. I was going to enjoy myself here; it was my kind of town.

4

*T*he next morning I rolled out of bed and powered my mobile up for the first time since just before boarding the plane. Sadie was still fast asleep, she moaned softly and turned over pulling the duvet up to her chin. It took a couple of seconds before the mobile was fully operational. Almost immediately my phone flashed at me telling me I had voicemail messages. I squinted in the half light. There were six messages to be exact. I had never had one message left on my voicemail in all the years I'd had my phone, so for someone to leave six of them was worrying. I reached for my jeans that were sprawled like a drunk on the floor at the side of the bed, pulling them on quickly, tucking my phone in the front pocket as I did so. I didn't want to wake Sadie, so I pulled my zip hoodie from where I'd draped it the night before whilst unpacking and headed out the door.

The hotel like almost every other building in Holland was tall and narrow; the interior layout was just a series of corridors squared with rooms coming off them in both directions facing inwards and outwards. Our room faced onto a courtyard, we were four stories up.

I closed the door quietly behind me and headed for the walkway we had discovered on the way up to the room the night before. As we staggered from the lift we took a wrong turn and ended up on a balcony/walkway that linked our building to the main body of the hotel—more convenient for us, it saved us about forty extra steps. It was also a designated smoking area, which suited me fine. I fished around in my pockets for my cigarettes after locating them I shook one out, lit it and then dialled my voicemail with the cigarette dangling from my mouth. I squinted as smoke blew into my eyes while I was waiting for the connection. The airwave silence was broken by a female's automated voice. She explained that I had six new messages from a number I did not recognise and that if I wanted to listen to them I had to press one. I pressed one and took a big hit off the cigarette whilst the connection was made. There was a brief pause of white noise and then Dim's unmistakable Russian robotic growl filled my ears, with dread. He sounded panicky which if I wasn't already would have woken me up with a short sharp slap.

"Kev, my friend, I got bad news for you. Mik's gone, the Chinese took him out in retaliation to our little operation. His dismembered body was found in a skip last night on a building site on the outskirts of Leeds. We don't know if they got anythin' out of him, or if he stayed quiet, he was tough but there is only so much one man can take. The fact that he was cut up into pieces could be a good omen for you."

There was another couple of seconds pause, where the only noise was white.

"Just watch your back is all I'm saying my friend, they seem to be pissed and they want the people responsible. You're okay you where you are, nobody knows where that is, so as long as you keep it that way, you got no problems. Batty is flying out of the country today so he should be okay. I don't know when it will be safe for you to come back. I'll be in touch as and when. See you my friend."

There was a click, and then he was gone.

I tucked the phone away whilst tossing this new development around my head to see if I could get an angle on it. But no matter how many times I tossed it around, or how many leaps and twists it took I just could not get my head round it, no matter how hard I tried. Mik was dead, tortured by the Chinese, allegedly. I couldn't believe it, or want to; the man had survived Afghanistan, and in my eyes he was invincible. On the one and only time I had met with him he had a look of calm about him but at the same time you got the sense he was calculating. He was an ambush predator, and he used his calmness as a form of camouflage. Well in the end whatever methods he had incorporated into the techniques he was taught during his twelve year stint in the Red Army did him no good. He was gone, and he wasn't coming back.

I stubbed the cigarette out in a foot long trough half full of sand hung on the inside of the balcony, and immediately lit another. I needed to think, and for that I needed fuel. Time for food. I checked the other voicemails while I stood on the balcony finishing my second cigarette of the day. It was now twenty six minutes past eight. The voicemails were all from Dim, all much the same, although on the last one he did ask me to get in touch as soon as possible. He sounded worried. So I rang the number he had left on one of the voicemails. It was a new number, one I didn't know. I stubbed the cigarette out in the trough while I waited for the connection. I had my arms resting on the balcony as the automated voice told me the number I had dialled was not recognisable. I felt like pitching the phone as far as I could but stopped myself due to the fact that I was four stories up and would probably do someone some serious damage if I hit them with it. Low profile I reminded myself as I shut the phone down and stuffed it back in my pocket.

I stood there staring into space for a while not really taking anything in, just enjoying the tranquillity that being eighty feet up in the air can sometimes give you. There was just a thin sliver of street visible from my view point. Amsterdam was back on life support again, until dusk, when its other side reared its ugly head, and came out snarling from the shadows.

Down below normal people were doing normal things, everyday tasks and whatever else popped into their heads during the course of the day. I watched as three guys wearing overalls came into view, followed by two more guys in overalls carrying jet spray nozzles which were connected to a water tank which was being pushed by a sixth. The first three were on litter detail, picking up any stray rubbish on the street; the second two were hosing down the footpaths and anyone who didn't happen to hear their warnings and got in their way. I laughed as a man in a business suit got drenched, I measured his anger by his frantic hand gestures and my conclusion was he was very angry. The street cleaners disappeared from view, so I turned away from the street and shuffled my way back to the room.

On the way I passed the cleaner with her trolley piled high—fluffy towels and starched sheets on the top shelf and cleaning products on the shelf underneath. She was a dead ringer for the black housekeeper in the old Tom and Jerry cartoons. Well I say dead ringer, I was just guessing as you never got to see the housekeeper in the cartoon other than below the waist, you only got to see leg shots of her and that was good enough for me; their legs were identical. She was the real life version; or rather the woman from the cartoons was her caricature. I nodded to her as I passed by and bid her good morning. She returned my greeting with a shy smile that belied her size and a perfect set of even white teeth that lay behind a thick set skull and two hundred and twenty two pounds of flesh, bone, body fluids and fat. She got on with her business and I went on my way with mine.

When I got back to the room Sadie was up and showering. I could hear the muffled sound of running water like some distant waterfall from under the sliding door. It was twenty minutes before she appeared like a mirage from behind the steam. Her face was pink and fresh from the shower and her hair was dry and tied back and down to her left side in a haphazard ponytail. A fluffy white towel was tucked up under her armpits and tied at the side. It was drooping slightly in the middle of her torso so that a glimpse of cleavage was showing. The only other bare flesh on show was her shoulders and the bottom half of her legs. The towel stopped mid-thigh leaving a little to the imagination and that was enough to start my mind wandering.

She looked up and saw me as soon as she entered the room, pretending to be shy, putting her hand on her chest to half cover her modesty.

I was now perched on the edge of the bed. Lost in thought but trying not to look distracted. I made a mental note to not chew my bottom lip. Anybody who got close to me would soon find out that was one of the first signs that something was on my mind.

She sat down on the bed next to me; the bed sank a fraction with the weight of her petite frame. She smelt nice and fresh, I breathed in deeply to inhale her scent.

"You okay?"

"Yeah not bad, you?" I replied.

"Bang on." she replied in a husky whisper that seemed to escape from those gorgeous full lips. Whenever her lips moved they seemed to put me in a trance, they produced a hypnotic rhythm.

"Did you sleep well?"

"Like a baby." she replied.

I looked at her quizzically.

"I wet the bed twice and woke up at five o'clock screaming."

My brow furrowed and I jerked my head back in response to what she had said. I must have looked a sight because she burst out laughing before managing two words inbetween bouts of uncontrollable giggles.

"I'm joking." was all she could utter for at least ten minutes due to her continuing fits of laughter. "How about you, did you sleep well?" she finally managed.

"Pretty much." I replied. "I had to double the pillow up. Hey, din't the brochure say they had memory foam pillows?"

"Yes. why?" Sadie replied.

"'Cos mine must have dementia, it's all floppy." I replied, picking my pillow up, examining it and then tossing it at her.

Sadie laughed and reached over for my pillow where it had bounced off her onto the bed, and then pitching it back at me. I dodged it and it crashed against the wall, sliding down like a felled drunk in a bar room brawl.

I left her towelling herself dry and went to get a shower and a shave, making sure I kept the image of her in the bath towel vivid in my mind. I came out of the en-suite wet room some thirteen minutes later feeling refreshed and smooth of face. Sadie was busy straightening the few strands of hair that had kinked during the night. She had dressed whilst I was in the shower; she had on a pair of khaki three-quarter-length cargo pants, trainer socks, and a pair of white

Lacoste low tops. T-shirt wise she had on a sexy tight white one with 'born to fcuk' in a freestyle black script printed across her chest. The b and the k in the script sat right on her nipples, making it look like those two particular letters were somehow in 3D. To finish off the whole look she had on a thin red all in one hoodie. Her choice of clothes was casual, but somehow she made them look elegant, as though she had spent hours on her appearance, when in reality she was fresh from the shower.

I would be ready in minutes, literally, all I had to do was roll on some deodorant, pull on a pair of jeans, a T-shirt and a hoodie, run my hands through my hair and hey presto that was me done. So I did what I had to do and ended up sitting on the edge of the bed for eighteen minutes waiting for Sadie to finish her daily rituals. I even went out onto the balcony for a cigarette while I waited. It gave me precious time to think about the news I had just received, and what if anything I could do to guard us both from danger. In the end I decided it was no use worrying we had done all we could do, and that was to get the fuck out of Dodge. Only time would tell if we had left Dodge and moved on to Tombstone.

5

It was twenty to twelve before the lift door opened out onto the hotel's foyer. Our emotions had got the better of us, and we had ended up sticky and sweaty needing another shower each to wash away our sins. We breezed into the hotel foyer; I had a stupid grin on my face that I couldn't shift. It was definitely the cat that had got the cream smile. I nodded to the clerk behind the checking-in desk as we walked past; he looked up for a second and nodded back.

"Have a nice day." he shouted after us.

I gave him a wave without looking back with one hand while the other cupped Sadie's left buttock. I could feel the muscle movement as it contracted and expanded, contracted and expanded. It was the best stress ball I've ever used.

We hit the street and turned right. To our left was the grand old red brick building Centraal Station—just a sliver of it was visible, the far right spire and tower.

"So what do you want to do today?" Sadie asked as we threaded our way through the already crowded streets.

"First things first." I replied. "We need a coffee shop so we can we refuel, and then we can decide where we want to go from there, if that's okay with you."

"Yes fine by me." Sadie replied, nodding her head in agreement as we made eye contact. "It sounds like a plan."

There are well over a hundred coffee shops in Amsterdam, dotted all around the city, so you are never far from one. We took the first right and headed down a short connector street. There were two coffee shops on this street alone, but we didn't like the look of them so we carried on. The streets like the buildings themselves were all narrow, narrow but clean. Some of the buildings looked like they could topple over at any minute, and some of them looked they had half sunk already.

We settled on a coffee shop ten minutes walk from our hotel. We had orange bud for breakfast and a slab of chocolate cake, washed down with two cups of filter coffee each.

It was now a quarter past one and I did not want to get off the seat I was so comfortable on, even though it was just a hard bench designed for one thing only, to get people out of the coffee shop as soon as possible—more customers equals more money. At this moment in time that bench was my best friend in the whole wide world, so it was with great reluctance that I parted from its company.

After being in a dark room for so long my eyes burned when we finally made it back on the street. We had decided to go to Anne Frank's house, so after first consulting a street map of Amsterdam we headed in the general direction of where we thought it was. After consulting the map a few more times and a couple of minor adjustments to the route we had chosen we finally arrived at Anne's house. The queue was about thirty strong, mainly groups of school kids and young adults. The house itself wasn't what I expected at all. I was expecting an old rickety gable house in a poor state of repair, patched up and rendered. But what we found was a modern glass fronted gable house. From where we stood it looked like it wouldn't look out of place in the opening credits to Dallas the soap opera. But it did look out of place here.

After half an hour queuing we finally paid our entry fee, and I picked up a few more weapons in the lobby and stuffed them into Sadie's handbag.

We shuffled our way through the house; it was a series of empty rooms with glass cabinets exhibiting items from the era. A few photos of the Franks and the other people who shared the small space they called home for almost two years adorned the walls. At first I thought it was a rip off that the inside of the house was just a shell, but as we made our way through it, squeezing past the book case which separated the shop downstairs from the secret hiding area upstairs my opinion changed. Especially as I realised that we were standing on the exact same floorboards that they had tip-toed on nearly seven decades earlier. Also, when you take into account that almost all of the people in the photos—including the Germans—would most probably have died agonising lonely deaths, it was thought provoking to say the least. Sadie was reduced to tears at one of the photos on the wall near the attic. It was one that was taken from across the street by a dentist who had seen the German soldiers rounding up his friends and neighbours, and had decided to document it. The photo itself was black and white and had lost some of its shine over the years, but no matter how many years passed by it would never lose the dramatic impact it had on us and whoever else happened to see it in the years to come. The dentist had captured the scene perfectly; even though it had been taken from across the street and from the other side of the canal it still showed the urgency in the German soldiers' actions, and the confusion and terror in the faces of their captives. It depicted a sombre scene, one that was real, and one that had happened in this exact spot. I shuddered at the very thought of it. Pure evil had stalked these streets and the terror from the people who lived here was imprinted on it forever.

As we stepped back out onto the street from the foyer after spending just over an hour musing through dusty empty rooms I had to agree with Otto Frank's decision to leave the rooms bare. Instead of looking at props you got to use your imagination to build the room up to something what it would have been like all those years ago, using the photos as a sort of template. And with my imagination capable of running riot at times it suited me down to the ground. I could see Sadie was still upset over the photo and in need of cheering up plus I could feel my stomach growling. We headed back in the general direction we had come, pausing round the corner from the Frank's house to pose for a photograph at the side of Anne's life-size statue.

"Should we try and find somewhere nice to get something to eat and drink?" I asked her as we linked arms. It was one of those rare times that I actually broke the silence.

"Yes okay that would be good. I could call home, see if there are any developments with the house."

I nodded in reply.

After her rescue Sadie had managed to wangle seventeen days off work, she had five days off on the sick to recover from her ordeal, which she explained away to women's problems. What had really happened to her was kept on the down low, nobody at work knew what really happened that day. Her official holidays were due to start on the day we flew in to Amsterdam, so she had sixteen vacation days left. During her time off on the sick she had put her house on the market, and instructed her sister to act on her behalf to deal with any offers that should come in while she was away. I had tried to persuade her not to do anything rash, but she had come up with a good argument. She told me that she had wanted to move out of the area for a while, and what had happened to her had given her the kick up the backside she needed. Who was I to argue, so I just left it at that. What else could I do? I just didn't want her to make any impulsive decisions that would have a detrimental effect for the rest of her life. It was bad enough knowing that I had turned her life upside down by just entering it. But moving house wasn't an option, it was a necessity. The Chinese knew where she lived therefore it wasn't deemed safe to go back there, ever. The sooner it was sold the better as far as I was concerned, it would cut all connections. And if that happened while we were away, all well and good. My rented property was an easier solution; I just gave the estate agent a month's notice and paid the bill in full, end of problem. I was as free as a bird, well almost.

We sauntered back down the route we'd taken some two hours earlier calling in a tiny box room coffee shop on the way. We ordered two coffees and I rolled a joint whilst Sadie went to the toilet and then made the phone call from outside. She came back into the coffee shop just as I was licking the Rizla. She was sporting a worried look on her face. She came and sat down next to me, her brow furrowed like a farmer's field. I passed her the joint to light.

"Problems?", I asked.

Sadie paused for a second then took a deep breath, and exhaled slowly.

"It could be something and nothing. I've just rung our Stella's phone and it was switched off and I know for a fact she never turns it off, not even when she's at work, she just switches it to silent. It's just got me wondering, you know with what happened to me." She paused for a split second, before carrying on, only this time her voice was faltering, wavering, her bottom lip was trembling slightly with emotion. "Oh I hope nothing has happened to her, I will never forgive myself or you. You don't think anything could have happened do you?"

"I don't think you should worry too much, it's probably run out of charge. I'm sure everythin's okay. I guarantee by ten o'clock tonight she will have got in touch."

"Yes, you're probably right." she said as she lit the joint, taking a big hit off it, sucking the excess smoke back into her mouth through her slightly parted lips. "I suppose I'm over-reacting."

The cannabis did its job and eased away Sadie's worries, for the time being at least. But this new development did have me wondering, what with Mik's body being found last night and now Sadie's sister was potentially missing. Was it connected or was it a coincidence. Well I don't believe in coincidences, not with things like this anyway, but I was prepared to wait it out and hope for the best. There was nothing we could do at the moment anyway; all we could do was dig in and hold fort until we knew for sure either way. Sadie passed the joint to the left hand side and I took it. It got passed back and forth until I crushed it out into the novelty Rastafarian ash tray.

"Are we ready?"

Sadie nodded and then finished off her coffee, pushing the cup and saucer towards the middle of the table.

I glanced at the clock on the wall behind the bar; it was now twenty to four in the afternoon. I slurped the dregs of my coffee, leaving behind what change there was and mud in the bottom of the cup.

The afternoon rush was in full swing, so I cleared a path for us through the queue at the bar and made for the door, opening it for Sadie, and sweeping my arm out for her in a left to right arc, as though she were royalty.

"Mademoiselle, your carriage waits." I joked.

Outside the weather had changed, for the worse. Big black rain clouds were hovering above us, like a police helicopter chasing a fugitive, only we were the fugitives, and it wasn't looking good. Sadie had on only a thin T-shirt and hoodie, and I wasn't equipped as well as I would have liked. All I had to rely on was two layers of insulation. I was wearing a T-shirt and a zip-up hoodie. I quickly zipped it up and shrugged my shoulders back and tucked my chin in to fight against the ice cold wind that was now whipping up the rain clouds into weird aggressive shapes.

"Come on." I said, grabbing hold of Sadie's hand as I made use of the gap in traffic and made a run for the other side of the road. "Let's find somewhere quick before it pisses it down."

We made it in one piece across the road, just; we left a crescendo of horn blasts in our wake. One thing you have to remember about crossing the road in Amsterdam is that if you think you're safely over the road then you'd better think again, because there is a bike lane to contend with as well. And eight times out of ten the bikes are going faster than the cars, and with no credible stopping mechanism in place to boot you'd better watch out. That is exactly what happened to me, thinking I'd reached the safety of the other side I let my guard down. Bad move, I was nearly ploughed over by an elderly woman on a ramshackle bike, she expertly swerved round me and carried on her merry way giving me a dirty look as she drew almost level with me and chuntering away to herself in some foreign tongue, which could have been Dutch, or possibly Flemish. It sounded like gibberish to me.

"Phew, that was close."

"I know, can you imagine getting run over by an old woman, on a bike like that?" Sadie replied.

"Oh, the shame of it." I joked.

I could see Sadie was still distracted by the lack of news from home and I was doing my best to take her mind off it. It wasn't working; I had to revise my plan.

"I'm sure she'll be okay, you'll see." I said trying my best to reassure her and to let her know I hadn't forgotten about it.

"I know, I know, I just can't stop myself from thinking something's up."

"Let's go get something to eat, wherever we find it should be quiet enough to make the call from inside, save us gettin' wet."

Sadie nodded again in reply, and then tucked her chin into her hoodie collar.

6

We found a little bistro down a side street about ten minutes walk from our hotel. It had stopped raining almost, slowing to a slight drizzle. So we spent a couple of minutes studying the menu from the window outside. It offered a steak dinner complete with an alcoholic drink for only twenty guilders, which in any city in the world was a bargain. So we took the plunge and pushed through the door. Like every establishment we had so far frequented it was dark, and it was long and narrow with dim wall-lights scattered on the walls above the tables. There was dowdy brown wallpaper on the walls, and underfoot were darkly stained, scuffed floorboards. There was a bar made from dark wood stretching along the left hand wall, behind which there stood a woman, behind her was a row of optics on a rack, bottles upturned like drunken sailors. In front of the optics were a selection of wines, and a large box of Cuban cigars. The woman was dressed in a regulation look work uniform consisting of a white shirt open at the neck revealing a thin gold rope chain, a black ruffled skirt which stopped just short of her knees and a pair of black tights. She had unruly dark brown hair just a bit longer than shoulder-length. She was in her early thirties. She held her arms out in front of her, palms up as if to say you can sit wherever you like. I nodded and smiled and we made for the table furthest from the door, it was one of those decisions borne from primeval instinct, one derived from when men ate in caves and there were no doors to protect you. Whenever, whatever, it works for me. It was a table nestled in the far left corner of the room beyond the bar, a table for two, silverware already set out and gleaming. A cut crystal glass held serviettes; there was a tea light in a small decorative metal lamp and shade dead centre of the table with star shapes cut into the shade. It was fluttering slightly from the wind our arrival had created, throwing rippled stars all across the polished surface. Apart from that the table was empty. There were about twelve tables in all in the T-shaped room, all made from the same dark wood as the bar. Three tables were placed along the right hand side wall opposite the bar. The rest of the tables were in the open area where we were, located deeper in the T-shaped part of the room.

I scraped a chair out from under the table and gestured to Sadie with a sweeping arm and hand arc to take a seat. I held onto the back of the chair while she sat down and scooched the chair closer to the table leaning on it a little to help with the process. I took my seat opposite Sadie, draping my hoodie over the back of the chair before sitting.

We sat for a couple of minutes before the woman behind the bar made her way listlessly over to us, pausing on the way to pick up a couple of menus that were propped up in a pile up against the edge of the bar and the wall. She handed over the menus with a forced smile, and then returned to her default position behind the bar. Apart from us there were no other customers in the place. There was a doorway to my left which opened up into a kitchen area in which a fat man was busying himself cleaning the worktops. He was in his late fifties with jet black frizzy hair round the back and sides; and bald on the top. He had on a pair of gray slacks, a plain blue shirt with the sleeves rolled up to his elbows, and a pair of scuffed brown brogues. If I did judge the book by the cover I would have left there and then, but I decided to stay and give them a chance to prove themselves. Beside the open kitchen door was a closed wood panelled door, it two was made from some dark wood as the bar, tables, skirting boards and coving, keeping with the mood. The letters W.C. were centred on it about three quarters of the way up.

After about ten minutes' deliberation over the menus we decided to go for the special, I had the steak dinner, rare, with a bottle of Budweiser. Sadie chose the grilled chicken breast with a glass of house red. I caught the waitress's attention and gestured to her that we were ready to order. She made a play of cleaning the bar before eventually sauntering over with a small notepad in her left hand and a ballpoint pen in her right.

"What can I get you?" she said, in a whiny voice, with only a hint of Hispanic to it.

"Er, can we have one steak special, and one grilled chicken breast please." I said folding the menu shut and placing it on the table in front of me.

"How would you like the steak?"

"Rare."

"And what would you like to drink with those sir?"

"A glass of house red, and a bottle of Budweiser please."

"Okay, I'll be back with the drinks." she said tearing the order page from the notepad and spinning one eighty on her heels and headed towards the kitchen area.

The man in the kitchen area greeted her with a series of frantic hand gestures and a slap to his own forehead and what I figured could only be a barrage of expletives in their mother tongue. It had to be a family business, got to be, and they were father and daughter, no other explanation. Because no employer would get away with talking to an employee like that, outbursts like those I guessed were reserved for family and family only. The woman slapped the sheet of paper with our order on it onto the top of a gleaming three tiered metal gurney, span round and headed back the way she came, speedwalking past us and towards the bar.

I heard a padded thud from the kitchen area; well at least the meat was fresh.

"Hope the food's better than the service." I whispered to Sadie as soon as the waitress was back behind the bar and out of earshot.

Sadie gave a little giggle before resting her index finger on those luscious lips of hers.

"Ssshhh." she whispered back to me. "They'll kick us out if you're not careful."

I feigned a look of surprise and then held my hands up in a mock surrender and said,

"Okay, okay, I'll come quietly." I said and then laughed.

Just a normal couple on a romantic break.

We made small talk for a couple of minutes while the drinks arrived. As the waitress was bringing them over to us, the door opened and a family unit entered consisting of three adults and three children, two boys of about four and seven years old, a girl of about ten, and two male adults and one female. They were all dressed up in their Sunday best; this was probably the highlight of their trip, a meal out, a novelty. Only the eldest boy wasn't singing from the same hymn sheet as the rest of them, he had his own agenda, and he wasn't budging an inch, whatever it was he was after.

"Mum, I want it." he ranted, stomping both feet on the floor one after the other, standing stock still in front of her, blocking his mother's path. She responded by lifting him up off his feet by his coat's hood and frog-marching him through the restaurant, his poor little feet dragging behind him. I felt sorry for the little man, although it was a comical sight.

They took over the residency of two tables just in front of us and to the right. Their two tables occupied the space next to the right hand wall in the T-shaped part. The little man struggled against his mother's grip all the way to his seat; he flopped down onto it his shoulders slumped in disgust. I figured the unit consisted of a mother, father, the children, and uncle. My guess the uncle being there was probably a product of a relationship breakdown. As he was sullen, as was the father, they both looked hen-pecked and brow-beaten. Nagged to death at twenty nine, what a way to go.

The waitress placed our drinks on the table in front of us, and then she made her way over to the family unit, calling at the bar on the way to pick up her notepad and pen.

I could hear sizzling coming from the kitchen area, and I could smell the meat searing from where I was sat which put me in a good mood. My stomach was growling constantly now and I was feeling a little shaky as though my blood sugar had dropped as fast as B.P. shares after the oil spill.

I watched as Sadie fished out her mobile from her handbag and pressed the green button twice to re-dial the last known number. I didn't have to ask her the outcome, I knew, as her face turned from hopeful to distraught in a millisecond; it was like watching one of those tricks you used to do as a kid, when you'd wave your hand over your face and change from smiling to frowning, just like that.

"No luck?" I asked in hope.

"No it is still switched off." she replied, tucking the phone back into her handbag.

"What time does she finish work?"

"Erm, half past five. why?"

"Well I was thinking if her phone has run out of charge, I would give it until about six-ish, then ring her she should be back home by then." I said reaching for her hand and squeezing it.

It was a role reversal, I was returning the favour, she had molly coddled me through the flight and now it was my turn to help her through this. You scratch my back and I'll scratch yours. I would scratch it anyway.

"What about your mam and dad, do they live anywhere near?"

She looked up at me with her puppy dog eyes and shook her head saying,

"No they retired to the south of France a couple of years ago."

Shit, that avenue closed quickly. I thought rather than the agonising wait we had in store Sadie could have rung her folks and asked them to call round to her sisters. Then we would know either way a lot sooner if there was anything wrong than we would if we played this waiting game. Besides if something had happened to her the only real chance of finding her would be to act quickly. I hoped and prayed she would be okay and that it was just her phone out of charge. But my gut feeling was something had happened to her. Needless to say I kept this to myself for the time being.

I had another thought.

"What about any friends who live near?"

"Well I don't want to worry anybody unnecessarily, do I?" she said, pausing to take a sip of the claret before continuing. "If what you think has happened and her phone has run out of charge then it would be a waste of time."

"I suppose you're right." I said. "Best to wait 'til later."

But the more I thought about it the worse I felt. I needed fuel to help me through the next hour and half. On cue, the fat man shouted something from the kitchen area and the waitress duly dropped everything and made her way over to him. There was another heated exchange, and the fat man turned his back on the waitress and threw his hands up in the air. The waitress responded by picking up two plates from the worktop she was stood in front of and made her way over to our table.

"One steak special, rare." she said as she placed the plate in front of me. "And one grilled chicken breast." she said as she did the same for Sadie. "Can I get you anythin' else, a drink perhaps."

"Not just yet thanks." I replied.

With that she was gone, back to her default position behind the bar. Her palms propping her chin up while she flicked through the pages of a magazine.

I cut a piece of meat from the corner of the fourteen ounce steak and popped it in my mouth, it was absolutely divine. It just melted in my mouth. My eyes rolled and I sighed longingly.

"How's the chicken?"

"It's really nice."

"So is the steak, wonders will never cease."

We finished off our meals; my plate looked like I had licked it clean such was the culinary delight. We ordered another drink then decided we should find somewhere closer to the hotel to have a few more drinks. It was now half past five. Half an hour to D-hour.

We left a ten percent tip and made our way back to the street our hotel was on. Sadie had seen what looked like a nice bar; she said it was just round the corner. So we headed for it. We hit the doors to the bar at ten minutes to six, ten minutes to D-hour.

7

*I*nside, the bar was virtually a carbon copy of the bistro, a long narrow room which opened up at the far end. It had a dark wood bar across the left hand wall that stretched a quarter of the way in. There were a couple of stools stationed around the bar. Two old men occupied two of the seats, the third was empty. As we walked past the old men I picked up what they were saying, not the actual words, but I recognised the accent. One was a Geordie, the other was Scottish, they were both slurring. They were both dressed in typical northern attire (old style), they both had on a pair of thin work trousers complete with creases down the middle. The Geordie had on a white cotton shirt with two light blue vertical stripes at either side of the neck, with the top two buttons undone, while his Scottish counterpart had on a plain white cotton shirt and only the top button was undone. They both had cheap polyester coats draped over the two stools they were sprawled on. I nodded to them as I got level, only the Geordie nodded back. I noticed little black puffballs of lint clinging to the collar of his shirt and I cringed.

There wasn't much of a jump in decor between the bar and the bistro either. It was all dark wood and wall lights. There was a ceiling fan without a light gently spinning round, like a samara caught on a gentle breeze. Underfoot was rough terracotta tiling, our trainers slapped on the surface as opposed to their scuffed thuds in the bistro. I motioned for Sadie to find a table further in the room; again it was borne from instinct, programmed deep into the subconscious. I didn't even after think about it, I just did it. It was now six minutes to six, six minutes to D-hour.

The barmaid was plain looking with mousey brown hair; I caught her side profile as she served the two old men at the bar. She had a cute elfish face, with a button nose. As I got within intimate proximity to the barmaid she looked up to greet me, and as soon as she caught sight of me her pupils contracted ever so slightly and her face flickered in recognition, she dropped the glass she was holding onto the floor smashing it into pieces. I stopped dead in my tracks, she did the same, she just stood there where she was staring at me shaking her head and pulling a face. Then she regained her composure and disappeared from view for a couple of seconds. I heard the tinny sound of a soft brush on hard wood and the tinkle of glass as she swept the debris up, and then the crash as she tipped it into a silver pedal bin that was behind the bar stood against the left hand wall.

She popped back up from down under, like a Punch and Judy puppet. Her composure regained enough to utter a few words. She smiled and said,

"Hi, sorry about that, what can I get you?"

I asked for a bottle of house red and as soon as she heard my accent she visibly relaxed. I watched her face go from concerned to passive the instant I opened my mouth. The mind boggles.

She wore a plain T-shirt and a pair of faded blue denims; on her feet she wore a pair of battered black Nike low tops. She had her hair tucked up in a convenience ponytail. She was pleasant enough, smiling when she took my money, smiling when she handed my change over, and absolutely beaming when I left her a ten percent tip on every round. I ordered a bottle of red and two glasses. She took her time serving me, but I didn't mind because she was constantly smiling, service with a smile gets you everywhere; well it gets you a ten percent tip at least.

By the time I joined Sadie with the wine it was two minutes to six, two minutes to D-hour.

There was a clock on the wall directly opposite the table Sadie had chosen. I found myself staring at it, but instead of it looking like it was going backwards, which it normally did if you were waiting on something, it looked as though it had somehow sped up, as though an invisible finger was pushing it round and round, faster and faster. I looked around, I like to acclimatise myself to places, the more familiar you are with your surroundings the safer you feel. Not only that, you never know when you might need to make a speedy exit. I like to know where both the official and unofficial exits are in any building I'm in. On the back wall there were three doorways, one which was open that led into a kitchen area and two closed. I presumed that the two closed doors were toilets. There looked to be only one exit, the front way. But I was sure there had to be one in the kitchen area. I don't know much about Dutch regulations but it was common sense to have an emergency exit in the room most likely to catch fire.

There was various Irish paraphernalia adorning the walls, from U2 picture discs, to pictures of Hothouse Flowers, the Pogues and the Corrs. There were also a couple of landscape pictures of the emerald isle, and one of the Giant's Causeway. At the side of the table there was a gigantic upside down top hat vase engraved with a filigreed pattern, inside it there were dried and sprayed twigs and fibre-optic flowers that changed colour from Irish green to misty pink intermittently.

Directly behind us there was a thin box room with half and half wooden panelling and glass for walls; it was partitioned off from the rest of the room by a sliding door. My guess was that it was a smoking area. I guessed right, as the barmaid checked that everybody had a drink who wanted one, then made for the partitioned off room pulling her cigarettes out of her front jeans pocket as she did so. She smiled as she passed us.

It was now six o'clock; D-hour had arrived.

I nodded and looked up at the clock which was positioned right above Sadie's head and somehow looked like it was growing from it and said,

"It's six o'clock; do you wanna try your Stella again?"

She nodded in reply and began a thorough search of her bag to retrieve the mobile. After cordoning off the corners of her bag Sadie finally pulled out the phone and proceeded to press the green button twice and lifted it to her ear.

I waited for the connection with baited breath, as did she. Again I didn't have to ask, but I did saying,

"No answer?"

She shook her head and replied,

"No."

I pulled a face, and dry scrubbed my face with my hands and then ran my hands through my hair, messing it up even more than it already was. I kissed my canines, these were all actions I were doing in response to the bad news. But all wasn't lost, not yet anyway. There could be an innocent explanation; I hoped that proved to be the case here and now.

"Kev, what do you think has happened? Honestly." Sadie whispered to me from across the table. The barmaid had just finished her cigarette, blowing the smoke upwards while crushing the end out in one of the ashtrays provided. She was behind me and to the left; I could just make out her shape in my peripheral vision. She disappeared from my view, and then a couple of seconds later I heard the distinct shuffling noise of the sliding door scraping along the wooden tracks on its stiff wheels. I waited until she was back behind the bar again and out of earshot before I replied.

"Honestly, I don't know, I hope nothin' has happened for her sake, but I've gotta horrible feeling."

Her head and shoulders sunk as I spoke.

"Do you think it's the same people who took me?" she asked.

I shook my head. I didn't want to worry her unnecessarily and said,

"I don't think so; this is all pie in the sky until we know for definite that somethin's happened so let's try not to think like that, hey."

She nodded once and said,

"So what do you suggest?"

"Have you left her a voicemail?

Sadie shook her head saying,

"Not yet I haven't."

"I reckon we should wait until ten o'clock tonight, and then ring her again. If she doesn't answer leave her a message on her voicemail. Then if she doesn't get back to you by start of play tomorrow were goin' to have to assume the worst. For what it's worth, 'am sorry."

Sadie pursed her lips together tight and looked down at her hands that she was nervously wringing and said,

"I'd like to tell you it's not your fault, but it is isn't it. I mean if I would never have bumped into you in the shop that night then none of this would have happened would it?"

I figured the question was rhetorical so I didn't offer an answer. When Sadie looked up again she had tears in her eyes, one of them over filled and a tear spilled out over the rim and ran in a line down her cheek. Her lips were trembling, I wanted to jump up and put my arm round her to protect her and reassure her that everything was going to turn out alright, but I also knew Sadie was a private person and that such a profound display in public would attract attention to us and neither of us wanted that. It would also label Sadie as being vulnerable and defenceless, it would be like emitting a signal to a tracker, leaving trampled blades of grass in your wake, or a snapped twig on the floor, it would be a bad idea anywhere but more so round here with the characters we'd encountered so far. So I exercised self control and held my impulses in check for the time being and stayed where I was, giving her hand another squeeze which would tell her the same things but without the theatrics. I topped up both glasses and took a sip of the blood-red liquid. There was an awkward silence between us for a long period.

I broke the silence saying,

"I know it's hard but let's try not worry about it, 'til we know for sure what's happened."

Sadie looked up and gave me a shy smile, wiping away the tear trail from her cheek.

We finished off the glass of wine and headed for the smoking area. The door struggled against its tracks for a couple of seconds before giving way. We entered. No sooner had I slid the door closed behind us then the air conditioner kicked in noisily, whirring and rattling. It was a small oblong room of about twelve feet by eight; there were three small tables on each side laid out in single file.

Each table had two chairs tucked under it. At the far end of the room there was a bench that occupied the whole of the back wall; at either side of the bench were two small tables. The bench had a cushion on it, some old floral design that had faded and become blurred with age. We made for the bench. Sadie sat to the extreme right; I sat in the middle to give her a little space.

"Do you want me to make one or . . ." I started to ask Sadie, but she cut me off.

"I'll make one; it might help to take my mind off things."

Sadie located the materials needed in her tardis/bag and proceeded to make an extra large joint. It was thin at one end, fat at the other, like a deformed sausage. I held my hand out for her; I had the tip of the lighter virtually level with my thumb and index finger so it looked as though the naked flame was in fact coming from my hand. The fat end of it erupted in flame then glowed with intensity, popping and crackling as it took hold.

"I need a piss." I said.

Sadie pulled a face as I made for the door, grabbing hold of my hand and pulling me back so that I was facing her.

"Kev, I know it's not entirely your fault, but I don't think you've been honest with me have you?"

I shook my head in response and looked to the floor, like a naughty school kid being told off.

"If this is going to work—I mean us—then you need to tell me exactly what's going on, leaving nothing out."

"Let me go to the toilet and I will tell you everythin'" I said, wiping my hand across my mouth then dragging it over my chin and cheek.

I had to give myself time to think.

What do I tell her?

Do I tell her everything? If not, which bits do I leave out? And which bits do I tell her?

I spun round on my Nikes and headed for the sliding door, I left it half open, to avoid the struggle of opening it again. As soon as the toilet door was closed behind me I dug out my mobile and powered it up. I nipped into a cubicle closing the door behind me and locking it. I pushed the lid down and sat on it and waited patiently while my mobile found its bearings, pulling the metaphoric hood from its head and re-orientating itself with its global position. Once it had re-booted I waited another couple of minutes to see if any messages came through. There were none. I pressed the green button twice to dial the last known number, which was the number Dim had left on the voicemail. Again the automated voice told me I had dialled an incorrect number. I turned the phone off and returned it to its resting place in my pocket. I decided to tell Sadie the whole truth and nothing but the truth it was the only way.

After washing my hands, and pausing at the rusting mirror to examine my appearance, satisfied I returned to the bar and then on to the smoking area joining Sadie, pausing at the table we had first sat to pick up what was left of the wine and the two glasses. We needed privacy for what I was about to spill so I kicked the door shut behind me. I picked up the half smoked joint which was propped on the side of an ashtray as I sat down next to her. I needed some Dutch courage so I took a big hit off it, then another, then another, and then a double hit before returning it to the ash tray smouldering.

"I don't know where to begin."

"At the start is universally accepted, so how about we take it from there and see how it goes."

I nodded, paused for a split second, took a deep breath and made the plunge, I knew this was a make or break time for Sadie and me. After this we would either part company here and now or form a formidable partnership that would last forever. I hoped it was the latter; I'd spent far too much time already being a victim, all alone with no back-up I'd succumbed to my fears and allowed them to dictate how I lived my life, well no more. This was it. No more fears, no more tears.

"Can you remember the prank?" I asked Sadie.

"Prank, what prank?" she replied. "What, you mean the one Ally and who was it with him? Pulled on you all those years ago."

"The very one, and it was Ian and Craig who orchestrated it with him. I'm surprised you remember it."

"Why wouldn't I, it kick-started the beginning of the end for us. Didn't it?"

"What? You mean you knew the reason why I was so moody?"

"It wasn't a secret Kev, everybody knew about it, the prank I mean and it doesn't take a genius to work out what happened to you after it. You changed, from a nice person into a horrible one overnight, I didn't think you'd ever be the same again, and I wasn't about to take that shit from you or anyone. So I thought it best to part company before you did something you would regret." She paused for a second; something had grabbed her attention.

I followed her gaze; the barmaid was heading towards the smoke room, pulling her cigarettes from her pocket as she strolled across the room. The cigarette was dangling from her mouth as she reached the door and she had it lit before she had closed it behind her. She was full of beans, happy, bubbly. No matter what you said to her she just laughed.

"I need the little girl's room; will you watch my bag for me please?"

I nodded in reply.

Sadie exchanged pleasantries with the barmaid as she passed her. The barmaid laughed. Sadie struggled with the door, I was just about to jump up to help her when the door dutifully scraped its way past the problem part of the track and slid open enough for her to squeeze through. I watched as she glided across the room and over to the ladies, and then disappeared behind the door.

I picked up the remainder of the joint stuck it between my lips, lit it and took another double hit off it. I held the smoke in for a couple of seconds before blowing it out through my nostrils. I pictured myself as a cartoon bull, just before it's about to charge, snorting and kicking up dust. Ahhh, not long now and I would be approaching my own little nirvana, and nobody else was invited apart from Sadie, she had a V.I.P. pass to access all areas. I took another hit off it and gestured to the barmaid to take the spliff. She leap-frogged two chairs and took the joint off me before sitting back to front on the last chair on the left. She took a couple of hits off it then passed it back laughing. Now I understood why she was constantly laughing, it was because she was constantly stoned. I bowed my head in genuflection. If only I had a job like hers. I took one last hit off the joint and crushed it out into the ashtray. The barmaid laughed and then returned to her post behind the bar. I glanced at the clock on the wall; it was now ten minutes to eight. A hundred and thirty minutes until the second most important phone call of my life. The most important one will be the one in the morning to Stella's phone if there was still no answer tonight.

A couple of minutes later Sadie reappeared like a magician's glamorous apprentice, all that was missing was the smoke and the blinding flash. She was positively glowing, looking all freshened up, fresh lipstick applied, and a quick spray from a bullet sized perfume bottle and there she was gliding across the rough oak laminate, like a toy ballerina on a music box.

She squeezed back through the door, sliding it shut behind her. Surprisingly enough it shut without too much of a struggle. She sauntered over and sat back down beside me, gave a quick look to the barmaid (who was back behind the bar laughing at every one) to make sure we wouldn't be interrupted again, and then she gave me a shy smile and said,

"It's okay, whatever you tell me won't change anything between us."

I nodded then looked to my feet saying,

"You sure about that Sadie?" I said.

Thoughts were ricocheting around in my head like bullets. I mean, would Sadie still feel the same if her sister was never found, disappeared without trace? An absolute nightmare for family members, because it meant no closure, and no closure means no peace, not ever. And then there was the small matter of my involvement in Ally's death, plus there were the three Chinese kidnappers, I didn't know for sure how much of it Sadie remembered and in a way I'm glad she was out of it. The last thing she remembers is talking to me on the phone and then everything is blank until she woke up later that night with me asleep laid on the floor beside her bed, and the rest as they say is history. Which on the plus side meant three less things to confess—swings and roundabouts.

"As sure as I can be without actually knowing what it is you're going to tell me." she replied.

"As I was saying, the prank changed me and I held Ally responsible. So when I got made redundant I got this idea in my head that if I came back and put a few ghosts to rest then I would be able to put it all behind me and get on with my life."

"So that night we met at the shop, you were telling the truth, initially."

"Yeah, yeah, I swear to you, I didn't think you'd still feel the same way, I thought it was gonna be a one night thing and that would be it, maybe a couple of dates if I was lucky. And then when I got back to your house and the way we were all over each other I realised it was somethin' deeper. You've gotta believe me Sadie, there were things happening that were out of my control, I got involved with some people who helped me get my own back on Ally, and I couldn't get out of it they had me by the bollocks. Plus the money they offered was too much to turn down. But then you came along and things changed—I had somethin' to lose and that's how these people work if they can't get at you they take someone close to you instead."

"How did you get your own back on Ally?"

"You don't wanna know."

"Er, yes I do."

"I got hold of a gun through a friend and I turned up at Ally's one night. Late on when I knew he'd be on his own and I don't know what I was gonna do, I just wanted to make him pay."

"And what happened when you got there?"

"They were both there waitin' for me, both Ally and Craig. They set the trap, laid the bait, dug in and waited for me. They knew I would turn up that night 'cos somehow they had set me up, they knew I was on to them. Don't ask me how, 'cos I an't gotta clue." I paused, a chance to compose myself. My thoughts were running all over the place like bacteria under a microscope. I was sweating freely; it must have looked like I was thawing out, like a cartoon snowman. Rivulets were slaloming down my face and scooting off my chin, in a constant drip, drip, drip, like a tap in a police cell.

"They sprayed somethin' in my eyes to temporarily blind me, then they stun-gunned me. When I come round they had me tied to a chair."

"And then what?"

"Well they tortured me, I kept passing out. It was daft o'clock when they finally made me drive my car while Craig went on ahead in his."

"Where were they taking you?"

"They own a house out in the sticks; they were takin' me there to dispose of."

"What you mean?"

I nodded my head in a glum response.

"Only we didn't get there, a police car came behind us put its siren on wanting to pull us. Ally told me to lose it, so I did. It ended up on its roof down Old Moor Lane."

Sadie lifted her hand to her now opening mouth. She was shaking her head, which wasn't a good sign.

"I can remember that." She said. "I didn't think for a minute you were connected."

"Why would you?" I said and shrugged.

"They made me take the back roads to the house and then just as we were about to turn into the village where the house is we saw another couple of police cars. They spun round and began chasin' us again. Ally told me to dump the car near the house and that we'd go by foot the rest of the way. Believe me Sadie if they had got me to that house that would've been it."

"So what happened then?"

"Well instead of doin' what Ally told me to do, I just carried on right into the street and smashed the car into their house. Ally collided with the windscreen . . . an' well, y'know the rest."

"No I don't, you're goin' to tell me."

"Well Ally was pronounced dead at the scene, and Craig got arrested for cultivation with intent to supply. I did a runner; I got to a shed about a mile away from the scene of the accident and didn't know what else to do. There were police dogs searchin' the immediate area and I was stuck there with no transport. So I phoned one of the guys who I bought the gun off and he came and picked me up. Plus he arranged an alibi for me." I paused for breath and also to allow Sadie a little time to take everything in. When all was said and done with what I had just spilt, it was hardly an everyday confession; there was a lot to take in, a lot of factors to muse over and consider.

"Who are these guys who you bought the gun off? Do you think it could be those who have taken Stella?"

I proceeded to fill Sadie in where I could where Mik and Dim were concerned, after all I had only met Dim twice, and Mik the once. What did I know? I told her about the job offer, the formula, Batty the crazy bastard, and the double cross somewhere en route, I told her about the voicemails Dim had left on my phone, and I told her about Mik's body being found. She sat and listened intently, like an overly keen student. She pursed her lips a couple of times and clucked her tongue on more than one occasion.

"So you see I don't think it could be Mik and Dim, it's more likely to be the Chinese, 'cos that's how they work, they take someone close like they did when they took you."

"What do they want, do you think?"

I tapped my index finger on my breast bone a couple of times and said, "Me."

"Just you?"

"I would've thought the Chinese want to get rid of everybody who knows their formula."

"And you know it?"

"No, but I acquired it with Batty remember, they just want me dead."

There was another awkward silence; I could see Sadie tossing and turning it, flipping it over and over in her head, like a pancake in a skillet on Shrove Tuesday. I could almost visualise the cogs turning, each part perfectly engineered and perfectly crafted to keep the momentum going.

"Sadie." I whispered.

She looked up and caught my eye, I maintained the contact for thirty seconds or so while I pleaded my case with her.

"That night when we first met, if I'd have thought then that there was any possibility that you or anyone else would be in danger through my actions then I would have stayed away. But how was I to know that any of this was goin' to happen." I paused for a second and scooted closer to her, putting my arm round her and giving her a gentle squeeze, letting go again straight after. "Listen to me Sadie."

She looked down; I scooted even closer still, until we were touching, thigh to thigh, knee to knee on the back bench in the smoke room in an Irish theme bar on the edge of Amsterdam's red light district. I gently lifted her head with the tip of my forefinger under her chin. As soon as we had eye contact I said,

"I promise you now as soon as we know for definite that she's gone and someone has taken her I will do whatever I can to get her back in one piece."

Her head dropped and she brought her hand up to it resting the palm of her hand on her forehead, the ball of her thumb sunk deep into her eye socket. She started rubbing it furiously, saying over and over again,

"I can't believe it, I can't believe it, I can't fucking believe it."

I stroked her cheek with the back of my hand and then scooted away from her.

"Should I get another bottle?" I asked her shaking the bottle so the dregs in the bottom kicked up a mini whirlpool.

She began to shake her head saying,

"No, can you get me a large Southern Comfort, lime and soda please, I think I need it."

I nodded and spun on my soles and made for the sliding door. True to form I started to struggle with the door but then stopped and took a step back, deep in thought. I had my forefinger and thumb resting on my chin in a V shape. I thought about it for ten seconds until it dawned on me everyone who struggled with it was grabbing hold of it by the handle and pushing all their weight onto the middle of the door, I worked out it was that what was the problem. Either the bottom or the top track was getting jammed when you opened it this way, whereas if you just gave the bottom a little tap with your foot . . . which I did and voila, it slid open as slick as the bridge door on the Starship Enterprise.

I sauntered over to the bar, the barmaid was busy pulling the Geordie two pints of lager and she had just tilted the second glass under the pump, the liquid looked golden in this poor light and it looked like honey being drizzled from a spoon. The smell of a stone baked pizza came wafting in from somewhere outside and I licked my lips in anticipation, I was starving again, my fuel light was on and I knew I had to replenish my energy supplies at least eight times if I was to get through the next couple of days or so.

I watched the barmaid as she served the Geordie, she smiled as she handed him the drinks, smiled as she took his money, smiled while she worked the till and deposited the cash, and beamed as he waved away the change. She turned to me and smiled tilting her head back a little and raising her eyebrows, which in universal body language means "What can I get you?"

I smiled back and said,

"Can I have a large Jack Daniel's and a large Southern Comfort, lime and soda please?"

She nodded and smiled back, turning her back to me to fix the drinks. She reached under the bar for two tumblers and slammed one under the Jack Daniels optic and one under the Southern Comfort optic and hit them three times. The optics dripped twice into the slop trays, the tears of a clown. She slid the tumbler with the Jack Daniel's in it gently across the bar towards me; it came to rest on the edge of a beer towel. I took a sip of the liquid fire and winced. I turned my back to the bar while she fixed Sadie's drink, leaving a ten guilder note on the bar, enough to cover the drinks and a generous tip.

I looked over to where Sadie was sat still in the smoke room; she was now wiping her eyes with the backs of her hands. She looked up saw me and managed a half smile; I just about managed one back. I snuck a look at the clock on the wall as I turned back towards the bar. It was now ten to ten.

I said to the barmaid "Keep the change." as I scooped the two tumblers up and spun back round and headed back towards the smoke room, towards Sadie and to whatever verdict she had reached with regards to my confession—and all that it entailed. I used my new found method on the sliding door; it was as though the tracks had been smeared with butter, it opened easily. I plonked the drinks onto the nearest table and sat down next to Sadie who was now examining her reflection in a little compact mirror she had pulled out from her handbag. As I sat down she closed the compact case and returned it to its place in her bag, just about anywhere seemed to be the preferred system. When she looked up she was smiling, I didn't know if it was a good omen or not, I'm sure time will tell.

"I've made a decision." she whispered, though there was no one else in the room, and only three people in the bar including the laughing barmaid.

I started to put some cigarette papers together—one large and one small, to do the cone thing.

Sadie spoke as she reached for her diluted spirit,

"I will give you the benefit of doubt for now. If and when we find out what has happened to Stella I will reassess the situation then. I just can't think at the minute, not with this hanging over my head. So what do you think?"

I took another sip and pulled another face and said,

"There's nothin' to think about 'am in."

Sadie pinched her nose between thumb and forefinger and downed the drink in one, when the taste hit her a split second after swallowing it she shook her head wildly from side to side a couple of times while saying,

"Blaaah".

"I think we should wait 'til tomorrow morning before we ring her, that way it will give her chance to get in touch of her own accord, no need to worry anyone unnecessarily. What you reckon?" I said, downing my own drink and wincing. I could feel the burning sensation travelling down my throat all the way into my stomach; it was like drinking erupting lava. What was it the Jack Daniel's advertising campaign said, "If you think burning charcoal to mellow Jack Daniel's is extravagant, well it is? Well I don't think it's extravagant, I think its madness.

"I need the toilet again." I said making for the sliding door.

"I'll wait for you in here, and finish this off shall I." I heard Sadie call after me; I think she meant finish the joint off. So when I looked back as I reached the door and saw she had her head bowed and sprinkling tobacco onto the papers I'd stuck together I just let her get on with it. I gave the door a tap with my foot and it opened easily. As I walked across the room towards the toilet I glanced at the clock on the wall, it was now ten past eleven.

I heard the main door of the bar open as I reached and opened the toilet door. I looked over my shoulder at the newcomer as I entered the bathroom; like I said before I don't like surprises, I like to be prepared. I only caught a passing glance just before the toilet door closed on me but that was enough, walking up to the bar were two tough looking thugs. The two men had trouble written all over them. One was in his late twenties early thirties with a skin head, and the other one was in his late forties with swept back jet black hair greying at the temples. They both had on three quarter length leather box jackets, both were wearing dark coloured jeans, the older one was wearing a pair of brown loafers, whereas the younger one had on a pair of black and white Converse sneakers. The skin headed one was wearing a plain white T-shirt, the older one had on a cream coloured shirt unbuttoned at the neck. Needless to say I did the do in the bathroom quicker than I have ever in my life, except perhaps the night of the prank, when I nearly pissed myself as the mystery shooter opened fire.

I was in and out of the bathroom in less than two minutes. As I closed the door and made my way across the room wiping my wet hands on the backs of my jeans I scoped the room looking for the two newcomers. They were stood at the bar right next to the two Brits, who were oblivious to what was happening around them, they were deep in conversation, from what I could gather from this distance is that they were arguing about football, primarily Newcastle and Celtic. The laughing barmaid wasn't laughing anymore and I could tell from her body language that something was up as she pulled the two newcomers their drinks. So instead of returning to the smoke room I tapped on the window to attract Sadie's attention, when she looked up I gestured two minutes to her with my index and middle finger. She nodded in response and then went back to making the finishing touches to the joint.

I made for the bar.

8

I got to the bar just as the laughing barmaid had finished pulling the first drink, she was now passing it to the older of the two, and age deserves respect I guess, but not in this case. As the barmaid released her grip on the glass in front of the man, instead of grabbing the glass and taking a big slug of it, he gripped hold of the laughing barmaid's wrist. I could see it hurt her as she creased her face up and shut her eyes tight in response. The man pulled her close so he could whisper something in her ear; she started to nod her head frantically in reply to what he had said to her. He let go of her wrist and pushed her backwards. She stumbled backwards a couple of steps until she came up against the row of optics strung across the wooden surround of the bar, jarring her back against one of the bottles and dislodging it. It crashed to the floor smashing into tiny pieces. She then turned back towards the pump rubbing her wrist as she did so, her trainers crunching on the broken glass. She had now made it to the pump, her damaged wrist resting on it pulling it down slowly and expertly, I could see that her wrist was already swollen and red raw. It looked like someone had given her an Indian rope burn.

While the barmaid was pulling the second drink I was sizing up the two men, trying to work out which one to go for first if it came to it. I had about thirty seconds to make up my mind, the time it took to pull the drink. Both men were clean shaven; though the skinhead had razor burn on his neck, little pin pricks of blood dotted along his neck just above the collar of his shirt. Out of the two men it was obvious the younger one was the more dangerous, he was about my age but he had about sixty pounds on me. The older one was about my weight, but not my physique. He had a skinny frame laden with a beer gut, I came to the conclusion if I took the younger guy out first the older one would fall in line no problem. It was the younger of the two who was worrying me as I took into account his massive arms, neck and shoulders. I weighed just short of thirteen stone, but I was cut up rather than bulky. He was the exact opposite, bulky and weighing in at about seventeen stone. He was solid though with not an ounce of fat anywhere on his body, a mini version of Dim. I had to be quick, and I had to be precise if I was to do him some damage and take him out of the game. So as the drink reached half way on the glass I was already psyching myself ready to explode if needed. The elder of the two reached for his glass and lifted it to his mouth it was then I remembered something I'd read about the Krays. They used to use a trick in their heyday to tackle people they thought represented a problem to them, size wise. What they did was offer the said person a cigarette and a soon as he had his mouth open they would hit him with a sucker punch aptly named the cigarette punch for obvious reasons. An open jaw is easier to break than a closed one. I was going to bring the Krays' chosen method of attack into play here. In a split second I had it arranged in my head what I was going to do. I would wait for the younger of the two to take a sip of his drink, wait until the glass was almost touching his lips and then—wham—I'd hit him with a right hook.

By now the drink had frothed a little, forming the perfect head on it, she handed it over to the younger of the two and as she did so the older one caught her eye and pointed to the till, and said,

"Get me a light as well will you."

So that's what this was all about, protection money.

I tried to catch the two Brits' eyes who were stood at the bar but they were still engrossed in their own little debate, and even if they wasn't, I didn't think they would be any use to me, too inebriated, too out of shape, too old.

The skinhead didn't take a drink at first, which was good in a way because I wanted to see what unfolded.

The barmaid tossed a book of matches onto the bar in front of the older man; they skidded for a second or so before colliding with a beer mat and coming to stop just to his left. The man picked them up and stuffed them into his jacket pocket.

I glanced over my shoulder to the smoke room where Sadie sat waiting, she gave me a smile and a quizzical look, and I just threw her another two minute gesture and shrugged my shoulders, and turned back towards the bar. The laughing barmaid was stalling, she and the older man were having a conversation in their native tongue, I presumed it was Dutch. This confirmed my suspicions that the older man was the leader, the boss, the local capo, the big cheese round these parts, and the skinhead was the back-up, the hired muscle. I'd made my mind up: I had to take the skinhead out of the equation and that was that. At the same time as the laughing barmaid worked the till and the cash drawer spilled out, the skinhead reached for his drink, time to get in character. Just as the glass touched his lips I made my move. I caught him with a crunching hook to the lower ball part of his jaw, and he dropped like somebody had pulled the rug from under his feet. It was like an old cartoon where a hole is cut into the floor under the character—now you see him, now you don't. I don't know if I broke his jaw or not but his eyes had rolled back in his head, and he was out cold. I turned to the older man and, while nodding to the floor where his accomplice lay convulsing, I said,

"If you don't want to end up like your friend I suggest you get the fuck outta here now."

He stood for a split second weighing up his options and then he turned and started to make for the exit.

"Take him with you, and if I ever see you in here again you're dead, understand? And leave the matches." I said calmly.

I didn't want any connection to him via the bar or anywhere.

The older man reached into his pocket and tossed the book of matches onto the bar and then he turned back towards his crumpled friend and tried his best to rouse him without any luck. He turned to me and shrugged his shoulders. I wasn't having any of it; I looked to the floor and shook my head and said,

"You've got two minutes to get that piece of shit outta here or I'll do the same to you, but worse."

The man nodded his shame complete, he couldn't work round here anymore and he knew it. With one punch I'd destroyed what had taken him a lifetime to build, his reputation. Protection gangs rule by fear, and once they've lost that, they've lost everything. The older man grabbed the skinhead by his jacket collar and unceremoniously started to drag him out of the door. The skinhead's mouth was flopping freely like a ventriloquist's dummy, and a bad one at that. The unorthodox pair looked like the act that didn't get through on Britain's Got Talent. No blood, no mess, no problems.

I turned to the now shocked barmaid. She had a look of total disbelief on her face.

"You don't know what you've done." the laughing barmaid said shaking her head, her pony-tail flopping from side to side.

"I thought I was doin' you a favour, but there you go." I replied.

I turned away from her and gestured to Sadie that we were ready to go; she nodded and started to gather her things up, pulling my hoodie from off the back of the chair and holding it up to let me know she had it. I nodded to her to let her know I'd seen her.

A second later she got to her feet and made for the sliding door. She struggled with the door so I walked over and gave it a gentle tap with my foot and it slid open. She passed through it and gave me a half smile that still managed somehow to reach her eyes. As we reached the bar the laughing barmaid beckoned me over with a waggle of her hand.

"Give me two minutes; just wait for me by the door, on the inside." I said to Sadie. "I need to have a word with the barmaid about somethin'."

"Oh okay." she replied walking over to the door and taking the seat closest to it.

I saw her rummage around in her bag for a couple of seconds before finally fishing out her mobile. I watched as she pushed the green button twice and lifted the phone to her ear, tucking a few strands of hair behind it as she did so. I caught her negative body language just as I made it to the bar, shoulders slumped and her head dropped, again there must have been no answer from her sister.

"You shouldn't have done that." the laughing barmaid said as I reached the bar, though she still wasn't laughing.

"Listen 'am sorry, you looked like you needed a hand so I gave you one."

"Ya well let's hope they don't come back in a hurry." she replied.

"Are we still okay to come here for a drink, my girlfriend likes the wine here? If there's a problem we'll find somewhere else to go—it's totally up to you."

She creased her face up in thought for a second before answering, saying,

"Yes, yes you can come have a drink here anytime you like, just keep your hands to yourself next time okay." she said and smiled for the first time in about three minutes, this time her smile created dimples in her cheeks.

"Okay." I replied and headed for the door.

Sadie got to her feet as I reached her.

"You ready?" I said.

She nodded in reply.

I opened the door for her, putting my hand on the small of her back resting it on the gentle curve between her buttocks and her back and ushered her outside. Once we were outside I searched the street for the two thugs. The fresh air hit me like a getaway car, I'd had a fair bit to drink, and so had Sadie. She swayed at the side of me. I grabbed a hold of the inside of her arm to steady both herself and me. The two thugs were to our right, the older one had stopped dragging the skinhead and had him propped up against the display window of a delicatessen slapping his face and shouting his name—Edgar, slap, Edgar, slap, Edgar, slap. The skinhead wasn't responding to his harsh paramedic method which was hardly surprising. The older of the two gave up the ghost for the time being, he let go of the skinhead's lapels and he just rolled over and bent over double like a Jack-in-a-box after activation. I steered Sadie to the left, fished out my cigarettes, shook two out, lit them both and handed one over to Sadie.

"You hungry?" I asked as we made our way down the poorly lit street.

"Er, no I don't think so; I think I just want to go back to the hotel." she said and gave me a wicked smile.

The moon poked through a broken cloud as we stepped over the threshold into the hotel foyer, it looked like an old silver coin, dirty round the edges. The clerk was sat behind her desk engrossed in whatever reading material she had brought to see her through the night. She momentarily looked up and welcomed us with a smile as we made our way through the foyer and to the lift. It was now twelve o'clock. Tomorrow was going to be a big day for the both of us, and I wondered what it would bring. One thing's for sure it would either bring a load of shit or not. Whichever, whatever, I was ready.

9

I woke the next day and immediately reached for my phone and turned it on, dry-scrubbing my face and hair while I waited for it to re-boot. I could hear the sound of running water coming from the adjoining wet room, the bed was empty on Sadie's side and the sheets were crumpled up.

I had no voicemails or texts left on my phone. It was seven thirty am Greenwich Mean Time, so that meant it was eight thirty here. Sadie was up and about already, which could only mean one thing she'd had some kind of news, either good or bad, either or. And in this case no news was bad news.

After rummaging through the wardrobe I found myself a clean set of clothes and laid the clothes on the bed ready to put on while I waited for Sadie to finish off in the shower. Again she emerged from the wet room pink and fresh and with a towel wrapped around her tanned midriff. Again she had managed somehow not to wet her hair.

I too emerged from the wet room some ten minutes later after showering and brushing my teeth, with sopping wet hair, a not so pink face and a white fluffy towel wrapped around my waist.

"Have you heard anythin' from your Stella?" I asked.

"Not yet. I was going to ring her after we'd had some breakfast—that is if you fancy some."

"I fancy somethin'" I said reaching out for her.

She fended me off with an arm block saying,

"Kev, we can't, Stella remember?"

"Yeah okay." I said.

I towelled myself dry and dressed whilst Sadie performed her daily rituals.

I had on a pair of dark blue Ecko Jeans, baggy fit, a plain white Nike Air T-shirt, and my trainers. It wasn't that cold for this time of year but I still decided to take a hoodie and tie it round my waist. Sadie had on a pair of shop faded boyfriend jeans, a tight pink T-shirt which looked to be struggling to keep her breasts at bay, and a thin white zip up hoodie. She also had on her white Lacoste low tops. Her hair was down and she looked anxious.

"Do you want to try the cafe next to the hotel on the corner or would you prefer to go somewhere else?" Sadie asked.

"Erm." I said and paused for a second to mull it over. "I think the cafe on the corner will suffice." I replied jokingly, even though this wasn't a time to be joking around. Right at this very moment her sister could be in grave danger and the look Sadie gave me told me not to mess around, she was ready for business.

We passed through the hotel, the hotel clerk momentarily looked up and nodded before going back to whatever it was that had her undivided attention. I nodded back, to no avail. By the time I nodded her head was back down.

There were two entrances to the cafe, a front entrance, and an inner one. The inner entrance was only to be used by guests at the hotel who wanted to eat in the cafe. The cafe was called Carla's; their slogan, Peace, Love, and Food. Everything in it was organic, even the assistants.

Inside it was clinically clean. As soon as a guest departed, an assistant would appear straight away as if by magic with a cloth in one hand and a spray bottle in the other to clear away the plates and cutlery and to wipe the table clean.

Again we used our cavemen instincts and chose the table furthest from both doors. The tables were pine, the chairs were pine with chequered cushions, and the counter was stainless steel and glass, polished so that it was gleaming. Underfoot were cream coloured foot square tiles, the walls were adorned with framed pictures of Carla's classics, or so the captions said underneath. On display inside the counter behind the glass were all types of nut yoghurts in small glass tumblers, carrot cakes, cheese cakes, and massive slabs of fruit cakes with nuts inside. There were a few savoury exhibits, if that's what you can call Quorn rolls and pies.

There seemed to be no dress code for the staff other than a shiny green pinafore with the word Carla's printed in a fancy black script across the chest, then underneath that it said Peace, Love, and Food in a plain style script. There were three assistants working in the shop. One was a woman of about twenty eight with a shiny face and mousey brown hair pulled back so tight in a ponytail it looked like she was undergoing a homemade face-lift. She wore faded stone washed denims, a blue striped T-shirt and battered pair of hippy style sandals. Her toenails were a freshly painted turquoise.

The other two assistants were both male, and both in their early twenties. But that was where the similarities ended. One was black with dreadlocks half way down his back, scooped up into a loose ponytail, the other was Caucasian with a receding hairline shaved close to the bone. The Rasta had on a pair of blue nylon track pants and a Zimbabwe national football shirt, the white guy had on a pair of grey chinos and a blue shirt unbuttoned at the neck. The Rasta wore a plain pair of sneakers, and the white guy wore brown moccasins, both represented two opposite ends of the realm.

I walked to the counter.

"Can I have two breakfasts please?"

"Are you guests from the hotel?" the Rasta asked.

"Yeah we are." I answered.

He must have seen us enter from the hotel entrance.

"Can I take your room number?" he asked as he reached under the counter and retrieved a long black plate with an organic platter on it. The platter consisted of nut yoghurt, a slab of fruit and nut cake, a chunk of spicy cheese, a slice of cold meat, a crusty bap and a singular serving of butter.

"One—two—four." I said. "There's two of us."

"Okay." he said and retrieved another plate of platter from underneath the counter. He placed the two plates on top of the counter; and then he turned away from me and marked off the number 124 in a register next to the till. "There is bacon and eggs over there if you want them and tea and coffee over here." He pointed to two areas, one directly behind me and one behind me and to the left.

"Okay thanks." I replied scooping the two long plates up and making my way over to the table where Sadie was waiting with a smile.

I plonked the two plates on to the table and asked Sadie which she preferred, tea or coffee. Then I walked back over to the tea and coffee serving area. I spooned some ground coffee into a flask and filled it with hot water. The reaction from the ground coffee beans to the hot water filled my nostrils with a heavenly scent, and I love the smell of freshly brewing coffee in the morning. I waited a couple of minutes before deploying the plunger, scooped up two coffee cups with one forefinger. It was a big flask, so by my reckoning it would give us three cups each which would be enough stimulants for the time being. I didn't want caffeine to gatecrash my stoned buzz. I made my way back over to the table furthest from the doors and scooched in across from Sadie.

"This looks nice." she said as I made myself comfortable.

"Yeah it looks it." I said, eyeing the area the assistant had pointed to when referring to where the eggs and bacon were. It was a small pine table on wheels; the wheels were all scuffed and nicked from regular use. On top of the table was what looked like a metal box with a hinged lid on a metal grid platform. Underneath the platform there were about twenty tea lights, all lit, all fluttering gently.

I picked up the slice of spicy cheese and took a bite, mockingly crossing myself as I bit into it. It surprised me, it was nice, the spicy chunks inside the cheese were hot and that was fine by me. With food, the hotter the better as far as I'm concerned. I took a bite out of everything just to try it, it wasn't for me, I like my plates to look like a massacre has happened when I have finished eating, not just a few crumbs. So I excused myself and went over to where the bacon was hiding and helped myself to three rashers and a small plate full of scrambled eggs.

I trudged back over to where Sadie was busily gnawing away at the vegetarian platter.

"So you've heard nothin' from your Stella?" I asked her as I sat back down, directly across from her.

She shook her head in reply as she took a bite out of the sandwich she had concocted from the bap, the piece of cheese, and the slice of cold meat.

"No voicemail, nothing." she replied, covering her mouth with her delicate fingers in between words. After swallowing the mouthful she carried on. "I don't know what to think Kev, do you?"

I shook my head and started to concoct my own sandwich out of the rashers of the bap, the bacon and the scrambled egg, saying,

"Neither do I, but if it's totally out of character . . ."

"Which it is." Sadie interrupted.

"Which it is," I echoed, "then something must have happened to her. I don't like coincidences, especially not when they turn up in scenarios like this one, y' know what I mean."

Sadie nodded.

I wolfed down the remainder of my breakfast, washing it down with the dregs from the flask. I waited until the assistant had cleared and wiped the table before I spoke again.

"So what do you think we should do?" I was thinking out loud.

"I don't know, I mean, where do you start with something like this?"

I shrugged my shoulders.

"How did you find me?" she asked me and then looked away, the pain of it all still too close to even contemplate thinking about.

"I had a little help." I replied.

Sadie gave me a look that said I'm waiting.

"Well you know the two Russians I told you about, Mik and Dim."

She nodded.

"When you went missin' I didn't know where to start so I followed the only clue I had, which was a Chinese takeaway I knew had connections with the gang who had taken you. So I went to it and searched the place. It was empty, just a shell. Nothing in it that would lead me to you except a phone started ringing so

I waited for it to stop, dialled one-four-seven-one and took the number down. When it became clear I wasn't goin' to find any leads inside the house I used the number left on the phone to find you."

"How?"

There it was. The sixty-four thousand dollar, one word, mono-syllable question, the question I couldn't answer, not even if a million dollars were up for grabs.

"I rang one of the Russians and gave him the phone number and he did all the rest."

"How?" she asked again.

"I don't know for sure, well I do know that you can buy a device that can listen in to phone calls, provided you're within range. But for someone to locate a phone out of the blue like that, that's some pretty sophisticated equipment you'd need. The only people I know of that can do stuff like that are the police or the military."

"So you think your friends involved the police to find me?"

"I don't know for sure, both of them are ex-military. Maybe they still have connections. Other than that I haven't gotta clue."

"Can you ring them and ask them to locate Stella's phone?"

"I've tried a couple of times to contact them since we arrived. No luck. And anyway if something has happened the phone has got to be on to be able to track it. Which it wouldn't be if they had her. When you went missing I used their number, remember."

Sadie said she remembered.

There was a couple of minutes silence as we both thought about our options. I came to the conclusion we didn't have any. There was only one way to go from here and that was to go back home and find her, simple as that. How we did it was another matter, it needed planning properly or we would just be running around like Mike the headless chicken, and not get anywhere with it.

I needed my phone; I searched for it in my various pockets without success.

"What are you looking for?" Sadie asked.

"My phone." I answered patting everywhere there was a pocket, double checking. "I must have left it back in the room. Give me five minutes. I'll make some calls and I'll be back down."

"Okay. I need the toilet, so say we meet up back in the hotel foyer in five minutes."

"Make it ten." I said as I scraped the chair back on the tiles and headed for the door. I needed a shit.

10

I saw the maid from the cartoons again on my way up to the room. I nodded to her, she nodded back as I passed her in the long corridor between the lift and the door to the room. She was in exactly the same position as before which I thought was a bit weird.

Once behind the door I retrieved my phone from where it was—laid on the bed. I had six missed calls from an unknown number and the icon in the top left hand corner of the screen told me I had at least one voicemail. I dialled my voicemail to hear the automated voice tell me I had one voice message. It was Dim. His now familiar Russian robotic growl filled the airwaves with menace, and my ears with dread.

"It'z me, you don't have to worry about the Chinese any more we took the whole lot of them out last night for Mik." Dim said. Now Dim was a lot of things but I never had him down as the bearer of glad tidings. Wonders will never cease. He went on, "This number will be in operation for two weeks. If I don't hear from you in that time then this is goodbye my friend. If you want work when you arrive back in country then keep in touch."

The phone went dead; the message was short but so very sweet. I looked at the screen. It was back to its default setting.

I blew out a huge sigh. Now with that out of the way there was one less thing to worry about; now I was free to concentrate on trying to find Sadie's sister. I hurried down to the foyer and was greeted by a beaming Sadie. Her whole face was lit up like the Manhattan sky-line at midnight.

"She's just got in touch now, she lost her phone." she said as I reached her.

I exhaled loudly. Phew, thank fuck for that I thought.

"Thank God for that." I said.

I was off the hook for the time being.

"Oh yes I almost forgot." Sadie said, linking arms with me and walking me out onto the street. "Someone has rung up about the house; they have arranged a viewing for tomorrow night. Stella said they sounded pretty keen, so hopefully if everything goes alright they might put a bid in straight away. By this time Friday I could be house and debt free."

"Are you sure you want to do this Sadie?" I said and passed on the message Dim had left me on my voicemail.

I let her digest it for a while as we walked.

I broke the silence.

"Now you have an option, you don't have to sell if you don't want to." I said.

"Like I said before, it gave me the kick up the back-side I needed. There's no reason for me to be there. None of my family lives there anymore. Plus I don't want to live in an area where that kind of thing is happening right under my nose and yet know nothing about it. It's not a place where I want be, if you know what I mean."

"Nobody ever knows what happens behind closed doors do they?" I said cryptically.

"That's true." Sadie replied.

We were now walking down the street where the little Irish bar was located. I was thirsty and in need of a drink, alcoholic or otherwise I wasn't fussed. Plus as well as being close, the Irish bar had another thing going for it, it was one of the few bars in the city that allowed you to consume cannabis inside their establishment. It goes without saying we wasn't planning on straying far.

"I don't know about you but I could do with a good drink." Sadie said as we drew level with the Irish bar. It was as though she was reading my mind.

The bar was open but you could only just tell, what with it being sparsely lit. I had to duck down, cast my hand over my brow and squint to see if there was any movement inside. I saw that there was some movement behind the bar, but between the bar's gloomy light and the glare on the glass outside I couldn't tell if it was the laughing barmaid from the previous night or not. I bit the bullet and pushed the door open. Sadie followed close behind. I made for the bar with a delectable shadow in tow.

A couple of steps in and we'd left the noise of the street behind—the chatter and the rustle of fabric, the diesel clatter of taxis and buses, the electric whine of the trams, the footsteps and the constant tinny thud, thud, thud as bikes passed by with their tyres bumping up and down on the flagstone slabs, the footsteps, like soldiers marching at the end of a long tab and the occasional jingle of a bike's bell—they were all gone as soon as the door swung shut behind us. It was like walking into a cowboy movie, except the place was empty apart from the barmaid, and I'd traded boots and Stetsons for a pair of Nikes and a hoodie.

It wasn't the barmaid from the night before. The new barmaid was of similar age as the laughing barmaid but that was it as far as similarities went, the two barmaids were like chalk and cheese, yin and yang.

There was no way of knowing without asking her—and attracting unwanted attention to ourselves—about how much she knew about the protection racket that was operating in the area, plus there was no way of knowing if she knew about the trouble the night before. I quickly decided she was here on a need to know basis and it was best for all concerned if I said nothing.

She greeted me with a smile as I approached the bar. Sadie carried on walking, and I guessed she was making her way to the smoke room. I watched as her peaches wiggled and jiggled as the weight shifted from her left leg to her right. It was with great reluctance that I turned away. I sighed as my fingertips touched the bar because it was such a heavenly sight I'd turned away from. I turned my attention back towards the barmaid as Sadie struggled with the sliding door.

"Hi, can I have a bottle of house red please and two glasses?"

She nodded and smiled then spun away to retrieve the wine.

Sadie was inside the smoke room now and was making her way to the bench at the far end of the room. The one that was situated the furthest from the door, again pre-historic instincts subconsciously making the decisions without consulting as it came natural, without thought.

The new barmaid was slim with very curly, auburn hair, either it was natural or she spent hours every morning getting it just right. I would put my money on it being natural, because it isn't justifiable that a working girl has that much time to spend on herself, let alone her hair. She had on a pair of woodland camouflage cargo pants, a simple ribbed blue T-shirt with a V-neck, and she wore two gold sleepers in each ear. She put her index finger to her lips while she studied the wine bottles, she settled on a bottle of Stowells. After she had reached underneath the bar and retrieved two multi-faceted cut crystal wine glasses and plonked them on the bar in front of me she proceeded to open the wine. After she had opened it she gestured to me with the bottle to ask whether or not I wanted her to pour it.

"No that's okay." I replied. "I'll do it." Meaning I would pour the drinks.

"That will be seven guilders please."

I gave her a twenty guilder note and told her to keep the change. I was in a particularly good mood, and I wanted to spread the happiness with small bills. I spun away from the bar and headed towards the smoke room. I heard some background music open up as I reached the door to the smoking room. It was U2's Trip Through Your Wires, one of my all time favourites.

"I was broken, bent outta shape, I was naked in the clothes you made." Bono crooned as I reached the door. "Lips were dry, throat like rust, you gave me shelter from the heat and the dust."

In the background The Edge was weaving his magic.

It was now ten o'clock, at least that's what the clock on the wall was saying. I gave the door a gentle tap with my foot and it slid open easily, I had it cracked, backed up and ready to roll.

Sadie looked up from her task in hand, which was at this moment in time sprinkling tobacco onto the rolling papers, and with a quizzical look on her face asked "How do you do that? Everybody struggles with it, even the staff, yet you walk up to it and it slides open." Her brow furrowed as she echoed "How do you do it?"

"Instead of struggling with the handle I just give it a gentle kick like this." I said spinning round and closing the door with a deft flick of the foot.

"Oh right, I see now." Sadie said as I made my way down what constituted a long narrow wooden box that was partitioned off from the rest of the bar. It might be the management passing on a subtle message, something along the lines of keep smoking in this long wooden box and you will end up in one, I thought to myself as I plonked the two glasses and the bottle of wine onto the nearest table to us. I shrugged off my hoodie and draped it over the nearest chair and then sprawled on the bench. I was half laid, half sat up. Sadie was just putting the finishing touches to the joint as I poured the drinks.

I scooched over to Sadie on the bench at the back and handed her one of the three-quarter full glasses of wine. We chinked glasses, making a toast to the both of us, and I took a long slug on the thick red liquid. Not the way you are supposed to drink it, granted, but I needed it after the twenty-four hours we'd just had. I felt like a death row prisoner given a last minute stay of execution.

"Here's to us." I said, as I took another slug.

"To us." Sadie echoed and took a sip.

I watched her as her head ducked down, and she jammed two hands into her handbag. Her hair fell forward partly obscuring her profile. Just the tip of her nose and the bumps of her lips were visible. It was enough to make me shudder like someone had just walked over my grave. When she came back up for much needed air after scouring her handbag for the lighter she had the joint dangling from those luscious lips. She gave me a wink as she lit the joint, the baggy end bit flared for a second until the tobacco and weed caught on. She took a long hard pull on it, letting the smoke bellow out of her mouth before sucking it back in.

"I've been thinking." Sadie said, taking another pull on the joint. "About what I said when we thought Stella had been kidnapped."

"Or yeah." I said. "I've been dreadin' this." I paused for a second to take the joint from Sadie's outstretched hand. "Go on."

I double pulled on the joint, enough to start it off spitting and popping, the thin paper fizzing as it burnt evenly down both sides. I was in my element here; let's hope Sadie's news was good news.

"I'm prepared to go with the flow for now. But I am telling you if you ever put me or any of my family in danger again either directly or indirectly it's over, no ifs no buts, it's over, okay."

"Okay." I replied.

I took another hit and relaxed my stomach muscles as I sprawled out again. Ah this was the life. I love that period in-between the smoking of a joint and feeling the effects of it. It's a mixture of anticipation, excitement, and the fear of the unknown.

During the ten years of my voluntary solitary confinement my inhibitions had laid foundations and built solid walls to defend, but as the weed crept up on me those foundations they started to weaken, and the walls began to crumble. Within three and a half minutes the weed had my inhibitions wrestled to the ground, hooded, and tied up and tucked up in the boot of its car. I wasn't going to move very far over the next six hours or so, that was clear.

I passed the joint back over to Sadie. Pretty normal day then, up to now.

11

*T*he minute hand had just completed a full circuit on the clock on the wall, I watched it as it made its way round, it was now one minute past ten, things were about to change, I could feel it in the air and in my bones, I could sense it, I could reach out and almost touch it.

It was the sudden ceasing of the pedestrian traffic outside that initially alerted me to the fact that something was going down outside. From where I was sat I could see very little of the street outside as there was a net curtain covering the bottom half of the bars one and only window. All I could see were the top halves of people bobbing up and down as they walked by. Some looked inside, and some didn't. The pedestrian traffic went from being constant to non-existent in a split second, a sure sign that there was something about to happen. My spider senses were tingling, and I had a bad feeling about the whole situation as it started to unfold in front of my eyes.

At first it was just two men entering the bar. Both of them walked in together, one after the other, in single file. I spotted them straight away for what they were, plain clothed policemen. They're as easy to spot in Holland as they are in England. They stuck out like sore thumbs the minute they stepped over the threshold and into the bar. It was like they were still wearing a uniform even though they were supposed to be out of one.

The two men walked up to the bar and engaged in a conversation with the barmaid.

"Everything okay."

It was Sadie.

"Yeah, yeah I'm fine." I replied, still maintaining visual contact with the two men. "So what's the plan for today. Are we planning on doin' anythin' or are we just gonna get drunk. 'cos either way suits me fine."

The door swung open again, this time a man and a woman entered the bar. Same routine as the two men who came before them, one after the other, in single file—only this time the man stayed by the door with his back to it. He stood at ease and with his hands clasped behind his back. The group looked to be all similar in age, all late twenties early thirties, except for the man stood near the door, he was in his late forties with dishevelled, greying, receding hair. He was also dressed different to the others; it was as though he'd given up the fight trying to blend in, knowing it was a lost cause, and just decided to dress like a stereotypical plain-clothed cop. He had on beige slacks, brown loafers and a plain white shirt unbuttoned at the neck, there was a loosely tied tie dangling from the collar, and he was wearing a Columbo style rain mac, minus the creases.

The first two who came in were similarly dressed in black jeans and black jumpers, and black Doc Martens. The woman had on a pair of beige cargo pants and a red Adidas hoodie, her hair was tied back in a bun, on her feet were a pair Nike high tops that looked too clean to be street. All these factors kept on piling up, enough for me to be switched on to the situation in hand. I quickly weighed up my options. I didn't have any. The only exit I was sure of was now being guarded by the man by the door, and there were three people between me and him, so escape and evade if need to wasn't an option. I had to stand and fight my corner.

I saw the barmaid first, and then the two men look in my direction. Fuck, what did they want? Surely this whole set-up wasn't for me? One of the men turned away and nodded to the man guarding the door. The man guarding the door nodded back.

"What do you think Kev?" Sadie said, though I had no idea what she was on about. With my full undivided attention on the goings on in the bar I had only caught the tail-end of what she had said.

I turned to her and said, "Sorry I was miles away, what did you say?"

"I said we could go on one of those moonlit canal boat tours later if you fancy it."

"Yeah, yeah, that would be good." I replied distractedly not really knowing what she had said or what I was signing myself up for. I was too engrossed in the scene playing out in the bar.

The barmaid and the first two through the door were talking again; one of the men was leaning on the bar and blatantly staring at the contours of her breasts through her T-shirt, the other one was scribbling something down in a little black notebook. The man finished whatever he was scribbling and tucked his notepad into the back pocket of his jeans. He turned to where we were sat in the smoke room, said something to his partner, and they both made for us.

Here we go.

They struggled with the door, until they finally had it open wide enough to squeeze through. As they reached us the lead man pulled out a black leather wallet and flipped it open. It had his warrant card and photo on one side and a gold badge with scrolling around an illustrated centre circle; it had two scrolls wrapped around the top and one scroll wrapped around the bottom.

There was no doubt in my mind that it was a police badge of some sort, possibly a detective one.

"I'm Jan Smit; this is Edgar Van de Berg." the man said in broken English, with an unmistakeable Dutch twang to it.

The second man flipped out his own ID. It was as though it had been rehearsed a thousand times, which it probably had, as well as another thousand times for real, like now.

"We're investigating a murder that happened not far from here last night. Were you in the area?" Smit asked.

The second man stayed silent.

I looked over to Sadie and raised my eyebrows at her before answering,

"Yes, yes, we were, we were drinking in here last night." I said. "'Til about half past ten, and then we made our way back to the hotel. You don't think we have anythin' to do with it do you?" I said as calmly as I could.

"I don't know do I, but I'm afraid I'm going to have to ask you to make a statement. We can either do it here or at the station it's entirely up to you. Don't worry, we're interviewing everyone in the area, and this is natural for us to be able to eliminate you from our enquiries." Smit said.

"What, both of us?" I asked.

"I'm afraid so." Smit said sullenly.

I definitely didn't want to go to the station, so I said,

"Here's fine."

"My partner will take your . . ." Smit paused looking over to Sadie, allowing me to fill in the gap for him.

"Girlfriend." I said.

He continued, "My partner will take your girlfriend's statement and I will take yours. Do you mind if I take a seat?"

"No, go ahead." I said. "Be my guest."

He scraped a chair out from under the table closest to me, while his partner ushered Sadie to the other end of the smoke room and sat across from her at the first table on the left hand side. I saw him reach into his jeans pocket and pull out two Polaroid photographs and then my attention was grabbed by Smit.

"I'd like you to have a look at these photographs to see if you recognise any of the men in them." Smit said.

He too retrieved two Polaroids from his back pocket; they were slightly creased in the middle and round the edges. He placed them on the table, fanning them out slightly so I could see both faces clearly. The images of the two men's faces hit me like a buck shot to the brain. It was the two racketeers from the night before, the skinhead who I'd hit and his boss. Shit. Surely the skinhead hadn't died from his injuries. If he had I was fucked.

I pretended to muse over the photographs before saying,

"No, I've never seen them before." I lied, knowing Sadie would say the same thing as a sort of back up. The only difference was she was telling the truth, I wasn't. I knew I was taking a big gamble, lying. But it was one I was willing to take given the circumstances.

"Are you sure?"

I gave the photographs another once over laying my index finger at the bottom of each one before saying,

"Yeah, I'm sure." I said flicking each photograph towards him.

I saw Sadie shaking her head; probably in response to the same question I had just been asked.

I played dumb, and stayed silent while he pulled his black notebook from the opposite pocket to where he had pulled the photographs from. He left the photographs where they were, with the two men's eyes staring up at me. He freed the little pencil which was held in place by a loop of elastic and then said,

"You said you were drinking in here 'til about . . . , what time did you say you left?"

Automatically my eyes shifted to the left, and then I looked down whilst stroking my chin.

"I think we got back to the hotel around eleven, so I guess it would have been a quarter to when we left here." I replied.

"Which hotel?"

"Belle View, the one on the corner near . . ."

"It's okay." Smit said nodding. "I know it."

I saw his pupils dilate ever so slightly as he realised we were in the area at the time of the murder. I saw him pick up the scent literally and then follow its lead.

"You didn't go anywhere else?"

"What do you mean?"

"From here, did you go straight to the hotel?"

"Yeah." I said. "We did."

"And your . . . girlfriend will say the same will she?" Smit said.

Our eyes locked, and I saw another flicker of recognition in his. He was switched on, I could tell. He was young, and he still had that steely determination about him which some of his older counterparts lose after years of dealing with the terrible things human beings do to each other, it comes with the job and with the territory.

"Why wouldn't she?" I said.

He scribbled something down, probably the name of the hotel or something else, I couldn't see as he had his arm curved round the pad.

"As well as your girlfriend, the clerk at the hotel will verify your story will she?" Smit said, his eyes locking onto mine like heat seeking missiles.

I nodded in reply.

"What nationality are you? British?" Smit said. He spat the word British out as though it was somehow tainting his mouth.

"English" I said, not breaking eye contact.

"How long are you here for?"

"Two weeks."

"Two weeks." he echoed and scribbled something else down.

There was a couple of minutes' silence, a chance for me to collect my thoughts. What implications if any would this new development have on me? If the skinhead had died of his injuries then I was sure I would be doing jail time before long. I played it cool and relaxed a little. See, I'd realised the only person that could make the connection between me and the dead guy was the laughing barmaid and the local boss. And I was sure that given the right incentive I could persuade her to forget all about the night before. All I had to do was keep calm, answer the questions in a polite manner and that would be phase one completed. Phase two would be to locate the laughing barmaid; phase three would be to persuade her.

The local boss was a different kettle of fish altogether, either he would seek revenge or he would slink back under the stone he had crawled from. I hoped it would be the latter.

"What is the nature of your visit?" Smit said, breaking the relative silence.

I shifted my eyes to the left again, just in case he was as switched on as I thought he was.

"Pleasure." I replied.

I glanced over to Sadie and the other detective, they were just finishing up, and the cop was rising to his feet. Sadie stayed where she was, she looked over to me and I gave her a reassuring wink and a shrug of my shoulders, as if to say what the fuck is happening here? She threw back an equally quizzical look, as if to say I don't know. Though she didn't know it, she was my alibi.

Smit flipped his notepad shut, secured the pencil in the little elastic loop at the side, and said,

"I think that will do for now." he said and got to his feet, nodding to his partner, who started to make his way over to us.

"Have you got a cellphone I can contact you on if I need to?" Smit asked.

I gave him my number; he programmed it into his phone. In the background the air conditioning kicked in, whining at first before settling into a steady flow. Almost instantly the air turned icy cold. I shivered as I erupted in gooseflesh.

I wanted to take advantage of the slack laws regarding soft drug use and seeing as though the interview was over I thought to myself why not.

"Do you mind if I . . ." I said and gestured to the materials scattered messily on the table.

Smit looked puzzled. Van de Berg had reached him now and was hanging on his shoulder.

I mimed rolling a joint using both hands so there was no mistaking what I meant.

Smit nodded sternly and then turned to his partner. He pulled Van de Berg to one side and they conferred for a couple of minutes, while I busied myself sticking the Rizlas together. It was a weird feeling, rolling a joint in front of a copper but it was something I felt compelled to do. I watched the two detectives out of the corner of my eye; they were like ventriloquist and dummy, Smit being the ventriloquist and Van de Berg the dummy. Smit talked and Van de Berg nodded, then Van de Berg talked whilst Smit nodded. Together they made a good double act, like Ray Allen and Lord Charles.

I snapped about three quarters of the cigarette off, leaving about half an inch on the filter, licked it down the crease and peeled a thin strip of paper off to allow me to get to the tobacco. I sprinkled it evenly over the Rizla paper whilst watching the two detectives. They seemed to be disagreeing over something. There were no raised voices or anything, I just got a gut feeling. Their body language and eye contact with each other spoke volumes.

As Smit turned back to face my way I saw Van de Berg mouth the words "It's your call". Smit nodded and then made a move back towards where I was sat. Sadie was still sat at the table at the far end of the smoke room. She had her phone out and it was stuck to her ear. She was smiling, which is always a good sign. I was just putting the finishing touches to the joint as Smit reached me. Sadie caught my eye and mouthed the words Stella and smiled. I smiled back and then turned slightly to face Smit as he reached me.

"We're going to need to talk to you again at some point, to verify your statement, then as long as it holds up you're in the clear." he said as he reached me.

I nodded to him in response. I lit the joint and disappeared momentarily from his view, consumed by the smoke cloud I'd created. I was in my element here, anywhere else in the world the very thought of what I was doing would be ludicrous, but here it was as normal as bacon and eggs.

"Yeah, yeah, whatever." I replied. "You've got my number."

Smit then rejoined Van de Berg and they left the smoke room. They both nodded to Sadie as they passed her. She smiled at them both, placing her palm over the mic while she did so. Sadie stayed where she was for a couple of more minutes talking on the phone. I smoked while I waited for her to return, taking big hits and double drags until it was half way down. The air conditioning struggled to cope with the influx of smoke, until finally the room was clear again and the joint was propped in the ashtray waiting for its owner.

Sadie joined me at the table where I was sat at the far end of the room. She picked up the half smoked joint, lit it and took a hit off it.

"That was a bit weird wasn't it?"

"You can say that again" I replied.

She had one hand palm flat on my shoulder; the other was draped around my neck. She was so close I could feel her warm breath on my neck as she nuzzled in, kissing and teasing my neck and ear with her lips and tongue. I turned to face her and I could feel a warmness inside.

Little did I know her life would be on the line again, in less than forty eight hours and counting.

12

I picked up the nip bag of weed between thumb and forefinger and shook it to reveal its meagre contents, the few buds that were left danced around in the bag like tumbleweeds caught in a prairie twister.

"We need to replenish our supplies." I said.

Sadie nodded in response and then said,

"Oh by the way, that was Stella on the phone. Just letting me know the house is spic and span ready for tonight's viewing. She said the potential buyers are due to arrive around seven. So we should know how it went by about a quarter to nine our time." She paused for a second to take another hit, sucked the excess smoke back into her mouth, and held it in for a couple of seconds before blowing it out upwards towards the vents. She giggled to herself and then said, "She has even baked bread so the house smells welcoming. And she has took her percolator to make coffee for when they arrive, can you believe it?"

I shook my head in response.

We had hardly touched the bottle of wine, plus it was a screw-top not a cork so on our way out I asked the barmaid if she would put it to one side while we did a bit of sightseeing. I slipped her ten guilders as a softener; she gathered up the note and slipped it into the big side pocket of her cargo pants, smiled and then tucked the bottle away somewhere under the bar.

* * *

As we stepped back out onto the street a whale's skeleton stretched out in front of us across the sky in the form of clouds, it was one of the most beautiful cloud formations I have ever seen, beautiful but savage and we stood there for a few seconds watching it stretch further and further until it resembled nothing at all, only candy floss.

It was all hustle and bustle out here, so we fought our way to the nearest coffee shop, which turned out to be only two streets away. Result.

Another thing struck me whilst in Amsterdam was that while every coffee shop sold their own strains of cannabis, and in some cases different breeds altogether, when you walked past a coffee shop you got the same generic weed smell no matter where you were. I pondered on my notion while we walked the short distance from the bar to the coffee shop, but I couldn't come up with a reasonable explanation to satisfy my curious mind, so I tossed it to one side for the time being.

This new coffee shop was more like a sports bar, with two rows of tables running down both left hand, and right hand walls. Each booth had its own little flat screen TV embedded in the wall. There was nothing on the table apart from a cheap silver disposable ashtray, it had two grooves opposite each other on the rim, and there were a few roach ends crushed in it.

All the paintwork in the place was old and dated, and chipped. All the wood-work in the place was peppered in nicks, and it was in need of a sixty minute makeover but I thought it best to keep that to myself. But apart from that it was clean and tidy, and it was virtually empty, another good reason to choose it.

The table furthest from the door had already been taken, so I got hold of Sadie's hand and we made for the next one in, at the far end of the room, on the left hand side. The seats were bolted to the floor, and then attached to the table so I waited for Sadie to make herself comfortable, and then I slid in next to her part flustered and part shocked by the goings on in the bar earlier. I still couldn't believe the skinhead had died from his injuries. Something must have happened to him after leaving the bar, and if it had I was determined to find out what it was. My freedom counted on it. I needed Sadie on side to stand any chance of finding anything out, that was for sure. I had to bite the bullet and tell her about the shenanigans in the bar the night before. This wasn't going to be easy. Here I am in the last chance saloon as far as Sadie is concerned and already confessing to manslaughter.

After we made ourselves comfortable I said,

"Do you want a coffee? Or a hot chocolate?"

"I think I'm going to try a hot chocolate please." Sadie replied, smiling, that cheeky, gorgeous smile of hers. The one where her whole face lights up and her eyes twinkle.

"Do you want squirty cream on it?" I said hoping, she got the euphemism.

"Yes please." she said nodding, and smiling. There was a glint in her eye you couldn't mistake—she had got it alright.

I made my way over to the counter/bar; I could see it had a misted glass vase perched on the left hand side of it with a bunch of freshly cut Kingsblood tulips poking out from the top like blood spattered blades of grass.

Behind the counter/bar was the campest man I'd ever seen. I could only see him from the waist up, but that was enough. He had on a pink silk shirt; open necked, with at least three of the buttons undone. Poking out from behind his shirt was a white cravat. His head was shaved close to the bone, and he had two studs in either eyebrow, and one in his left ear lobe.

He smiled, maybe he was hoping for some action, or maybe he was just glad of the passing business. Again I hoped it was the latter.

"Hi." he said.

And as soon as he opened his mouth my suspicions were confirmed. I would stake my life that he was gay.

I nodded as I reached the counter/bar.

"I'm the proprietor, my friends call me Jan."

He paused for a second so I said, "Hi Jan."

"What can I get you?"

"I'll have two hot chocolates with the squirty cream, and can I have a look at your weed menu please?"

"Yes sure." he said, and slid a piece of laminated A4 paper to me. He then turned round and busied himself making our hot chocolates. He was singing while he worked, I caught the tune; it was Alexander O'Neal's Criticize. As he turned round he belted out, "All you wanna do is criticize."

He then smiled as he plonked the two cups onto the counter/bar in front of me.

He lifted his chin and eyebrows up as if to say what else would you like? His stud glinted in the light as it caught it momentarily.

I glanced down to look at the menu, and didn't need to look far, I said tossing the menu back to him,

"Can I have three grams of blueberry please?"

Jan nodded and spun on his heels to retrieve the correct Tupperware box with the blueberry in it. There was a shelf behind the counter/bar with about twenty five reasonably sized Tupperware boxes all stacked on top of each other, five rows, all of them were five deep.

All the Tupperware boxes were half full of different types of weed. Amsterdam is a smoker's paradise. See here they can legally grow it, which in turn means they have been able to learn from their mistakes within the growing process. Whereas in England say, where it is illegal to cultivate it, the growers have to keep looking over their shoulders the whole time, plus they have to up sticks and move camp regularly—they have to so they can keep one step ahead of the authorities. Unless you're lucky enough to set something up like Ally and Craig did—they were virtually untouchable, until I arrived on the scene and fucked things up for them both.

Jan retrieved the correct Tupperware box with the blueberry in it, spun back round, popped the lid off the box then proceeded to shake the buds from the box onto a set of electronic scales, which were positioned underneath the Tupperware boxes and next to the till on the shiny work top. He stopped shaking the buds a little over the three gram mark. He stood back with his hands out as if to say here take a look. So I leant in to have a look at the blood red digits. I nodded to him, to let him know I'd seen that it was the correct weight. Jan then picked up the scales and awkwardly tipped the buds into a medium sized nip bag. That was another thing about Amsterdam—nobody touched the weed with their fingers. It made sense to me because the more it was handled the less of the pollen remained on the buds for the consumer to smoke.

He placed the nip bag on the counter/bar and slid it over to me with his fingertips still resting on it.

"That will be twenty seven guilders please." Jan said.

I dipped my hand into my pocket and pulled out a small bill fold, peeled off three ten guilder notes and handed them over to Jan. He spun round again and minced his way over to the till still singing,

"You've just closed your mind, ooh oooh ooooh . . . criticize."

Jan spun back round and tried to hand me my three guilders change. I waved him away.

He thanked me and I headed back to Sadie with the two mugs of hot chocolate and the nip bag of weed. The two mugs wobbled in the saucers and as I walked they rattled and chinked, the squirty cream was piled high and spilling over the rim.

Sadie had already set the Rizlas up when I reached the table so I plonked the two mugs and saucers on the table and slid the nip bag over to her.

She looked up and said,

"Thanks."

I sat opposite Sadie, watching her concentrated face as she nipped and manipulated the Rizla. When she had finished rolling the joint, I reached for my cup and ran a finger round the outside of it to catch the overspill of cream. Sadie saw what I was doing and did the same thing, but she made it look sensuous. As she slipped her finger in and out of her mouth, I shuddered as I imagined that it was me and not her finger she was sucking.

I shook my head to rid myself of the image that was occupying precious head space, there was a time and a place for these type of thoughts; it was time to get in character.

"I need to tell you something." I said as I took the head off the froth.

Sadie handed me the joint saying,

"You light it babe, what's up?"

I took it and did the honours. It flared up for a second until the tobacco and cannabis mix caught on. The lit end of it was popping and fizzing, like a fly on a zapper. My hands were clammy, like I had just taken off rubber gloves, and I had butterflies in my stomach fluttering around and making me want to retch. I had goose bumps on my arms, and the hair on the back of my neck was standing on end. My tongue was stuck fast to the roof of my mouth, and the hot chocolate was still too hot to take a meaningful drink of it. I was in no man's land.

"You look like you've seen a ghost."

I laughed nervously.

"It's funny you should say that." I said and took another hit off the joint, holding the smoke in for a while, whilst I took another sip. I blew the smoke out after swallowing the scalding liquid and continued,

"Those two police officers who came to the bar just now."

"What about them?" As she spoke the words, she pulled a face in puzzlement.

I glanced to my right, just as the coffee shop door opened; three new age hippy types stepped over the threshold into the coffee shop. All were white males, middle class. Two out of the three had dreadlocks, or at least their poor attempts at dreadlocks. I don't know why but when white people wear their hair in dreadlocks to me it is a waste of time, it just looks dirty. The third one had his hair pulled back in a greasy pony tail. None of them looked as though they'd had the pleasure of acquainting with soap in the last six months. All of them had at least two weeks growth on their faces, but it was all for show. They were upper class rich kids on a kick. It was their footwear that gave it away for me. For they all had on top of the range Timberland boots, and they were all brand new, straight from the shop, you could tell. Dreadlock One had on a pair of black skinny jeans and a grey and orange tie-dyed saggy T-shirt. To top off his dowdy range he was wearing a green and blue checked tweed jacket, the type farmers wear. Dreadlock Two had on a pair of three-quarter urban camouflage cargo pants, and a pair of thick woollen walking socks rolled down to the tip of his boots, a plain black T-shirt, and a thick black and grey flecked cashmere type cardigan. The cardigan was old and ragged, like a tramps beard. The ponytailed new age hippy was wearing a pair of shredded Levi's, and a fluffy black knitted jumper, with a non-descript T-shirt underneath.

They shuffled their way listlessly to the counter/bar, that's when I lost interest in them and turned back to Sadie. She was smiling with her chin propped up in the palms of her hands. She didn't deserve this, and I didn't deserve her.

"The two men in the photographs."

Sadie was nodding slightly in recognition.

"They showed up at the bar last night." I said and paused letting her slowly digest what I had just told her.

After a couple of seconds contemplation she said,

"When? I didn't see them."

"Just before we left. Can you remember, I went to the toilet, and then when I came out I knocked on the window and said I'd be two minutes. I think you were doing the crossword or reading one of those leaflets."

"Yes, yes I remember that."

"Well, the two men, like I said showed up at the bar. They were giving the barmaid a hard time; they wanted money from the till. I don't know if it was a regular arrangement or they were just tryin' their luck."

I took another double drag, and then propped the joint in the ash tray and slid it over to Sadie. This wasn't going to be easy, not by a long shot.

She had a couple of hits off it and then she too propped it in the ash tray. There were two different colours of smoke curling up into the air from the joint. Blue, and white, the blue smoke was curling up in tendrils from the lit end, and the white was drifting upwards from the roach end, the blue smoke equalled cannabis, and the white equalled nicotine, cannabis good, nicotine bad.

"What're you trying to say? What happened?" Sadie said and looked to the floor. A solitary tear spilled over the rim and hurtled down her cheek and then dropped onto her cargo pants, leaving a perfect sphere-shaped damp patch.

I blew out a huge sigh and then carried on with my confession.

"Listen, I know I shouldn't have got involved."

"You're damn right you shouldn't have got involved."

"What else could I do?"

"Stay out of it; it was none of your business to get involved in the first place."

"I know, I know, but I couldn't just stand there could I, if I hadn't intervened God knows what would have happened. I mean the barmaid was reluctant to pay the money, she was stalling."

"You should've walked away. So what happened then?"

"Well, I hit the youngest and biggest of the two, the one with the skinhead."

Sadie nodded her head in recognition.

"I can't believe I never saw it, what were you thinking Kev?"

I looked down to my trainers and ultimately the floor.

"I don't know, I didn't think did I, I just hit him."

"Yes, and now he's dead. I can't believe it; I can't believe what you've done, especially after what we talked about last night."

She looked disappointed, as she lit the joint and took a hit off it.

Things weren't going to plan; this wasn't the way it was supposed to be.

"What did they ask you? The police I mean." Sadie asked.

"Probably the same as you, only they mentioned that they might want to talk to me again, that's if my story doesn't stand up. And there's no reason why it shouldn't, is there. I mean you have verified part of it, 'cos it's the truth as far as you're concerned. The clerk at the hotel will verify it further. I can't see there being a problem."

Sadie took another hit, now it was her turn to look to the floor. She held the smoke in for a couple of seconds and then blew it downwards, as soon as it hit the floor it gathered a life of its own as it started to spread along the dark wood, like morning mist on a dew soaked field.

"That's not the point though is it? You've been lying to me again, and if it's one thing I can't stand, it's liars."

Sadie took another hit off the joint and then crushed the end out into the ashtray, even though it was a couple of inches from the roach. A clear indicator she wasn't happy with the situation—or me for that matter.

"I'm sorry, I won't do it again, I promise." I said and took her hand in mine. "I mean it, no more secrets, no more lies."

Sadie shook her head, another sign that she wasn't happy, she wasn't happy at all.

I let the news sink in for a couple of minutes, until I could wait no longer. I broke the silence.

"This isn't gonna change anythin' between us is it?" I asked tentatively.

She answered without looking up,

"I don't know Kev; I can't keep going on like this."

She pulled her hand away from mine.

"I need some time to think, I will meet you back at the hotel at four if that's okay?" Sadie said gathering her things and making to get up.

"Yeah, whatever you want." I replied. "What time is it now?"

Sadie lifted her arm up and flicked her wrist so that she was able to see the watch on her wrist.

"It's quarter to twelve." she replied.

She reached out her hand and gave mine a little squeeze and said,

"I just need some space, it's a lot to take in you know."

"Yeah, I know." I replied to her back.

And with that she was gone, out of the door and melting away into the near midday crowds.

13

What to do, I had around four hours to kill.

After Sadie had left the coffee shop, I ordered another hot chocolate, and another gram of blueberry, as Sadie had left with the other deal. I made myself a joint and just chilled with it, taking in the pedestrians who were either going about their daily business or just plain sight seeing.

Jan was busy wiping the surfaces clean with a clean rag squirting them first with a spray bottle, all the time he was singing,

"I just called to say, I love you, I just called to say I care, and I mean it from the bottom of my heart."

I made for the counter. Jan had just finished, now he was leant on the counter sideways on, staring into space thinking about God knows what.

I nodded to him as I reached the counter/bar and said,

"Hey."

He nodded back.

"I don't suppose you could recommend anywhere to go? I'm at a loose end for a couple of hours and I haven't gotta clue what to do."

"Depends on what you like?" he said inspecting his manicured nails.

"Well I've been to Anne Frank's house, so I don't really fancy anythin' historic, or arty for that matter, so what do you reckon?"

"There's the sex museum or the cannabis museum, like I said it depends on what you like."

Well I didn't want to egg him on so I said,

"The cannabis museum sounds okay, whereabouts is it from here?"

He paused for a second and looked up to his left, and then started to say something but was interrupted by the door opening.

PART 2

The Laughing Barmaid
and Her Secret

14

*I*t was the laughing barmaid who had just closed the door and was now making her way towards us; by some strange coincidence we had chosen the very same coffee shop she bought her daily dosage from. What a stroke of luck. Good for me because it saved me a lot of time and trouble, bad for her because I was on to her from the get-go.

She showed visible signs of shock on her face as she walked up to where we were conversing either side of the counter/bar. She side-stepped me and looked to Jan and said,

"Can I have two grams of blueberry please Jan, and a coffee?"

Jan nodded and spun on his heels and busied himself sorting out the laughing barmaid's order.

I caught the laughing barmaid's attention and nodded to her. She nodded back but I could tell she was uncomfortable in my presence, something had her spooked and I wanted to know what it was. I waited until Jan had finished serving her and when he spun around to deposit her cash in the till I caught hold of her arm and whispered in her ear.

"I need a word in private before you go, it's about last night."

She nodded and then made a move to go sit at one of the empty tables, but couldn't because I still had a hold of her arm. She didn't say anything, she just looked down her nose at where my hand was and the look she gave me was enough, I immediately let go of her arm. If looks could kill I would be dead now. I let go. I didn't want to cause a fuss.

She made for a table without another word.

I watched her as she made her way down the narrow slip between tables. Nice arse, jiggle jiggle. She was wearing her hair down today, and she looked almost human, as opposed to elfish when her hair was up.

She was wearing dark blue jeans, which had faded patches on the front and back in a bleached oval shape; on her feet she wore a pair of leather gladiator type sandals, and to top it all off she had on a white shirt with white lace piping and a black leather motorcycle jacket, no studs or writing, just plain black leather. On her shoulder she clutched a battered black leather shoulder bag which jiggled as she walked. Just like her arse.

I waited for Jan to assume his position on the bar, and I said,

"It doesn't matter now Jan about the directions. I don't think I will be needing them, somethin's come up. Thanks anyway."

I gave him a half hearted smile.

Jan nodded and I spun around and made my way to the laughing barmaid's table. She had taken the table closest to the door. Maybe her subconscious was calling the shots too—no doubt she was rattled by my appearance in the coffee shop, and if need be she wanted an escape plan in place, two steps and she was out of the door, end of story, gone. She could melt away camouflaged by her surroundings and she knew her way around. It was her neighbourhood.

I smiled to myself as I settled in across from her. She was already half way through the rolling process and she looked up as I sat down. She wasn't laughing anymore, she wasn't even smiling. Gone was the happy go lucky girl from yesterday, replaced by a poker-faced, all business and no play girl today.

She was using ultra thin papers, the silver kind, so her nose was creased up, and her lips were pursed together in concentration as she twisted the papers enough to roll. I did the decent thing and waited until she had the joint dangling from her lips and rummaging through her bag for a light of some sort to spark it up before I opened my mouth. She cut me off straight away leaving me with my hand held up in the air, like a school kid wanting the toilet.

I patted my pants pocket and after locating my own lighter I pulled it out and offered it to her, safe end first. She looked at me like she had just found me wedged in-between the grooves on the soles of her sandals. Charming, I thought to myself, that's gratitude for you, you help someone out and this is how they repay you. I made a mental note to mind my business from now on.

She took the lighter and lit the joint tossing the lighter onto the table that separated us; it skidded for a couple of seconds on the dull wood surface before colliding with the ashtray and then spun round a couple more revolutions before stopping. She lit it and took a couple of hits off the joint and then held the smoke in for a couple of seconds before blowing it out in my general direction. Her eyes levelled on mine and she tilted her head sideways on and said, blowing the last of the smoke out with the words,

"You shouldn't have done what you did last night. There will be repercussions."

It wasn't a question; it was a statement so I kept my mouth shut and kept quiet, shrugging my shoulders as a reply and an attempt at nonchalance.

She pursed her lips together and looked to the floor shaking her head.

"It's ok for you, you don't ever have to go in the bar again, not if you don't want to. I have to work there. It will be me taking all the shit not you." She said.

Her voice was strangely hypnotic, I don't know if it was her accent or the weed, or a combination of the two. But I was feeling very sleepy.

Up to a couple of months ago my life had just plodded on, for years all I did was go to work, read and keep fit. I was living in my own personal groundhog day, until I decided enough was enough and did something about it. And then of course I found Sadie, well bumped into her by chance, literally. Since that moment my life had really taken off, I had cut loose all the shit that was dragging me down and the inevitable happened, I fell head over heels in love, and my life had changed forever. And there was no way I going to throw it all away, not now, not ever.

I hadn't really had the time to think about the skinhead's death, so it hadn't sunk in yet. To be honest at the moment I was more concerned about losing Sadie than I was with what had happened to him. He had brought it all on himself, whereas I had brought it all on Sadie yet again, the story of my life so far.

"I could hang around the bar and offer some protection, if you like?" I said even though I would rather not.

"You're just as bad as they are." she said, spitting the words at me like they were bullets.

"I'm only tryin' to help."

"Well if your idea of helping is like last night, I don't need it thank you very much."

"I need to talk to you about last night." I said, just before the silence became uncomfortable.

She took another hit off the joint and then passed it over to me. The silver Rizlas had all stained black with oil around the roach which was starting to creep up towards the lit end in a zig-zag pattern.

"You've got two minutes." she said, again blowing the smoke out with the words.

I took a hit off it, waving the smoke away, then another, then a double hit, then another. Smoke was coming out of my nose, mouth, ears, and tear ducts, virtually everywhere. I had immersed myself in a personal cannabis fog just to piss her off. I wasn't going to let her or anyone dictate terms to me. I crushed the end out into the ashtray, and sat back in my seat and just stared at her, without saying a word. My strategy was to intimidate her first before speaking. But she was just sat there staring right back at me with added venom.

I broke what had now turned into an uncomfortable silence.

"The skinhead from last night, he's dead." I said and watched for any outward signs on her face or in her eyes that she already knew something about it. I was confident that I would detect any signs no matter how subtle they were.

Her face showed some signs, but I wasn't sure what they were. They had me baffled. Her eyes and face only flashed for a second before she regained her composure enough to rebuild her defences. Her eyes contracted and her face twitched slightly, it was subtle but it was there. If I wasn't looking I would have missed it. Like I said the signs were there to see I just couldn't figure them or her out, not at the moment anyway. The signs could have been bewilderment, surprise or shock, anger, hurt or a mixture of all five. I just didn't know. She was a puzzle I had to work out—and fast.

The laughing barmaid began to build another joint.

I had positioned myself so I could see the comings and goings through the door, which was just a couple of feet away. I didn't want to be caught off guard in any situation, not here, not now, not ever, not after what I'd seen and done.

Now the door opened and a smartly dressed woman breezed into the coffee shop. I put her in her late thirties/early forties. She had blonde hair, the type you get from a bottle as opposed to natural. She was nice looking but not my type. I could see her roots had been freshly done, maybe even en-route to the coffee shop. She had an elegant face, but time was catching her up. There were the beginnings of crow's feet starting around both eyes, though they were more prominent on her left side. She was wearing a pleated tartan skirt, black leather boots that stopped just below the knee, a thin white roll neck top, and a dressy three-quarter length sheepskin jacket. She had a few different sized thick gold necklaces bouncing on her chest in time with her breasts, as though the breasts had set the rhythm and the necklaces had to stick to it. Her fingers were laden with stones and gems of all colours and sizes. She made her way passed us and onto the counter/bar.

"Did you hear what I said?" I asked the mute elf sat across from me.

She shook her head as if to say she couldn't believe what she had just heard.

"Yes, yes, give me a minute will you. I can't believe it." she said, still shaking her head. Or she was good, but not good enough. I could see right through her, there was something up and I was determined to find out what it was.

I left her alone with her thoughts for a couple of minutes, and chanced a look over my shoulders to see if I could locate the newcomer. She had struck up conversation with Jan while she waited as a fresh pot of coffee brewed on a hot plate. It was only small talk between them I could tell; there were no tell tale facial expressions, or unnecessary eye contact, nothing. As far as I could see and was concerned they were just passing the time until the coffee was ready to serve.

I turned back to face the laughing barmaid, she was just reaching for my lighter which was still where she had tossed it, joint dangling from her lips, like an old washer woman. It was then that I noticed the swelling and bruising around her wrist from where the older man had grabbed her last night. It could have been mistaken for a ganglion cyst, but I knew better.

"How do you know this?" she asked me still looking down, it didn't come across as a question, it was more like a taunt.

"Because I've just been back to the bar and the police turned up wanting to talk to anyone who was in the area last night, so I made a statement alright, that's how I know." I spat back.

She was beginning to do my head in, big time; it was like getting blood out of a stone, or pulling teeth. She wasn't going to give away nothing, nothing without a fight that is. Or maybe . . .

I tried a different approach.

"Listen, the way I see it is we're both in this together, you help me and I will help you." I said cajoling her.

"What is it you want from me?" she said to the table and not to me.

"Well, we both need each other, I need an alibi, and you need protection. You can be my alibi, and I will be your protection, simple equation." I said to the top of her head.

She finally looked up, still shaking her head and pulling a face, as if to say I don't know.

"What do I have to do?" she finally asked.

I breathed a sigh of relief.

"The police will want you to make a statement seeing as though you were working in the bar last night. They will show you two photographs, the skinhead and his boss. All you have to say is that neither of them came into the bar last night and that's it."

"And what exactly do I get out of this arrangement?"

"I've just told you, protection."

"That was just the B-team muscle you took out last night, the street crew. Believe me when they've found out what you've done they will send someone to sort it out."

Look into my eyes, my eyes, not around the eyes, the eyes, the eyes. I felt something pulling me down maybe it was just plain tiredness, or just maybe it was guilt finally catching up on me and weighing me down. Whatever it was, it was as heavy as fuck.

The laughing barmaid finally looked up; her eyes were moist, welling up at the sides. That's when I knew that whatever was going to come out of her mouth next was going to be a lie, for sure, guaranteed, 100 per cent, odds on.

How did I know?

She had no reason to be upset, why would she cry over someone who came into her work regularly demanding money by menace; if anything she should be overjoyed with what had happened, instead here she was turning the waterworks on over nothing. It was a dead giveaway.

Or was there something else on her mind? I didn't know as yet I was struggling to break through her initial line of defence.

Her nosed creased a little at the sides; it was probably something she used everyday with certain men to get her own way, but it wasn't going to work with me, not this time, not here, not now, not ever. Her card was marked as far as I was concerned.

She fluttered her eyelashes, another daily tool she probably used to get her own way. Like I said, it wasn't working. For what good it was doing her she could have daubed shit on her eyelashes instead of mascara.

She paused for effect before finally speaking.

I was convinced it was all a show, but I decided to hear her out. What choice did I have? I needed her and she needed me.

"I'm not sure about this." she said and paused again.

"What are you not sure about exactly?" I asked.

The door opened again, this time a Caucasian male in his mid thirties sauntered in off the street. He had short dirty blonde hair, combed forward then ruffled. Clothes-wise he was wearing a baggy grey T-shirt which had a pair of earphones as a design pattern, making it look like the wearer of the T-shirt had a pair of earphones around his neck, a pair of urban camouflage three-quarter length combat shorts, trainer socks, and a pair of blue and white Nike Air low tops. He looked like a sinister version of Jasper Carrott, only younger. He had a Nike tick scar on his right shin, starting just below his knee and heading downwards. Our eyes locked for a split second as he passed our table and I saw in his eyes the same thing I saw in Dim's, Batty's, and the late Mik's, which was a wanton disregard to anybody or anything, and a vacant, distant look that only killers or those acquainted with them can pull off. I wondered to myself if other killers spotted the same thing in my eyes, I hoped not. I wanted to be able to move about undetected, low profile, under the radar and not advertise the things I'd done.

"All this with the police, the implications and everything it brings if I get caught lying." she whined.

She was good I'll give her that, but like I said just not good enough. Nowhere near.

"You won't get caught though will you, the only people in the bar were the skinhead and his boss, you, me, and the two pissed up old codgers propping up the bar, none of which will say anythin.'"

"What about the woman who was with you?"

"Let's leave her out of it." I said in a quick fire reply. "Besides she ain't gonna say nothin' trust me, the police have already spoken to her and she has said the same as I did, that they didn't come into the bar last night. All you have to do is stick to the same story and were home and dry. You look after me, and I will look after you." I caught her gaze and held it lifting my eyebrows up as if to say "well it's up to you?"

She shook her head again, and blew out a huge sigh; she was pretending to think about it, weighing up her options. I could tell it was just a facade, that she wore a mask on her face, the tears were fake and so was her concern for breaking the law, I would put my life on it. She had a hidden agenda and I was going to find out exactly what it was.

"How are you going to be able to protect me, I mean you can't be in the bar every minute of every day can you?"

"No, you're right I can't, but I will give you my number, if they show up and I'm not there you call me and I will be there within minutes, I promise."

"Yeah right." she said. "How do I know I can trust you?"

"You don't, but what other option is there, you're not exactly spoilt for choice are you?"

The laughing barmaid pulled another face, and said,

"Give me your number."

Thank fuck for that, it was a great weight off my mind which was only going to get heavier the longer it went on. But the laughing barmaid turned out to be my saviour and she now held my ticket to freedom in her well manicured hand.

I gave her my number; she punched it into her own mobile then stuffed the phone back into her shoulder bag and zipped it shut. I then remembered that I had given my number to the police and they were going to contact me when they needed to speak to me again so I fished my mobile out and powered it up. I waited until it had re-booted properly and checked to see if I had any messages or not before stuffing it back into my pocket.

There were no messages from the police or anyone else.

"Listen, I gotta go, what time are you due in work today?" I asked the laughing barmaid, who so far hadn't even managed as much as a smile today.

"Today." She paused for a beat whilst she racked her brain, her eyes shifted to the right.

I made a mental note of the fact; it may come in handy some day soon.

"I'm in two 'til closing, whatever that time is." she replied.

It was now twenty to one. I had done nothing so far other than get stoned and side-tracked.

"What I suggest you do is . . ." I paused for a beat. "Are you goin' to work straight from here?" I asked her.

She pulled a cute face and said,

"No I have a few things to do before work, so I will be leaving here in about twenty minutes."

"Right, right." I said. "Do whatever it is you have to do, then go into work as normal, don't say anything to anybody. Wait for the police to come to you, and when they show you the photographs of the two men remember to tell them that they do call in from time to time to the bar but they haven't been in for a while, and definitely not last night. I'm sure you know what to say, use your imagination. You got that."

The laughing barmaid nodded.

"Right." I said. "You've got my number? In fact give me yours as well so I know it's you when you ring."

The laughing barmaid nodded again and recited her mobile number to me from memory, her eyes shifted to the right as she recalled it; to her memory bank.

I punched her phone number into my phone under "laughing barmaid" and stuffed it back into my pocket.

"I will find a coffee shop near to the bar and hole up there until the police have been to speak with you. Meantime if anyone shows up causin' grief, ring me and I will be there within minutes."

The laughing barmaid nodded for a third time and said,

"Okay, I hope you know what you're doing."

I got to my feet and without another word spun on my heels and made for the door.

I didn't but I'm sure I would cope.

15

I couldn't trust the laughing barmaid at all that I was sure of, there was something else going on and I was going to find out what because I was sure it would help my cause. So instead of going on my merry way I stepped out of the door and turned left, crossed the street and after a couple of steps I waited out of sight on the corner of the street. And waited, it was now ten to one.

The laughing barmaid strolled out of the coffee shop at sixteen minutes past one; she was accompanied by Sinister Carrott and the well dressed woman. This new development set my mind racing. Who were they? And more to the point, what were they doing with the laughing barmaid? The trio stood conversing on the pavement outside the coffee shop for another couple of minutes until sinister walked away, towards me on the opposite side of the street. The two women walked the opposite way to sinister, and away from me. I waited for Sinister to vacate the area before I set off in pursuit of the laughing barmaid and the well dressed woman.

I followed the two women keeping the distance between us. I used the various alcoves, shop fronts, and pedestrians for cover. They reached the end of the street and turned right. I went to cross the road so I was on the same side as they were and nearly collided with a cyclist. I stepped back onto the pavement and held my hands up in mock surrender. The cyclist flashed past me in a flurry of hand gestures and what I can only guess at as being Dutch expletives. I checked both ways before crossing the road, the streets were packed but I reached the corner in time. I peered round the corner and saw the two women still walking on the same side of the road, about thirty yards ahead. I held my position for a beat, and then started off after them at a steady pace. Every time it looked like I was gaining on them I would stop and pretend to browse in a shop window. I kept an eye on the signs of the various shops I passed so I knew if it was suitable or not to stop or not—it would be no good stopping in front of a shop if it was selling say, old women's knickers. True there were some signs that you would never be able to guess what the shop actually sold from it. If that happened I would just carry on to the next suitable shop window, this was going to be as easy as shelling peas.

16

I shadowed the two women for approximately twenty minutes, both their heads bobbed up and down in unison as they walked and dodged tourists and natives alike. It was mayhem on the streets. They had taken a series of left hand turns and right hand turns to the point where I didn't have a clue where we were, I was lost. But I figured that the laughing barmaid would head to work eventually as it was nearly quarter to two and she had told me that she was scheduled to start work at two.

I started to recognise the surrounding neighbourhood at about eight minutes to two; in fact I knew exactly where we were. We were a couple of blocks from the Irish bar. The two women paused at a crossroads. The laughing barmaid wrestled a pack of cigarettes from her handbag, they were some foreign brand, she shook one out and lit it. The well dressed woman took the time out to locate her mobile and check it. Satisfied, she stuffed it back into her coat pocket. Both women checked both ways before crossing the road. I followed suit when I hit the cross roads some ten or so seconds later. The coast was clear traffic-wise so I crossed the road in slow pursuit.

Now I was on the corner again, loitering. The two women were stood outside the Irish bar, talking. It was now four minutes to two. They talked for a few more minutes and then the laughing barmaid disappeared into the bar. The well dressed woman carried on walking and eventually turned the corner and out of sight.

I heard a commotion behind me so I turned to look; two natives were standing, swaying on the pavement, about thirty yards away staggering towards me. Both had long hair, the one on the left had a blue and white striped bandana wrapped around his head, while the one on the right had his locks dangling loose, like greasy curtains in a cheap motel room. Both men looked the worse for wear. They were both dressed in three quarter length woollen jackets; both jackets were a dirty brown colour. The one on the left had on a pair of dark blue jeans, and a pair of black cowboy boots, the ones with the silver toe caps. Though the boots were old and scuffed, and the toe caps pitted with rust. The one on the right had a pair of black cargo pants, and a pair of scruffy Reebok classics on his feet, the laces were filthy, stained brown, and snapped off and tied into tight little knots. They were now both doubled up and laughing uncontrollably. Every passing pedestrian gave them a wide birth. People were walking past and rubber necking back at them all the way up the street. They started towards me, still laughing, and zig-zagging their way across the full width of the pavement and back again. As they got closer I could hear what they were saying, I couldn't make out the words of course, as they were speaking in their native tongue. But as they got just about level with me I heard the bandana clad one say as he switched from talking in Dutch to English,

"I've forgotten how to use these things."

"What things?" his mate asked him.

"These." he said, nipping hold of the material on his cargo pants and lifting his legs off the floor. "My legs, I have forgotten how to use my legs."

His mate almost collapsed on the floor with laughter, the only thing that was keeping him upright was the lamp post he was leaning on. Their pupils were like saucers, hardly any colour at all behind them they were that big.

They staggered on past me with the gait of thunderbird puppets; I could still hear the slaps of their footwear on the pavement half-way up the street.

I found a coffee shop to hole up in about a third of the way down the street on the opposite side of the road to the Irish bar. I strolled through the door and made my way up to the counter. This coffee shop was a similar shaped room to most of the establishments I'd so far frequented, long and narrow. It had a long dark wood bar alongside the left hand wall, which dominated the first quarter. There were about six dark wood tables scattered along the right hand wall, the first one of which sat next to a window. Each table had two chairs facing it, tucked underneath neatly. There was a dark wooden bench that ran the length of the right hand wall. The total seating capacity looked to be around twenty. There were only eight people sat at or around the tables, and most of those were situated further on in the room.

I ordered a coffee, black, and one sugar. The assistant spun on his heels and busied himself making a fresh pot. While the coffee machine coughed and spluttered the assistant spun back around so he was facing me and said with a smile,

"That will be two guilders please."

As soon as the words spilled out of his mouth I knew he was English.

I had some change in my pocket so I dug in and foraged out enough to give him a one guilder tip.

"Have you got a weed menu I can take a look at please?" I said.

"Yes sure." the assistant replied and bent down to retrieve a laminated piece of A4 paper from a shelf underneath the bar. He slid it across the bar to me and I studied its contents.

I found my salvation in the Indica section, in the form of two grammes of Black Domina. I hoped it wouldn't affect my judgement when it came down to it.

"Can I have two grammes of Black Domina please?"

"Yes sure." the assistant replied and spun around to retrieve my order.

Again I noticed that the assistant's hands and the weed never came into contact, not once.

He sealed the bag with his forefinger and thumb and tossed it onto the counter in front of me.

"Let me see." he said and looked up and right as he did the mental arithmetic. "That'll be twelve guilders exactly please."

I handed over twenty guilders and told him to keep the change. He smiled, spun round and poured my freshly brewed coffee and placed it onto the counter in front of me. The thick black liquid sloshed about in the cup leaving a trail of residue all the way round that slowly made its way back to the main reservoir.

I nodded to the assistant and made for the table closest to the door with my coffee and my weed. It was the only one in the room with a window view. I was ignoring the primal scream within me telling me to head deeper into the room and the relative safety it offered. I had to keep an eye on the entrance to the Irish bar, I wanted to know exactly when the police arrived and left. That way I would be able to tell if the laughing barmaid was on my side or not. If she rang me straight away I would give her the benefit of doubt, if she didn't I would watch her like a hawk.

I settled down on the bench and got myself as comfortable as the hard wood allowed. I had a perfect view of the Irish bar from my current position, the only obstructions were when gangs of pedestrians walked passed. Which was happening right now as an entourage of oriental tourists shuffled past, so I hunted out the materials from my various pockets to make a joint. I wanted to try the Black Domina as soon as possible. I did the deed as quickly as I could and then fumbled my lighter from my pocket, joint dangling from my lips and eyes locked firmly on the Irish bar across the street. I lit the joint taking my eyes off the bar for a second. The joint flared up so I remedied it by wafting it about until it stopped. I took a double hit off it, sucking the smoke in deep and holding it there for a while. I felt nothing for the first four hits or so, and then boom, it hit me. I felt like the floor was swallowing me up whole and all of a sudden my mouth was bone dry. I blew out a huge sigh and propped the joint in the ashtray, I'd had enough of that for now. I noticed that there was writing on the nip bag so I spun it round on the table so I could read it. It was in Dutch. So I could only guess at what it actually said. But I got the gist; smoking is harmful, over eighteens only and so on. What it should say on the bag is don't make any fucking plans.

I clocked the two detectives at 2.32pm precisely. They made their way down the street dodging pedestrians all the way to the Irish bar. They crossed the threshold at 2.33pm.

I picked up the joint, lit it, took one hit off it and thought better of it. I was wasted so I propped it back in the ash tray. I needed some sort of re-fuel or quick jolt so I necked the dregs of the coffee and willed the caffeine to try and do its best to revive me. I knew it faced an uphill battle and I held out little hope for it. But it did do something, I couldn't quite put my finger on what it was but it was there, subtle, hanging in the background, like an inspirational phone call. It was weird, I was still fucked, and my legs felt like lead weights bolted to the bench, but yet my mind had been gently lifted. I felt as though I could float away and leave my body behind.

I caught the assistant's attention and held a finger up in the air and mimed the words "Can I have a refill please?"

He nodded and set to work.

If I didn't move now then I wouldn't have moved at all, so reluctantly I struggled to my feet and took my empty cup over to the counter. By the time I had reached it the assistant had finished pouring and was just placing the fresh cup of coffee on the counter in front of me.

"Two guilders please."

I gave him ten guilders and spun back round and headed back to my view point.

I gave the street the once over, all the way up and back down again on both sides, to make sure the detectives were still in the bar. I saw no sign of them on either side of the street so I had to conclude that they were still inside interviewing the laughing barmaid. Let's hope she sticks to her lines and doesn't fuck up under pressure, if only things were that simple.

An endless stream of pedestrians trickled constantly down the street, on both sides, making it hard to keep track on the door to the bar, but I kept my mind on the job. I had to, it was either that or fall asleep where I was. It was now ten to three. Time was running out, I sat up straight and dry scrubbed my face with my hands to try and bring myself round. I had to meet Sadie in our hotel foyer at 4.00 pm. That left an hour and ten minutes, and I would prefer to have this thing done and dusted when I did go to meet her.

The two detectives left the bar at two minutes to three, and walked back the way they came, round the corner and out of sight. I took my phone out of my pocket and sat it on the table and waited for it to start vibrating. After two minutes I decided to ring her mobile. It was engaged. I pulled a face, it was my turn to shake my head. I set the phone back on the table and waited. It took another three minutes for her to call me. I let it ring ten times before I answered it.

"Hello."

"It's me." said the seductive voice on the other end of the line.

"Who is it?"

"It's Anna."

"Who?"

"The barmaid, from the Irish bar."

"Have the police been?" I asked, knowing the answer was yes.

"Yes, they have just left." came the reply.

"What did they have to say?"

"It went how you said it would, they showed me the two photographs and I told them I thought I recognised them, and that sometimes they popped in for a drink but not for a while."

"And they believed you?"

"Yes, I think so."

"Did they mention me?"

"Not specifically, no."

"What do you mean? Not specifically."

"Well, they asked me who was in the bar, and I told them."

"What exactly did you tell them?"

"I told them it was quiet, at the time they asked about."

"Which was?"

"Between half past ten and twelve."

"Mmmmm." I said. "Who did you say was in the bar?"

"I told them it was quiet, we only had a few customers all night, and at that time there were only four in the bar. I gave them a basic description of you, and the two old men. I said that there was a woman with you but that I didn't get a worthwhile look at her to give any kind of description."

"Good, anythin' else?"

"Well there is something else but I can't talk over the phone. I've got a proposition for you."

"What kind of proposition?"

"I haven't been straight with you."

No shit.

"Just come to the bar and I will explain everything."

"Okay, I'll be there shortly." I said and hung up.

I didn't go straight over to the bar. Instead, I ordered another coffee and smoked the last of the Domina joint. I sat with my thoughts watching the entrance to the bar and cradling the cup of coffee, spinning the cup slowly round and round, and taking the occasional hit off the joint. By my count three customers had entered the bar since my vigil had started. Three nondescript customers, three Mister Greys, three people who no matter how hard you tried to you can never conjure up an image of after the fact.

There I was—smoking, thinking, thinking, smoking, and brooding.

The air was thick with smoke inside the coffee shop and the generic smell of weed was all around. I was in my own little bubble, lost in thought trying to figure out what kind of proposition the laughing barmaid was going to offer me. And more to the point, why me?

After a few minutes deliberation, I could only come to one conclusion, which was that the laughing barmaid was going to offer me the job of protecting the bar. It made sense, why else would the owner shell out protection money every week if they didn't need to. This also told me that there were organised crime crews operating in the area, and I would be best to leave well alone. In theory all I wanted to do was what I had to and get out.

My bubble burst as the door opened and in walked a couple. Both were dressed smartly. The man was wearing a grey suit, you could tell it was expensive and well cut from the way it hung from his athletic frame, and on his feet he wore a pair of flat black shoes which had some kind of intricate stitching pattern on them. The woman was wearing a thick plain grey tweed trouser suit and a white lacy blouse, and black stilettos. They were both in their late forties and were starting to show signs of wear and tear. They passed out of my line of sight and onto the counter. I was content where I was, I didn't want to move, at all. If it wasn't for the fact I had more pressing matters at hand I would have stayed there all day. I was on my own planet just sat there in the window of this cosy little coffee shop watching the world go by. But like I said I had more pressing matters at hand. I downed the last of the coffee, stubbed the roach end out in the ashtray and made for the door. I was back out on the street some three seconds later. Now I know why they chose to sell coffee alongside weed, because if they didn't they would just have a bunch of stoners lounging around all day, which is not good for business.

Out on the street it was like stepping out into another world. The coffee shop was warm and cozy, outside there was a chill in the air that threatened to eat its way through my layers of clothing. I shuddered against the cold, pulled my hoodie up and crossed the road.

Our hotel was a five minute walk from the bar, which left about thirty three minutes to sort things out. I pulled down my hood and entered the Irish bar at twenty two minutes past three. The laughing barmaid was busying herself serving what could only be described as a derelict. She looked up as I walked into the room and gave me a half hearted smile. I looked over to the smoking area and then back to her as if to say I'll see you in there, don't be long.

She nodded to let me know she understood.

"Can you bring me a medium sized lager please?"

She nodded again and then returned her attention to the pump.

I made for the partitioned off smoking area. As I got level with the bar I saw how badly deteriorated the tramp was. He had a salt and pepper and mustard beard, the mustard area being concentrated around his top lip. The skin on his face was like a screwed up chamois leather. As I walked passed him I held my breath, I didn't want his eau de cologne invading my nasal cavities.

I did the trick with the door and slid it shut behind me. I made for the table and the bench at the far end of the make-shift smoke room, letting my instincts rule once again, and waited. The laughing barmaid entered the smoking area at thirty two minutes past three. In her left hand she held my drink, in her right hand she held a kingsize packet of Rizlas, and a carton of Marlboro Lights. She came and sat opposite me at the last table on the right, plonking my drink in front of me. She had turned her chair round so that she was facing me, and so she could use my table to rest on to build a joint.

I broke the silence.

"So what's this proposition you've got for me?" I asked her and then without letting her reply I fixed my eyes on hers and added, "And how come you haven't been straight with me?"

"I will explain all in good time."

I took the froth off the top of the lager while I waited for her to continue. Instead she carried on making the joint, virtually ignoring me. I didn't have time for this. I glanced at the clock on the wall, it was now nearly twenty to four.

I waited until she had finished rolling the joint before I broke the silence again.

"So are you goin' to tell me or what?"

She pulled a cute face, clicked the lighter and tugged on the joint to get it going. It took a couple of re-lights but soon it was burning perfectly. Already the beginnings of an oil spill had started to creep up the Rizla.

"It wasn't the skinhead who was killed last night." she said matter of factly, without a care in the world.

"What? How come?"

"It was the older man, the boss."

"I don't understand."

"It's a long story." she said and took a big hit off the joint and then held it out for me, right arm outstretched.

I took it and propped it in the ashtray. I'd had enough for the time being. I had adopted the Rastafarian philosophy of when you reach a certain high, chill with it.

"Well I haven't got time for a long story, gimme the edited version." I said.

"The gangster who was here last night, the one who is dead."

"Yeah, what about him?"

"I'm friends with his daughter."

"And."

"Well to cut a long story short his wife has suffered at his hands for years. Countless affairs, beatings, mental cruelty, you name it, he's done it."

"So."

"Well one night after having a lot to drink and smoke we hatched a plan to kill him."

I kissed my molars, which in itself said something; I wasn't impressed with what was coming out of her mouth.

"Go on." I said, urging her on.

"I went along with it that night because I was so drunk and stoned. I thought it was just a laugh, you know a way to let off steam. I didn't think for a minute that they were being serious."

"Which they were, obviously."

"Well yes, my friend's mum rang me the next day. So I put the wheels in motion, so to speak." she said reaching for the joint in the ashtray, lighting it and sucking on it hard to get it going again.

"How do you organise something like that? I'm curious." I said, conscious of the second hand ticking slowly round the clock on the wall in the other room; it was now quarter to four.

"I know people who know people." came her simplistic reply.

"So what, you know a hitman, and you phoned him."

"Not quite, but I know a fixer."

"A fixer?" I echoed.

"Yes somebody who can put you in touch with just about anyone, get any problem eradicated if you know what I mean." she said with a wink.

"So why didn't you get your friend the fixer to sort your problem out at the bar?"

"I did ask him, but he wouldn't go anywhere near. Said it would destroy the uneasy truce that the various organised crime crews in the area had adhered to for the last twenty years or so. So when the opportunity came up and I could make money out of it . . ."

"But he will arrange a killin', the same bloke as it goes."

"It's different."

"Is it?" I said and held my hand up in the air like a traffic warden.

This was a lot of shit to take in. I scratched my hairline, in puzzlement. Talk about being in the wrong place at the wrong time, it was becoming a habit, and one I didn't want.

"So then what?"

"My friend put me in touch with this guy, I phoned him, and he agreed to meet us. The meetings were always clandestine, you know, late at night, dodgy places. We met up at least four times before he agreed to do it. He asked for a photo on the last time we met, so I met him yesterday before work and gave him the photo."

"How much does something like that cost?"

"Three hundred thousand guilders."

I whistled. It sure was a lot of money.

"How come it cost that much?"

"He had connections; you don't mess with a man like that unless you have to, or are getting paid well."

I did the mental arithmetic quickly; with the exchange rate as it was, rounded off we were talking a hundred grand sterling.

Three hundred thousand guilders seemed a strange amount, so I probed further.

"Why three hundred thousand? Why not two fifty, or say half a million? There must be a reason?"

"Because the hitman is British, and his fee is a hundred thousand pounds sterling." the laughing barmaid replied.

"What's your share?"

"Five per cent."

Again I did the mental arithmetic; she would get fifteen thousand hundred guilders, which in turn worked out at around five thousand pounds, which wasn't a lot of money, but it was money for nothing. Yet there was something else on her mind, I could tell. She had pound signs for eyes, literally.

"I don't understand where I fit in all this?"

"I'm just getting to that, if you let me." she said and crushed what was left of her joint into the ashtray.

I took that as my cue, so I used her Rizla and cigarettes to skin a Domina based one up. I set to work, occasionally looking up to keep her attention on me.

She looked to the bar.

"I've got to go, someone needs serving, I will be back as soon as I can." she said getting to her feet.

I looked over to the bar, it was the derelict who wanted serving. He was swaying, staring in our general direction, swirling his drink round and round.

The laughing barmaid left the sliding door open and made her way over to the bar.

It was now eight minutes to four. I supposed I could set off at two minutes to and run back to the hotel. I rolled the joint, lit it, sucked the smoke in deep, held it in and waited for the laughing barmaid to return from serving the derelict.

At five minutes to four the laughing barmaid re-entered the smoking room and slid the door shut behind her. She glided across the room like a ghost, or a swan on a calm lake. She was strangely mesmerising to watch, the way her hips swayed from side to side. I felt like I was going under. I shook myself, and shivered. She sat in the same seat as before, this time she leant forward and pinched the joint from my fingers. She took a massive hit off it and sucked the smoke deep inside, handing the joint straight back to me, blowing the smoke in my face as she spoke the words.

"You're the exact double of the hitman."

"What do you mean, I look like him?"

"Yes." she said, nodding. "Everything about you, your mannerisms, the way you walk, your looks, you could be his twin."

There—she had said it, it was now out in the open, like a fart at an orgy, lingering. The ball was in my court so to speak. I glanced at the clock. I was going to be late, it was one minute to four and she looked like she wouldn't be finishing anytime soon.

"So what do you want from me?"

"If you're up for it, we can scam the hitman."

"How?"

"You meet my friend's mum; she gives you the cash, simple. I will tell the real hitman the wrong time, give you an hour's grace so you can do the meet and get the cash. You give me my share and I'm out of here, gone."

"What just like that? What about your friend's mum?"

"She got the job done; it's the hitman who ends up out of pocket."

I tipped my head to one side in a silent salute. I had to hand it to her, ruthless wasn't the word.

"Strangely enough it's that what's gnawing at me, having a hitman after me ain't my idea of a walk in the park. I need to stay low profile."

"Besides, she'll be okay. I'm the go-between, without me there isn't a connection, he won't be able to find her."

"What about your friend, the fixer."

"He's on our side. We're old friends."

"Still he's not gonna let it go, is he?"

The derelict was swirling his glass again, swaying in time to some distant tune in his head. The laughing barmaid made to get up. I grabbed her arm, not enough to hurt her but with just enough pressure to keep her where I wanted her, right where she was, sat opposite me, face to face. That way I could keep an eye on her body language. I had a hunch that she was telling the truth, even without the kinesics. Why would she lie about something like this?

"Leave him; he'll be okay for a couple of minutes." I said and kept a hold of her, squeezing her hard and then letting go. I had to keep control of the situation somehow.

"All you have to do is collect the money and leave."

"It's not as simple as that, not for me."

"Why isn't it?"

I paused for a couple of beats, scratching my head and running my fingers through my hair. It was time to go. I was now officially late.

"Go serve the tramp; I have to go somewhere, gimme sometime to think this over and I will be back later with an answer." I said getting to my feet and making for the sliding door.

I had to get out of there, I felt like the walls were closing in on me. The laughing barmaid shadowed me through the make-shift smoke room and on to the bar. The derelict was unsteady on his feet, I don't know what tune he had stuck in his head but it had a weird rhythm, one I'd never come across before. I side-stepped him and made my way to the door without looking back. Once out on the street I checked my phone for the time. It was now eight minutes past four. I started off in a slow jog which soon turned into a full-on sprint.

17

I reached the door to the hotel some two minutes later. Sadie was still sat in the hotel foyer, thank fuck. She looked annoyed and when she caught sight of me her eyes flashed in anger, but then they softened, which is always a good sign. I pushed the door open and made my way over to where she was, nodding to the clerk en route.

She smiled—another good sign. She had also changed clothes and looked only minutes from the shower. Her face was flushed pink from the hot water and the exertion of changing clothes, and then the walk down to the foyer from the room.

She looked stunning; she was wearing a beige ankle length skirt which flared slightly towards the hem and swished around her feet as she walked, like a shoal of fish on the shore of a tropical island. Boy she sure knew how to dress to impress, to top it all off she had on a simple white T-shirt under a beige coloured wrap around cardigan. On her feet she had on a pair of flimsy skin coloured sandals—why do women do that when it's freezing cold? I could tell she had even straightened her hair fresh from the shower which I guessed had helped to pump the colour into her cheeks.

"You alright." I asked. My heart was beating like a hardcore baseline. I felt as though an alien was about to burst out from my chest.

She nodded and looked down to the floor.

"So what do you want to do?" I asked the top of her head.

"We could go on a cruise we saw on one of those leaflets you picked up yesterday; it would give us a chance to talk." she said to her feet.

"Sounds like a plan." I said.

I held the door open for Sadie while she grabbed her handbag which was curled at her feet like a faithful dog.

Outside the cold air hit us like a steam train. Again I pulled my hood up, and Sadie wrapped herself around me and kissed my cheek. Another good sign, I was confident that all would end well. I had already decided to take the laughing barmaid up on her offer. And I was sure I could talk Sadie round to my way of thinking.

We stood on the corner of Centraal and looked over to the grand old building that was Amsterdam's Centraal station. At the side of the station was a dock. A few luxurious canal boats were moored at the jetty bobbing and swaying gently on a choppy surface.

The excursion did a tour of the canals through Amsterdam starting at the dock over the road, passing through the red light district, past Amsterdam's famous gable houses, Anne Frank's house, and through various other industrial and residential districts until finally arriving back at the dock again. The whole tour took an hour and fifteen minutes from start to finish, and they ran every two hours. Sadie dug out the relevant leaflet from her handbag and opened it up so we could study it. The next tour was due to start at five pm. It was now coming up half past four and I was getting hungry. My stomach growled to reiterate the fact. So we decided to go and have something to eat first and then catch the next available tour which would be the one scheduled to start at seven. We would also get chance to talk and sort out our differences out before the cruise, no need to spoil it.

"You wait here, I'll run over to the booth and get the tickets."

"Okay." Sadie said, taking a step back and leaning on the brownstone building behind her.

I waited for a break in traffic and made a run for it.

Inside the wooden office it smelt of coffee and stale sweat. There were various posters advertising local tourist attractions—the cannabis museum, the sex museum, Anne Frank's house—which occupied every bit of available wall space. The poor kid behind the glass was wearing a bored expression; he looked to have been in position since summer, at least. I waited patiently while he finished whatever it was he was reading, still reading it as he placed it onto the counter in front of him, and veering his attention to me a split second before the magazine hit the counter.

He smiled and nodded to me in greeting.

"Hi there." he said.

"Y'alright." I said. "Can I have two tickets for the seven o'clock cruise please?"

"Yes sure." he said doing a poor Sean Connery.

I watched him work the mouse. Click, scrape, scrape, click, and click. He tore off the two tickets and slid them under the glass partition and said,

"That will be ten guilders please. I have to inform you for an extra twenty five guilders you can have a bottle of champagne on the cruise, it's optional though." he said and smiled revealing a slightly crooked set of off white teeth.

"Yeah, put us down for that cheers." I said and counted out forty guilders.

I slid the money under the glass. He counted it out and deposited it in the till.

"Sir, your change." he said to my back. I was already half-way through the door.

"I fancy another steak." I said as I got back to Sadie.

"Same place as last night." Sadie replied.

"The very one." I said.

One of my many mottos is if it ain't broke don't fix it.

We set off for the bistro. It was about ten minutes steady walking from our current position. Perfect. By the time the cruise started dusk would just be drawing in, even more perfect.

The pedestrian crowd had thinned out a little so it was easy going and we made it to the bistro in less than fifteen minutes. Taking in a few of the sights along the way, stopping and sharing a cigarette between us at one particular pitstop/map-check.

Inside the bistro everything was just the same as yesterday, same staff, same waitress in the same work uniform of a frilly black shirt, a black swishy ankle dress, and flat black shoes, and the same sombre but welcoming atmosphere. The waitress greeted us and swept her arm outwards in an arc, as if to say pick a seat, any seat. Her eyes showed a flicker of recognition.

The place was empty which surprised me, especially when they dish up a steak like I'd had the night before. We chose the same table, the one furthest away from the door/cave entrance, instinct rules.

We ordered and as we waited for our food to be served I wondered how many of the other things we do subconsciously everyday are actually borne from pre-historic instinct. It's like when a chameleon hatches from its egg, it just knows what to do, without being told. Instinctively it knows to climb out of its underground lair, trampling on its siblings along the way, even if it doesn't have to. And instantly it knows how to stalk and catch a fly—line up, aim, fire, pull back, and chew. Very rarely do they fail to catch their first meal. Why? Because it's acting on its natural instincts. If it didn't it would just curl up and die, it probably wouldn't even make it out of the shell. Instinct is nature's blue-print implanted deep inside each and every one of us, beyond reach or thought. Some people choose to ignore their natural instincts. I don't. There was no way I was going to just curl up and die. I had everything going for me, for us. We were the modern day versions of Bonnie and Clyde.

We had agreed not to start our chat until the food had arrived, that way the waitress wouldn't interrupt what could be a delicate part of the conversation. So it was just small talk, this and that. Sadie mentioned that she had spent most of the afternoon in Van Gogh's Museum before returning to the hotel to shower and change. I mentioned that I'd had a wander round before chilling in one of the coffee shops near to our hotel.

Our drinks arrived within minutes of us taking our seats; I had ordered a large lager, Sadie a large glass of house red. The food arrived a little under fifteen minutes later. The steak was done to perfection, just enough to seal and then straight out of the pan to rest. It was just as good as yesterday if not better, as I found out when I hacked a corner off and speared it with my fork, stuffed it into my mouth and tasted it. My features went slack for a split second as again the steak melted in my mouth and then I began to chew it. All the juices were flooding my mouth, threatening to spill out and onto my chin. I swallowed to stop it from happening.

"So what's the verdict then?" I said as I cut another chunk of meat from the steak.

"Let me just say this, I am not happy with what's happened. Especially with it being just after we had our make or break talk last night. In fact you walked straight away from it and killed someone."

I held my hand up in the air to halt proceedings.

"I got it wrong." I said spearing the chunk of my meat with my fork and tossing it into my mouth. One chew, two chews. "It wasn't the skinhead who was murdered last night. It was the other one, his boss." I said rolling the food around my mouth so I could talk.

"What?" Sadie said as she popped a piece of chicken into her mouth.

I waited until I had swallowed what I had in my mouth before continuing.

"It wasn't the guy I hit who died; it was the other one with him."

"It's irrelevant; you still shouldn't have done it after what we talked about."

"I know, I've said I'm sorry, what else can I do?"

"Think, before you act in future or it's over."

"I will, I promise." I said.

"I mean it."

"So do I." I said gulping down what was left of my drink and waving the glass in the air to attract the waitress's attention. She nodded and smiled to let me know she was on her way.

"Can we have the same again please?" I said to the waitress, and then to Sadie, "Is that okay with you?"

Sadie nodded as she bent forward and popped a mixture of chicken and vegetables into her mouth. I turned back to the waitress, who was waiting on my words and nodded to her whilst smiling and said,

"Yes same again please."

Two minutes later the drinks were placed in front of us, the waitress backed away smiling. She took to her default position, behind the bar where she picked up a damp cloth and began to wipe down the bar's surface.

I could now enjoy the rest of the meal without being off put by words I didn't want to hear. I had to watch my step from now on but as far as Sadie was concerned I was home and dry.

I speared the last chunk of meat on my fork and twirled it round and round, staring lovingly at it as though I was an art critic staring at an exhibit on a rotating plinth in a gallery.

"I'd like to have known the cow." I said to the piece of meat.

"What cow?" asked Sadie looking up from her plate in puzzlement.

"The one this steak came from." I replied and laughed, stuffing the last remnants of a divine meal into my mouth. "It was absolutely gorgeous." I said in-between chews.

I pushed the plate away from me and blew out a huge sigh. There were long thin slash trails of blood all over the plate from where I'd used the sharp knife to hack off bite size chunks. Sadie was only half way through her meal so I held back on lighting up. Instead I got my phone out and checked it for any missed calls, texts, or voicemails. There was none of the above so I tucked my phone back in my pocket, and waited for the right moment to bring up the scam in conversation. How do you know when it's the right time to say something like that? When is the right time? When is the wrong time? The answer is there isn't one, like Nike say just do it.

I waited for the waitress to clear away both our plates before shattering the silence with what I had to say.

"Was everything okay?" the waitress asked as she balanced both plates on her forearm, swiping up the food menu and replacing it with one for desserts in a well practiced move.

"Yes." we both replied in unison.

Well at least we agreed on something.

"Can I get you anything else—a drink or a dessert." she said forcing a smile.

"I'm okay." I said to the waitress, and to Sadie, "Did you want anythin'?"

"No thanks." she replied. "I'm okay for now."

"I'll give you a shout when we need a top up, cheers."

The waitress backed off and returned to her default position behind the bar. This time she sat on a stool and started to flick through the pages of an unseen magazine.

Just like the laughing barmaid before her I noticed that Sadie had something on her mind, even though we had sorted out our differences. It was like a pained distant look that wasn't there before. She never said anything or brought the subject up so I followed suit and let it lie, for now.

Outside the sky was turning all different colours—red, orange, gold, black and grey. It looked like it had been put on the rack, tortured and left to die, but yet it was still beautiful. It was now coming up to six o'clock.

"Do you fancy another one in here and then we can take a steady walk back up to the dock."

Sadie nodded in reply so I turned to the waitress and caught her attention by waving my glass in the air and mouthed the words "Same again please."

She nodded and set to work fixing the drinks. They arrived on the table bubbling and still respectively, some four minutes later. The waitress returned to her default position, this time she sat on a stool examining her nails.

"Have you seen outside, the sky, it looks beautiful." Sadie said.

"Yeah I noticed it earlier, it'll make a nice setting for the cruise don't you think?" I replied.

Sadie nodded.

I took the lager's head off in one fowl slurp, breathing in deeply as I swallowed it. It hit the spot.

"I've got something to put to you."

There, I said it; it was out in the open now and there was no going back.

Sadie's brow creased for a second or so, before returning back to normal.

"What kind of something? Is it legal?"

"Well, no not really, but, if you give me a minute I'll explain."

"You've got two minutes and if I don't like what I hear I'm out of here." she said taking a little sip of the blood-red mixture in her glass.

She swallowed the liquid with her mouth open slightly to exaggerate the taste. Licking her stained lips clean after it had gone down.

"You know the guy who was killed last night? Not the skinhead, his boss—the one from the photo."

"Not really, but yes go on."

"Well it turns out it was a hit, organised by the man's wife."

"I don't want to hear this." Sadie said collecting her things.

"Sadie please, just hear me out. You said you'd give me two minutes, and by my reckoning you owe me at least one minute and fifty five seconds."

Sadie dropped her bag back on the floor and sat back down on the seat facing me, only she wasn't facing me any more. She was facing the door. She wasn't happy, not by any stretch of the imagination, and it was all my fault yet again.

She turned to face me and said,

"The clock is running, so to speak, you've got two minutes to convince me otherwise or like I say I'm gone, out of here and out of your life."

This wasn't going to be as easy as I first thought.

"The barmaid from the Irish bar, the one from the first night in the bar."

"What about her?"

"Apparently she is friends with the dead guy's daughter; anyway after years of shit and God knows what else the barmaid, the daughter and the dead guy's wife hatched a plan to kill him, in drink. It would have been okay if they left it at that only they went through with it, hired a hitman and well you know the rest."

Sadie shook her head and looked to the floor. Good sign/bad sign, I didn't know as yet.

"What's that got to do with you?"

"I'm getting to it now; the barmaid reckons the hitman is a dead ringer for me."

Sadie's face froze in horror and her hand shot up to her mouth to try and keep some of the shock to herself. It was too late, I had seen her reaction.

I tilted my hands outwards so that my palms were flat facing up, as if to say, "Are you going to tell me or what?" Sometimes actions speak louder than words.

Sadie wasn't forthcoming so I echoed my action with the actual words this time.

"Are you goin' to tell me what that was all about?"

"I've met him today."

"Who?"

"The hitman."

"How? When?"

"Today at the museum, I was stood admiring one of the paintings and I was aware someone had come and stood by my side. So I turned to look and nearly fainted."

It was my turn to look puzzled.

Sadie continued after taking a sip of her wine.

"I thought it was you, and I was so impressed you'd taken the time out to find me. I just slung my arms around the guy's neck and went to give him a great big sloppy kiss. It was only when I moved in close I noticed."

"Noticed what?"

"His eyes."

"What about his eyes."

"They're blue, yours are green."

"So what happened?"

"Well I unhooked my arms from around his neck for a start."

"And then what?"

"I apologised to the poor man profusely, told him that I had mistook him as my boyfriend as he was the double of you."

"So what did he say?"

"He said he would only accept my apology if I accepted his invitation for dinner."

"What did you say?"

"I told him I wouldn't be able to make dinner—that I was on my way to meet someone, but I could squeeze a coffee in. So we went to a nearby coffee shop."

"What, and that's it."

"Well we had coffee if that's what you're asking."

"What did you talk about?" I said, not wanting to sound pushy, but still probably did.

"Nothing really, he said that he was here on business for a couple of days. We talked about the museum, the weather, and then he walked me back so far to the hotel."

"You didn't tell him which hotel we are staying at did you?"

"I don't know." she said and looked to the left, her memory bank.

"Come on Sadie it's important I need to know."

"I'm thinking, just give me a second. No I didn't."

"You're sure."

"Yes I'm sure. Why, what is going on Kev?"

"The barmaid has come up with the idea to scam the hitman."

"Scam him. You're kidding. How?"

"As you have rightly pointed out he looks like me. She wants me to meet her friend's mum as though I am the hitman, collect the money and give her her half and then scarper."

Sadie looked down to the floor again, massaging her temples as she did so.

"How're you going to do it?"

"I don't know the ins and outs as yet. I haven't even agreed to do it. I wanted to see what you thought before I committed to anythin'. I don't think she has any kind of plan, it's just an idea at the minute."

"When is the collection taking place?"

"Sometime tomorrow, this gives us time to formulate some kind of plan." I said.

"I don't know Kev, I'm not so sure about this." Sadie replied.

"What's there to worry about? You wait with the barmaid, or at the hotel while I pick up the money, when it's done I come and get you and we get the fuck outta here." I said shaking my head a little and gesturing with my hands as if to say "That's it, simple."

"You're sure that's all there is to it?"

"Positive, the risk is minimal."

"I can't believe I'm agreeing to this." Sadie said blowing out a huge sigh. "How much money are we talking about?"

"We split it fifty fifty with the barmaid, which all in all amounts to fifty grand, not bad for a day's work." I said giving Sadie a wink. "This time tomorrow we will be on our way to wherever we want fifty grand richer. Think about it, can you afford not to, it's money for nothin'."

"Okay, okay, we're in." she said.

"To . . ." I said as I raised my glass.

Sadie looked up slightly and to the right and then paused for a beat before making a toast.

"To opportunities you simply cannot pass up."

"I'll go along with that." I said and we chinked glasses.

I swallowed what was left of the lager, in one. Sadie finished off her glass of wine with a little more elegance, taking sips until it was gone. The wine that had clung to the side of the glass started to slip slowly down making its way to the bottom, like watered down syrup.

I caught the waitress's attention and then mimed the action of writing in a pad. A little over three minutes later she placed the bill in front of me on a small ceramic plate. I counted out thirty guilders without even looking at the bill and tossed the three ten guilder notes on top of the receipt.

"Come on, let's go or we will be late." I said getting to my feet. It was now twenty to seven.

The waitress gave us a smile and a little wave on the way out. For me it's the little things that count. If things had turned out differently and we had stayed for the duration I reckon I could have easily munched my way through two full cows, at least. Alas we would be out of here by tomorrow night at the latest.

Outside on the street the wind had died down, but it was still bitterly cold. Night was drawing in fast; by eight o'clock it would be pitch black. Perfect.

"So have you thought about where you might want to go tomorrow? Anywhere, you name it." I said to Sadie.

"Anywhere?" she said letting out a squeal.

"Anywhere." I echoed.

Occasionally we had to let go of each other's hand so that we could thread a way through the crowded streets. Amsterdam was rearing its ugly head again; it was time to switch its life support machine off for the duration of the night. I had visions of doctors and nurses fussing round Dam square, charging up the defibrillator ready to bring it back to life. One, two, three, clear. No response, and in the background a high pitched whine as the machine recharges. One, two, three, clear. "Hurray we brought Amsterdam back from the dead."

We had reached the corner of Centraal and were waiting for a gap in traffic so we could cross the road. Strange things they are, traffic lights in Amsterdam. Back in Britain the system is simple the lights turn green and you go, they turn red and you stop. Over here the lights turn to green and you think it's safe to cross but it isn't—cars are still coming at you, it's crazy.

We started to edge our way out into the road. Sadie noticed a gap coming up in the traffic so she grabbed my hand ready. When it was safe she made a dash for it pulling me with her, shouting,

"Come on lets run."

But she tripped over a tram line just as she started running, letting go of my hand and only managed the "Come on lets r . . ." before she fell. And then she rolled over a couple of times before springing back to her feet, laughing.

"Oh my God Kev, I can't believe I've just done that."

We both doubled up laughing until our sides ached, stepping back onto the pavement before the lights turned red again. I joked with her, grabbing her arm and saying "Come on lets r-oll over." Making as though I was going to run across the road in a jokey kind of take-off of what she had just done. We laughed that much that eventually when we did stop laughing it still felt like we were, my stomach and face were killing me.

Eventually we crossed the road, and made our way over to the jetty. There were two barges moored up, only one had any lights on so we made a bee-line for it. As we drew level with the barge I noticed that there was somebody sat in the driving seat on the left hand side of the boat. Obviously it was the driver and/or the captain.

As we approached the door the man sat in the driver's seat bobbed his head down so he could see us without obstruction. I gave the interior the once over. As far as I could see there were only two other occupants on the barge, a couple who were sat half-way down on the opposite side of the boat, so they were looking out into the dock, as opposed to the jetty.

"Hi there." he hollered.

"Permission to come aboard, Captain?" I said jokingly standing to attention and offering the man in the driver's seat a mock salute.

His hand shot straight up, saluting back to me with vigour. He was obviously ex-military and like I said old habits die hard.

"Permission granted sailor." he replied.

I jumped onto the barge and then turned round and offered Sadie a hand; she took it gracefully and climbed aboard. There were three steps to a doorway so small I had to duck down to get in. Sadie didn't, she didn't even have to break stride she cleared it easily. Once inside the man in the driver's seat welcomed us.

"Thanks for choosing to cruise with us; I am the captain and driver. Back there is the one and only crew member, Vanessa. Anything you need whilst were moving don't hesitate to shout and Vanessa will do her best to help, won't you Van."

I turned to look down the boat and right at the very far end beyond the tables stood a figure, silhouetted and waving, and nodding vigorously.

"If you would like to find a table and take a seat we should be good to go in about ten minutes or so. Oh, one more thing I have to insist that while the boat is moving you must remain in your seats the whole time."

I nodded and started to make my way down the gangway. Sadie held on to my hand, tight.

I chose the last table on the right on the side with the jetty view.

We sat directly across from each other; I slung my hoodie on the floor behind me. Sadie tucked her bag neatly under the table. As soon as I sat down, I sank into the cushion, pretty soon I found myself sprawling without wanting to.

Once inside the barge we found it was lavishly decorated. Oak floorboards, cream walls, and pine tables with two matching pine easy/high chairs which were facing one another, tucked in under each table. In the space between each window hung a few of Michael Godard's early pieces, each one thought provoking and unique in its own weird way. Underneath each painting there were speakers screwed into the wall. Each table had its own window. There were eight in all, four on the left and four on the right, each window measured in at about two and a half foot square. On each table was a tiny standard lamp fixed to the table and nothing else. The tables were situated at staggered intervals along each wall—that way it gave the occupants a little privacy.

The engine spluttered into life and the whole barge started to vibrate building up momentum and then we were off. First stop the red light district and all its points of interest. The captain expertly steered the barge into the narrow canal that runs through the heart of the red light district. The speakers crackled and then they came alive with the sexy voice of the narrator. Her voice was so low it sounded almost animal like. Her narrative coincided with the various attractions along the way. She spoke first in English, then Dutch, German, and finally French. I wasn't really listening to what she had to say, I was happy staring out the window. I had to admit it was a beautiful city, even more so from our present vantage point. It was like travelling through a portal back in time to the eighteen nineties, but without the period clothes.

We passed under bridges lit up by strings of white lightbulbs, and passed by clusters of houseboats that ranged from brand new to old and rickety.

Sadie had snuggled up alongside me as close as she could get, this was nice. This was the calm before the storm.

18

The barge edged its way back into the dock at twenty past eight. I was feeling a little giddy from the champagne and the company. I was under the influence, intoxicated by her charms and the drink, double trouble. At that particular moment in time I felt like the luckiest man alive and I didn't want it to end.

We thanked the captain and then bobbed under the door and onto the steps leading off the barge. I took the small step from the barge to the jetty and then helped Sadie do the same.

"Are you sure about this?" I said. "We still have time to change our minds if that's what you want."

"No I'm not sure, but yes let's do it." she replied.

"C'mon then we'll go to the Irish bar and give the barmaid the good news."

We took the now familiar route to the Irish bar, eight minutes later and we had turned onto the street where it was situated.

A couple of minutes after that and we had threaded our way through the crowded street and were stood at the door, paused at the threshold knowing there was no turning backing out once we were in.

I paused for a beat and then said,

"Listen, I think it's best if we keep your rendezvous with the hitman between me and you, we don't want to complicate matters further do we?"

Sadie nodded in agreement.

I reached out for the door and opened it, holding it open, standing to one side as I ushered Sadie in, with the palm of my hand resting ever so gently on the small of her back.

"After you M'lady." I said jokingly.

"Why, thank you M'lord." she replied and chuckled to herself as she stepped inside the bar.

It was the same old story once we got inside. Three barflies were propping up the bar, and even though they were seated they still looked unsteady like they could fall over at any second. There was a fourth person stood at/leant on the bar chatting to the laughing barmaid who was expertly pulling him a large glass of lager, and as we got closer to the bar I could tell he was American, his east coast accent was a dead giveaway.

Hothouse Flowers were playing on the stereo, it was their top ten hit "Don't Go."

Okay I won't I thought to myself, not until I have passed go and collected fifty G's anyway.

I caught the laughing barmaid's attention and nodded to the smoke room and mimed the action of lifting a glass to my mouth.

She nodded back to let me know she understood.

We made for the smoke room. Once inside I kicked the door and slid it shut. We took our usual places, at the far end of the room, and waited.

It wasn't long before the door slid open and the laughing barmaid struggled through the door with our two glasses. I got to my feet and squeezed passed her to kick/slide the door shut.

The laughing barmaid sat in the same seat as she had sat in this afternoon, the one attached to the last table on the right. She reached over and plonked our drinks on her table. I reached past her and grabbed Sadie's drink first, handing it over to her, and then reaching for my own. I took the top off the lager. As soon as I had swallowed the froth and burped I turned to face the laughing barmaid and said,

"Okay I'll do it. How are we goin' to work it, 'cos presumably this hitman can speak Dutch, and I can't speak a word of it?"

"I'd not thought about that." the laughing barmaid admitted.

Now there's a surprise. If you want a job doing properly you do it yourself.

"I suppose all I need to learn are a few simple phrases. Do you think you're up to teaching me."

The laughing barmaid nodded.

Sadie was rooting through her bag; she had already successfully hunted out a pack of cigarettes, the nip bag of weed, and a lighter, and they were all piled up on the table next to her like some weird art exhibit. It was the Rizlas that were proving to be the hardest to find as she moved things back and forth, back and forth, and back again, until she finally pulled the degenerated pack of Rizlas from her bag. She smiled triumphantly and set to work building a joint.

"Right." I said. "What we have to do is work out what I need to say when I meet your friend's mum, translate it and then all I have to do is keep repeating the phrases over and over again 'til I know them off by heart." I paused for a beat before continuing. "Have you any idea what time the meet is to take place tomorrow and where?"

The laughing barmaid kissed her molars, took a deep breath in and said,

"The hitman is going to ring me at one o'clock tomorrow so it will be sometime after that. I haven't gotta clue where the meet will be, it's open to negotiation."

That left us with just over sixteen hours at least for me to memorise the phrases and be able to repeat them with a degree of authenticity. For someone like me with a photographic memory it would be a piece of piss.

Right, time to think.

It would be wise to keep the conversation to a minimum, so I had to come up with phrases that didn't invite any kind of answer, the kind where a nod of the head would suffice. Just short abrupt phrases that related to the matter in hand.

Think. Think. Think.

Ping, lightbulb time.

"How do you say, 'Have you got the paperwork?'"

The laughing barmaid paused for a beat, and then said,

"Heb je het papierwerk?"

That was simple enough; this was going to be easier than I thought. I repeated the phrase a couple of times. Ten minutes later I had it down to a tee, almost native like. All I would have to do to keep it memorised was to keep saying it over and over again in my head and under my breath at random times throughout the rest of the night, and then recap in the morning. Job done.

I needed something else to say, something that would warn her off, but in a polite way.

Think. Think. Think.

Sadie had finished rolling the joint, and had just lit it. She now sat back in her chair, chilling. Taking in everything and saying nothing, for the time being anyway.

Ping, it was lightbulb time again. I clicked my fingers. I had it now.

"Right." I said, "How do you say, 'After today do not try to contact me, that number is gone, I do not exist'?"

Same script as before, the laughing barmaid paused a beat before reciting the correct translation.

"Na vandaag niet proberen om mij te contacteren, dit aantal is verdwenen, ik besta niet."

This was a little harder, trickier to say, even more trickier to memorise.

She wrote it down on a scrap of paper and handed it over to me.

I tried repeating it a couple of times but kept on fucking up half way through. I was confident I could pull it off before tomorrow; a lot can happen in twenty-four hour period, as I can well vouch for.

"I have to go, someone needs serving. Keep practicing. Everything depends on it." she said, getting to her feet and making for the sliding door.

The laughing barmaid vacated the smoke room, she struggled with the door. I didn't get up to help. Fuck her, why should I? She was out for herself, if that was the case then so was I.

I went back to reciting the phrase in my head, like a mantra.

Sadie passed over the joint, I took it and took a double hit off it and then propped it in the ash tray. I wanted a clear head for the task in hand.

"Na vandaag niet proberen om mij te contacteren, dit aantal is verdwenen, ik besta niet."

Over and over again.

"Na vandaag niet proberen om mij te contacteren, dit aantal is verdwenen, ik besta niet."

Over and over again.

*   *   *

The laughing barmaid returned to the smoke box some fifteen minutes later. I don't know what kept her, I didn't ask.

She asked me to repeat the phrase in front of her.

"Na vandaag niet proberen om mij te contacteren, dit aantal is verdwenen, ik besta niet." I said.

"Wow that's really good, do you think you can keep it up till tomorrow?" the laughing barmaid asked taking her seat.

"I think I can." I replied and picked up the joint from the ashtray, the lighter from off the table and fired it up sucking the smoke deep inside and holding it in, blowing out after five or six seconds, upwards.

I was confident I could carry it off. In fact I knew I could, I just needed a little more practice.

An hour and a half later I had both phrases memorised and could almost recite them both perfectly, by tomorrow afternoon I would have them both nailed down.

By the time we got ready to leave it was knocking on, coming up to one o'clock in the morning. It was pitch black outside and the crowds had thinned down to the odd one or two people staggering about; I had clocked only one person walking past in the last half hour. It occurred to me that to be out on the streets at this time of night in this particular part of the world you would have to be extremely naive, stupid, or reckless, or criminally minded, or possibly just a native doing their thing picking up some milk on their way home from work, or scoring a gramme before bed, whatever, if you didn't fit in any of the above categories then it was best to stay indoors. I fit the criteria for two out of five of the groups. Reckless. And criminally minded.

The last customer had left a little over half an hour ago so we had moved into the main area locking the main door so we wouldn't be interrupted.

"Just say both phrases before you go, I want to hear you again." the laughing barmaid said as I shook on my hoodie.

"Right I'll walk up to her, just as I get to her I will say to her in an abrupt way, 'Heb je het papierwerk?' 'Have you got the paperwork?'".

"Oooh."

The laughing barmaid cooed and clapped her hands together a couple of times. "I cannot believe it, you sound just like him."

I nodded and then continued,

"She will either be A, too scared to talk, or B, stutter an answer, or C, a mixture of both. Whereby she will then pass me the package I will quickly flick through the money, make sure we're not bein' ripped off. When I am satisfied I will say to her, 'Na vandaag niet proberen om mij te contacteren, dit aantal is verdwenen, ik besta niet.' 'After today, do not try to contact me, this number is gone, I do not exist.' With that I will turn away and walk off. Where will you be waitin'?"

"Well it's my day off tomorrow so I will wait for you at my flat."

"Which is where?"

"Not far, about a twenty minute walk from here it's just round the corner from Anne Frank's house."

I glanced towards Sadie.

"Tomorrow we will sort a place out for the meet and then we will work out a route for me to take after the exchange as taken place." I said to the laughing barmaid.

I now turned my attention to Sadie and said,

"We will sort out a rendezvous for you to wait while I go and get the cash, somewhere en-route between the meet and her flat. Is that okay?"

I rubbed my hands together with anticipation and glee for what tomorrow would and should bring.

Sadie nodded.

"Right." I said. "If that's everythin' covered, we're off." I said to the laughing barmaid.

"Hang on." Sadie said. "I've thought of something, well a couple of things to be precise."

I raised my eyebrows in surprise. I thought we had everything covered.

"First things first." Sadie said as she picked up her bag and looped it over her shoulder. "We need an internet cafe, so we can book a flight out of here, but we can do that tomorrow."

I tipped my head and wagged my index finger once in a silent salute.

"There is one near my flat."

"What's the other thing?" I asked.

"Well, you might look like the hitman, walk like him and talk like him, but do you dress like him?"

I shrugged my shoulders and looked to the laughing barmaid for an answer.

"Well do I?" I said to her when an answer wasn't forthcoming quick enough for my liking.

The laughing barmaid pulled a face, shook her head and said,

"Yes and no, he wears all sorts of different clothes."

"Well, what kind of clothes does he wear? He must have a style." I said.

"I have only met with him four times and each time he was wearing something different." She paused for a second her eyes went up and left.

"The first time he came in a suit."

"Well that's out of the question." I said. "I've never worn a suit and am not about to start now."

"The second time he came in a pair of trousers, shirt, leather jacket and a pair of shoes."

"That's more like it." I said.

"The third time he came in jeans, trainers, T-shirt and leather jacket."

"Even better."

"The last time we met he was wearing jeans, trainers, and a sweatshirt with a hood."

"Well that's that then." I said shrugging my shoulders. "I'll just wear what I normally wear."

I looked over to the smoke room; we had left in a right mess. Discarded empty packets of crisps, and nuts were strewn across three tables; it looked like the aftermath of a child's party. That was only half of it, at least half a dozen empty glasses of all shapes and sizes were stacked on top of each other, and three almost overflowing ashtrays were piled up on the last table on the right. I smiled to myself; the laughing barmaid wasn't going anywhere anytime soon.

"What time do you normally get up?" I asked the laughing barmaid.

"Not early on my day off, say about ten."

"Okay, ring me when you get up and we can meet somewhere."

The laughing barmaid nodded.

Like Elvis, we left the building.

19

Once outside the bar I pulled Sadie to one side, there was no one else on the street. It was like a ghost town where nothing stirred, not even tumbleweeds, urban or otherwise. Everything was as still as a forest pool. The moon became visible for a split second before being swallowed whole by a monster cloud. Now you see it, now you don't.

"What do you think? Think we can pull it off?"

"I don't see why not." Sadie replied, pulling me close and kissing me full on the lips with an intensity that instantly got me hard. Her tongue searched and probed, and then she stopped and said, "It seems pretty straight forward to me, the way we've planned it I can't see anything going wrong."

"Me neither." I said returning the kiss with equal vigour.

I was in a good mood as we walked back to the hotel. What could possibly go wrong?

I wonder.

We dawdled our way through the empty streets, laughing and joking, stopping and kissing. This was the life; this was how it was meant to be . . .

20

The next morning I woke to someone tapping lightly on the door to our room. I struggled to sit up in bed reaching for my phone as I did so. I squinted at the screen. It was ten past nine am. I got out of bed, still naked and hard, and stretched, and stumbled over to the door and listened with my ear to the gap. My mind was still cloudy from the smoke and the drink the night before. But I soon came round when the tapping turned into banging. I quickly stood to the left of the door. At this point I didn't have a clue who it was on the other side so I wasn't taking any chances. That way if somebody did decide to smash their way through it I was tucked up to one side and out of the way. No bother. And if that did happen, their kinetic momentum would carry them off balance leaving me with the advantage. End of story, in a situation like that who gains the upper hand means everything.

Sadie sat up in bed rubbing her eyes.

"Who is it?" she said, her voice all croaky.

I put my finger to my lips, and listened. I could hear muffled voices and shuffling out in the corridor.

I counted to five, and then said,

"Hello."

"Housekeeping."

It was the sweetest voice I'd ever heard, like an angel sighing. If it was the housekeeper who looked like the old housekeeper from the Tom and Jerry cartoon then her voice as well as her smile belied her size.

I blew out a huge breath all in one and said,

"Can you come back later please?"

"Okay."

I heard some more shuffling, presumably as she moved her cart onto the next room.

My whole body relaxed. I had tensed up, ready for action. Instead I sat down on the edge of the bed, relieved. No sooner had I sat down then my phone started to vibrate. I checked the screen before answering. It just said "Call" on the screen. I gave it another three rings before I answered.

White noise.

"Hello." I said.

"Could I speak to a Kevin Naylor please?" said the metallic voice.

"Speaking."

"Detective Smit here."

"Okay." I said.

Sadie threw me a quizzical look.

I held an index finger up in the air as if to say, "Hang on, let me find out and I will tell you."

"I'm phoning you up about the enquiry I'm heading, we talked yesterday."

"Yes." I said. "I remember."

It seemed like an age ago since they first walked into the bar yesterday morning, mob handed.

"Just informing you that we won't be needing to speak to you again regarding the matter. Thank you for your help in our investigation and I hope the rest of your stay here is enjoyable."

Short but sweet.

"Oh right, I hope you catch the person that did it." I said, careful to make sure I said person and not man; I didn't want him getting any ideas where I was concerned.

"We're hopeful we will apprehend the suspect within the next twenty-four hours. Thank you again."

"Okay bye now, glad to be of help."

The line clicked and then went dead.

I looked at the default setting for a couple of seconds before a smile started to spread across my face; I then turned to Sadie and said,

"That was the police."

"And what did they say?"

"They said they wouldn't need to talk to me again. That's good news innit."

Sadie nodded.

"Did they say anything else?"

"Only that they were hoping to apprehend the suspect within the next twenty-four hours. That's even better for us don't you think?"

Sadie nodded and said,

"Well let's hope they don't catch him before the meet or its bye-bye money."

"That's a point, we can't scam him if he's locked up can we?"

Sadie shook her head.

All was good. Pretty normal day then, up to now.

"I need something to eat." I said. "I need fuel, we've gotta long day ahead of us not to mention the flight out of here tonight. I'm not looking forward to it at all."

"You'll be okay; I'll make sure of it."

"Let's just get through today, hey." I said making for the shower. We needed to be ready to move on a second's notice.

While I was in the shower the curtain opened slowly to reveal a naked Sadie wearing a mischievous smile. Without a word she dropped to her knees and I gasped as she went to work. It was a strange sensation to have the water cascading over my head and shoulders while she was licking and sucking, and nibbling, until finally I was past the point of no return. She made eye contact as I shot my load down her throat. It was too much for me, my knees almost gave way, and I had to reach out with both arms and hold onto whatever to keep my balance. It was still a struggle to stay upright as she cleaned me up with her tongue. She finally released me and licked her lips; I shuddered and pulled her up so we were virtually face to face. We locked lips; I kissed her full on the mouth.

She broke away and playfully pushed me and said,

"Now hurry up, I need a shower as well." she paused for a beat and then said, "Shellfish."

She had a wicked smile, and a dirty laugh, all in all she was good with her mouth, as she had just proven beyond any doubt. This was going to be a dream partnership, I could tell, one that could last forever, or not as the case may be.

While Sadie was in the shower I fished out the scrap of paper the laughing barmaid had written the two phrases on and transferred it to my new jeans. I would have to go over the phrases again and again, right up until the actual meet. That way they would be embedded deep into my memory, and there would be no way I would forget them, ever. Even months after the fact I would be able to recall them no bother.

21

After towelling myself dry I got dressed in attire similar to the hitman's. I was wearing a pair of Levi's, Nike Air, a non-descript T-shirt under a grey hoodie. I looked at myself in the mirror on the bathroom wall. I looked the part, even if I did say so myself.

Sadie was still in the shower so I decided to go for a smoke on the balcony. On the short walk down the corridor I checked my phone for any missed calls I might have had whilst I was in the shower. There were none. The time was coming up to quarter past ten; the laughing barmaid would be ringing any time now.

Once on the balcony I shook a cigarette out and lit it, as soon as I blew the smoke out the wind just gathered it all up and dispersed it into nothing. I leant on the balcony and watched the little people from Lilliput down below getting on with whatever it was they were doing. Some were in a rush barging into people to try and gain a few yards here and there, and some were just sauntering along as though they had all the time in the world. There was one tiny derelict on the opposite side of the road dressed in rags, with long hair shuffling his way down the street. He walked like Jack Nicholson in One Flew Over The Cuckoo's Nest after his electric shock treatment. People were actually flattening themselves against the wall as he passed; some were holding their noses or wafting newspapers in front of their faces to try and get rid of his stink. He was trying to talk to people as they passed him, but they were all ignoring him, he probably only wanted a couple of guilders for a coffee.

I stood there on the balcony for a good twenty minutes smoking and watched the day unfurl below. I was just about to light my third cigarette up when the door to my left opened and out stepped Sadie, looking drop dead gorgeous, dressed not to kill but to fleece. She was wearing a pink hoodie with a white T-shirt underneath, her white Lacoste low tops, and a pair of jeans. Simple, yet the effect it was having on me was complicated, in more ways than one.

"Has she rung yet?" Sadie said as she took her place at my side.

"Not yet." I said. "We should go grab some brekky before it's too late. By the time we have finished eating she should have rung by then."

"Come on then let's go." Sadie said as she hooked her arm around mine.

We headed for Carla's.

The breakfast was the same as yesterday. Not exactly the same, there were a few variants, but in general high fibre food, and nuts, and yoghurts. I skipped that shit and made myself a bacon and scrambled egg bap and happily munched my way through it, so much so I made myself another, and another. I needed fuel for the fire that was burning inside.

After we had finished eating and drinking, we had emptied three flasks; we left Carla's and made the short walk to Jan's coffee shop. We had run out of supplies and seeing as though Jan's seemed to be the laughing barmaid's local it seemed a good a place as any.

I pushed the door open to Jan's and stepped inside holding the door for Sadie. She smiled and stepped inside too. I let the door go and made for the counter/bar, Sadie made for a suitable table. The place was empty, deserted except for Jan; he was in his usual position sat looking up and left at a large screen fixed to the wall. Some domestic shit was on the flat screen with the sound turned down, I didn't have a clue what it was, and I didn't care less. That's how I like it.

I got to the counter/bar and leant on it.

Jan looked over to where I was stood/leant and smiled, and said,

"Hey, what can I get you?"

"Some more of that Blueberry please." I said nodding to the Tupperware boxes full of weed. "And two coffees, one black, one with cream please."

Jan nodded and spun on his heels.

I watched him as he filled the flask up with water and then filled the reservoir at the top of the machine with the water from the flask. He then tucked a brown paper filter into the drainage section and spooned some ground coffee into the filter, flicked a switch and then spun back on his heels so he was facing me again. The machine started to cough and splutter, softly at first, but then slowly gaining momentum, until it was going at it like an old smoker.

"How many grams of the Blueberry were you after?"

"You best make it five mate." I said.

He nodded and spun back on his heels and set to work weighing my order.

"You might as well go and sit down. I will bring it over to you when the coffee is done yes."

"Yes okay." I said and pointed to the table where Sadie had taken refuge. "I'll be over there."

Jan nodded.

Just as I sat down my phone started to vibrate in my pocket, so I stood back up again and dug it out. Looking at the caller's number before answering, it was a habit I would never grow out of, and never grow tired of doing. I recognised the laughing barmaid's number and pressed the button to answer.

"Hello."

"It's me."

"I know."

"Are you awake?"

"Well yes of course I am otherwise I wouldn't have answered would I?" I said, placing my hand over the mic and mouthing the words to Sadie, "It's the barmaid."

"Where are you?"

"We're at Jan's coffee shop where I saw you yesterday."

"Okay, wait there I will be half hour at the most."

The line clicked, and then went dead.

I didn't mind waiting here, it wasn't the worst place I could think of, and in fact it would rank at the very top of my 'best places to hang out in' list. Nice one.

"Where do you fancy flyin' to?" I asked Sadie while we waited for our coffees and the gear.

"I don't know it depends where they fly to from Schipol doesn't it?" she replied. "Find out the destinations and pick one."

"Sounds good to me." I said nodding towards the counter/bar from where Jan was making his way over to us, a cup and saucer in each hand and the nip bag clenched between his teeth. The crockery rattled with every step he took, scuff, chink, scuff, and chink.

"Here you go." Jan said as he placed our drinks in front of us. "One black coffee."

I put my index finger up in the air.

"That's me." I said.

"And one with cream." he said placing the drink in front of Sadie.

He paused for a beat and then said,

"Just call it forty five guilders." he said, tossing the nip bag on the table in front of me; it spun round a couple of revolutions then came to a halt.

I peeled off five notes, knowing that they were all ten guilder notes. It's a little quirk I have, I like to have notes of the same denomination in my pocket, that way you don't flash your bill fold about all the time, you just peel them off in your pocket and hand them over, no worries, and no unwanted attention.

"Keep the change." I said.

Jan beamed a smile at us and then spun back round and walked back over to the till to deposit the cash with an extra bounce in his step.

"Do you think he's gay?" Sadie asked just as Jan bumped the till shut with his backside.

I nodded and blew on the steaming surface of the coffee until it rippled; like some far off marsh shrouded in mist in a fairytale, the wells of the moon maybe.

"Oh, without a doubt." I said. "And I'd go as far as sayin' I'd put my balls on it."

"I wouldn't." she said and gave them a gentle squeeze.

I took the top of the coffee; it was nice, a lot nicer than yesterday. Hot. And strong. How I like my coffee and my women.

"Do you want to do the honours or shall I?" Sadie asked.

"You do it; I need to chill for a while." I said. "Oh that reminds me."

I dug around in my little Jonny pocket for the scrap of paper the laughing barmaid had written the two phrases on. I didn't think I would need it but I stared at the two phrases anyway.

"Heb je het papierwerk?"

"Have you got the paperwork?"

Over and over again.

Burying it deep inside.

Over and over again.

Locked away safe, in one of the many vaults my memory boasts.

"Na vandaag niet proberen om mij te contacteren, dit aantal is verdwenen, ik besta niet."

"After today do not try to contact me, that number is gone, I do not exist."

Over and over again.

"Na vandaag niet proberen om mij te contacteren, dit aantal is verdwenen, ik besta niet.

Under my breath, and out loud.

Not a question.

Or a threat.

It was a statement of intent.

Don't try and get in touch or else.

When I was satisfied I had re-familiarised myself with the phrases I recited them back to Sadie. I was a bit rusty at first, but I soon had it back to the same level as the night before. Perfect, we were good to go.

Sadie lit the joint and immediately passed it over to me; I accepted it gracefully and stuck it in my mouth and tugged on it holding the smoke inside while I took a sip of the coffee. I swallowed the liquid down but still held the smoke in for a little while longer. I wanted the full effects, and I wanted them now. Eventually I blew the smoke out and upwards. I could feel the weed's tendrils reaching out, trying to grasp a hold of my mind. I knew it wouldn't be long. I took another hit and then handed the joint back to Sadie. We played the hot potato with the joint, passing it back and forth and then back again, until Sadie crushed it out in the ashtray under a well manicured fingernail. The roach end still smouldered for a while in defiance, until it eventually petered out.

I finished off my coffee necking the two-tone dregs down in one. I could feel the caffeine working its way into my system, contradicting the weed. The weed was sprawled out saying chill out man, just sit back and relax. Whereas the coffee was stressed out in the corner shaking and twitching saying come on get up we've got things to do. I ignored them both and just went with the flow. Up one minute. Down the next. When you're up you're up. When you're down you're down. Cause and effect. I drink the coffee. I smoke the weed. Therefore I take the consequences whatever they may be. What goes around comes around, Karma, sod's law, however you dress it up it boils down to the same thing, a force working on its own with its own ends and its own means. Sometimes it's on your side, and sometimes it isn't, if it is—all well and good, if it isn't—fuck it I'll do what I have to do to tip the scales in my favour. That's how I like it, then if it all goes wrong there's only one person to blame, and that's me. I control my own destiny, with a little help from my friends of course.

Some twenty odd minutes later the door pushed open and in walked the laughing barmaid. She was dressed in a pair of faded jeans, and a non-descript T-shirt and jumper under a stonewashed parka. The parka was zipped up tight, but the hood was down. She had her hair up in a ponytail like on the first day we had met her. Like she could really do with washing it but couldn't be bothered, so instead she scraped it back and stuck a bobble on it, convenience triumphs over hygiene every time.

She nodded to us as she passed us and made her dainty way over to where Jan was sprawled on the bar. She said something and he set to work, weighing and pouring. Finally she spun around and made her way over to us, cup and saucer in one hand, nip bag of weed in the other. Why would you want to leave all this behind? The mind boggles. She plonked herself in alongside Sadie, opposite me, not directly just slightly to the left.

"Will the clothes do?" I asked the laughing barmaid.

She was more like herself today, less stressed, more relaxed, easy going and carefree, and smiling.

"Yes they're fine." she said, giving me the once over, looking me up and down, from head to toe, and back again. "I can't believe it, you look exactly like him. It's uncanny, weird."

"Anybody been in touch?" I asked her.

She shook her head and then took the froth of her cappuccino, leaving her with a foamy moustache, which she licked off slowly, and seductively, all the time maintaining eye to eye contact, with me.

I looked at Sadie, this was a complication I could do without for sure, and one I hadn't even accounted for, or even thought about for that matter. It was a spanner in the works, a curve ball. I raised my eyebrows at Sadie. I made sure the laughing barmaid wasn't looking before I did it—she had glanced over her shoulder at where Jan was, he was still in the same position sprawled over the counter/bar, his arms out in front of him, both palms were flat and his fingers were spread out and across the dark wood like two albino spiders. He was still staring up at the screen, I don't know if he was actually watching or it was just his way of coping with the boredom of having no one to wait on. Trance out at the screen, pass some time away.

Sadie looked hurt; she shook her head and looked to the barmaid who had now turned back round to face me. She was wearing a half smile and even that was half hearted.

I was going to ask the laughing barmaid to accompany Sadie to the internet cafe but that looked to be out of the question now. I would have to go with her myself, which wasn't ideal. I had hoped to fit in a bit of extra-curricular down filth alley. Bastard. We would have to wait now and see how the day panned out, whether or not it was viable. I kept my fingers crossed, metaphorically.

"We have to go to the internet cafe to book our flights outta here; as soon as I give you your cut then we split."

"I can walk up with you if you want. I will wait at my flat; as soon as he calls I will be in touch."

"We're ready now aren't we?" I asked Sadie.

She nodded in reply. I was in her bad books, I could tell.

"I just need to roll a spliff before we go, and finish my coffee."

We made small talk for the remainder of the time in the coffee shop, once we were out on the street the conversation turned serious.

"The police phoned me today." I said.

"What did they have to say?"

"Nothing really, just that they wouldn't need to speak to me again. So I guess I owe you."

She kissed her molars, and crinkled her nose. She had decided to turn up the heat. And that unfortunately meant bad news for me, for us, for the plan. It could jeopardise the whole thing, I had to nip it in the bud now or it could end up ruining everything. I have to admit I was tempted, but that was where it ended, at temptation's door. It might put bums on seats in cinemas but there was no place in real life for it, it was an unwanted distraction. One I wasn't prepared to go along with.

"They did say that they were confident they would catch the killer, soon. Within twenty-four hours."

I watched the laughing barmaid for any tell tale reactions.

Her lips pursed and she chewed on the inside of her mouth. A sure sign of stress.

I probed further.

"Let's hope it's later rather than sooner." I said first to Sadie, and then to the laughing barmaid.

Sadie nodded in agreement.

The laughing barmaid nodded once and looked down at her moving feet.

Guilty conscience.

Something to hide.

I let it go, for now.

We had turned down a series of side streets after leaving Jan's. A few lefts and rights keeping on the same side of the road, but this time I had an idea where we actually were. I visualised the street map of Amsterdam in my head, pinpointed where I thought Jan's coffee shop and Anne Frank's house was, and then did the relevant calculations to pinpoint where we were right now. By my reckoning we had covered half of the distance needed.

"Presumably your friend's mum has been questioned?" I said. "By the police."

The laughing barmaid's head bobbed up and down vigorously.

"Yes, she has, twice, but she's playing the part alright. She deserves an Oscar."

"What about her daughter?"

"Once."

"Everythin' okay?"

"So far so good." She replied.

"What about your friend the fixer? Has he had a tug yet?"

She looked puzzled.

"Has he been questioned by the police yet?"

"No he hasn't, but he did tell me that he had heard on the grapevine that the police are questioning everybody who had connections with the dead gangster, his friends, family, everyone."

"Mmmm." I said while stoking my chin. "They're bound to turn somethin' up, you shake something hard enough and things tend to fall out."

Again the laughing barmaid looked anxious whenever I spoke of the hitman's demise. And then it suddenly dawned on me that maybe they had slept together. Why not? It wasn't beyond the realm of possibility. He looked like me, and she hadn't exactly been backward at coming forward where I was concerned. She had practically thrown herself at me, in front of Sadie to boot.

We paused at a crossroads, waiting for a break in the traffic. And then we were off again.

"Do you think the skinhead will say something to the police, you know about the other night?" the laughing barmaid asked as we took another right turn.

"No." I answered.

"How can you be so sure?"

"I just am." I said smugly.

"How though? Because if he wanted to and was clever enough he could put you in the frame for the murder."

"Firstly, it's his word against ours. Secondly, he wouldn't want to lose anymore face than he already has. And thirdly, because if he had I wouldn't be here right now would I?"

"I guess not." she replied.

We took another right.

"The internet cafe is up here on the right." the laughing barmaid said. "My flat is about another five minute's walk. Up there."

She pointed; I followed her finger-line and glanced down the street. I could see a residential district looming in the background like some old horror flick back drop.

"When he rings I will come and meet you."

"Okay." I said. "Well we're not doin' anythin' really we're just gonna be passin' time."

Sadie stayed silent.

We parted company at the internet cafe. The laughing barmaid promised she would be in touch as soon as any new information came in.

I pushed the door and held it open for Sadie, side-stepping so she could squeeze through the gap I had created.

"Let's hope that we're not getting mixed up in anything we can't handle." Sadie said as she tried to step passed me.

I reached out both my arms to form a barrier around her, one hand on the door jamb and one hand on the door, so I was blocking her entry.

"Up to now." I said. "Touch wood."

While I spoke I took hold of Sadie's hand and rested it on my crotch.

Her eyes lit up and she scraped her teeth along her bottom lip.

"I have coped with everythin' that's been thrown at me, 'av even had to revert to plan B on the odd occasion. Don't worry I'm more than capable of looking after us." I said, doing my best to placate her fears.

Internet cafes were a new phenomenon, they were popping up all over the place, every continent, every major city, everywhere. And they were all the same generic design, both inside and out. Hi-tech places with shiny fascias and shiny signs with fancy scripts and weird names, and that was just the outside. On the inside it was shiny walls and even shinier floors, shiny counters with shiny people behind the counters, and so on. The point is they're all the same.

There were rows and rows of computers nestled into little pigeon-holed desks, each computer faced another one. If you looked at the room from above it would resemble a maze. Most of the bays were occupied by either nerdy students or just students. The whole place stank of stale sweat and bad breath.

"Do you really need me to go in there with you?" I said blowing a breath out of slightly parted lips.

"No not really why?"

"It's just I don't fancy it." I said pulling a face and looking away.

"Where are you going to wait while I book the flights?"

I scanned the street looking for an ideal place to loiter.

"Over there." I said pointing up the street where a modern marble bench stood unoccupied.

Sadie followed my finger-line and nodded when she found what I was pointing at.

"Okay, any preferences?"

"For what?"

"Der." Sadie said rolling her tongue up in front of her bottom set of teeth and pulling a face. "Destination, where do you want to go?" she said it as though she was spelling it out to a child.

"Anywhere baby." I said opening the door and stepping outside.

I motioned with my fingers for her to come outside.

She took a couple of steps closer to me.

"Google destinations from Schipol, and pick one from that. Whatever you choose I'll go with."

Sadie nodded and stepped back into the internet cafe. I walked away a couple of steps and she disappeared due to the glare on the glass. I made my way over to the bench and got myself comfortable. No sooner had I sat down then my phone started to vibrate in my pocket. I took it out and looked at the screen.

It was the laughing barmaid.

"Hello."

"It's me."

"I know, what's up?"

"My friend has just called to say that the police have just turned up again and took her mum in for questioning."

"That's okay."

"Is it?"

"Yes."

"How so?"

"It's just procedure, but it is worrying that they have come for her again."

"Tell me about it."

"Keep me informed." I said and cut her off.

I slipped the phone back in my pocket and shook out a cigarette. I left it dangling from my mouth while I jostled this new development around in my head, trying to get an angle on it. Was it worth precious head time or not? I thought not. Only time would tell.

I was just finishing my third cigarette off some twenty minutes later when the door to the internet cafe opened and out stepped a beaming Sadie. She clocked me straight away, and started to make her way over. She paused for a second while she waited for a break in the traffic, and then jogged over to my side of the road. When she got to me she was out of breath slightly, a big smile lit up her face, starting at her mouth and ending at her eyes. Her joy was evident. On her face. And in her eyes.

"So put me out of my misery, where are we goin'?"

She paused for a beat and then said,

"New York."

"You're kiddin' right?"

"No, I thought you'd be happy?"

"I am, in fact I'm more than happy. It was just a shock that's all. It's somewhere I've always wanted to go. How did you know?"

"I didn't know, how could I? I've been before and loved it. So when New York came up in the list of destinations and there just so happens to be a flight at eleven o'clock tonight I thought it was an omen. The fact that you like it is a bonus."

"Good choice." I said shaking a cigarette out for Sadie and handing it to her together with my lighter.

I sat for a while people watching.

"What's up?" Sadie asked the back of my head.

"Nothin'." I replied.

"There is I can tell."

"There in't honest."

"If you say so."

"Well." I said turning round to face her.

She was just stubbing the cigarette out on the ground dragging it backwards and forwards until it disintegrated.

"There is one thing, nothin' serious, just something niggling away at the back of my mind."

"What is it?"

"How long a flight is it to New York?"

"Well its seven and a half hours from England, so I would hazard a guess at around nine."

I blew out a huge sigh.

"It will only be my second time on a plane, I'm just worried."

"You will be okay; I will make sure of it."

"That's easier said than done. It's not that I don't like flyin', 'cos I do, the takin' off I love, the landin' I love, am not so keen on the bit in-between. It's my body that doesn't take to it well."

"We know now though don't we so we can counteract it."

"How?"

"We can get some pain-killers and some motion sickness tablets that will help."

"Yeah I suppose so." I said.

I looked at my phone; it was now twenty past twelve.

"While you go get the cash I can wait in the internet cafe for you. It's ideal if you think about it, it's en-route to the barmaid's flat. All I have to do is pay for a couple of hours airtime, surf the web and wait for you to show up." Sadie said.

I nodded in agreement.

"Yeah, we could organise the meet for Dam Square, it's public, somewhere safe for her piece of mind. Plus it's only a ten minute walk to where we are now. In fact the more I think about it the more I think it is the perfect place. Am gonna ring the barmaid now, she might even know a short cut." I said whipping my phone out of my pocket.

I pressed the green button twice without even looking; I knew the laughing barmaid's number would be the last one stored on the call register. So by pressing the green button twice it would recall the last number on the list and then re-dial it.

She answered after four rings.

"Hello."

"It's me." I said.

"He hasn't rung yet, I said I'd call you when he rang."

"I know, am just ringing to tell you to arrange the meet for Dam Square. Sadie is goin' to wait for me somewhere in-between yours and there."

I didn't want her to know where the rendezvous was, that way she couldn't double cross us. Fuck the short cuts, I'd make my own way there.

"Where?"

"We don't know yet, we're just lookin' now."

"I'll see what I can do."

"No make it happen, that's where I want to do the meet, so that's where it's gonna be. okay."

I cut the connection.

I looked to Sadie and said,

"He an't rung yet."

"What else did she say?"

"She asked me where you were goin' to wait while I picked up the cash. I said we didn't know we were just lookin' for a suitable spot now."

"I thought you were going to ask her about short cuts from Dam Square to the internet cafe?"

I shook my head.

"Thought better of it, if she dun't know anythin' she can't betray us can she?" I said with a wink.

"I don't like her, she could fuck everything up." Sadie said.

"I'm not particularly fond of her either; she's just a means to an end."

"I saw the way she was looking at you when she was licking that cream of her lips. If she tries anything on, I swear I will rip her eyes out."

"She won't." I said.

"She better not."

"Come on let's go find a coffee shop and wait for the call."

We both got to our feet and headed back the way we had came earlier with the laughing barmaid in search of a coffee shop. I had noticed one on the way up, so we headed in that direction. It was coming up to one o'clock in the afternoon.

PART 3

The Hunt and The Meet

22

*L*ess than a mile away, Van de Berg and Smit were sat in their squad room. They were dressed almost like identical twins. They looked like stereo-typical undercover cops, except they weren't undercover, they were plain-clothed detectives which meant they chose to dress this way, well Smit did, and Van de Berg followed his lead licking his arse.

Smit had on a pair of black denims, whereas Van de Berg had on a pair of thick black corduroys. Smit was wearing a thick black hoodie, whereas Van de Berg was sporting a plain black sweatshirt. Both men were wearing non-descript black T-shirts, a thin sliver of black was visible just above the collar lines of their respective jumpers, and both men were wearing Doc Marten boots. Smit's were eighteen holers, Van de Berg's fourteen. They both wore their jeans on the outside and both men had plain black bomber jackets draped over the backs of their chairs. Everything in the room was black, white or beige, even the detectives clothing mirrored the decor, and it was a bland place to work, one that lacked motivation and inspiration. But you didn't need any external stimulation when you were chasing a killer that came from within; it was personal for each and every one of them.

Meijer and Visser were in the interview room putting pressure on the dead man's wife. It was the third time they'd had her in for questioning since the murder the night before. It was obvious she hadn't pulled the trigger, but Meijer had a hunch and Smit who was the officer in charge of the investigation had learnt to trust Meijer's hunches and let him run with them. Meijer was the kind of detective who could sniff out a rat and he was definitely sniffing something where the woman was concerned. There was something going on with her, he didn't know what for sure but given time he would provide the proof needed to secure a conviction. All he needed to do was apply the right amount of pressure in the right areas and he was sure she would fold and flip on the man who had actually pulled the trigger. Job done, handshakes all around and a possible promotion?

The whole place stank of stale sweat and takeaway food, there were four air fresheners strategically placed around the room; and they were working flat out but were still coming off second best. A big round clock sat on the wall opposite them; it was institutional in appearance, like everything else in the building, white plastic casing with a see through face clipped onto it, its second hand was gliding round the face, like a lawn mower tied to a stick.

It was now coming up to one o'clock. Both detectives had been on the phone most of the morning. They were chasing up the only lead they had. It was an eye-witness statement; someone had seen the killer running away from the scene of the crime. The witness had got a pretty good look, and in turn was able to give a detailed description of the killer. It was that what was bothering the two detectives. The artist's sketch looked suspiciously like the Brit they had interviewed in the Irish bar yesterday. But he had a cast iron alibi. It had stood up to the test. The barmaid from the Irish bar had confirmed the two men had not been in the bar that night. She had also confirmed that the Brit had left the bar just before eleven with an unknown woman. The barmaid had claimed she hadn't got a good enough look at the woman to give a worthwhile description. Only that she was white, about five foot five, with long brown hair. The unknown woman had been at the bar yesterday when they had interviewed the Brit, she had confirmed that they left the bar just before eleven and headed straight back to the hotel. Both had claimed neither of the two men in the photographs they had been shown had been in the bar at all. Case closed. Or was it? Smit was prepared to give the Brit the benefit of his doubt for now.

Smit had the bit between his teeth, and he wasn't about to let go. He was staring at a computer screen as he had been doing for most of the morning. He moved the mouse around on the pad to his right so the cursor on the screen was at his beck and call. He was going down a list highlighting each segment in turn. It was a list of hotels in the area. The businesses were listed alphabetically. Van de Berg was doing the same, only he was checking out bed and breakfasts, and hostels. Smit was on L; he had a few call backs to make, namely the Grand Hotel Krasnapolsky and The Dam Hotel. Van de Berg was only on C due to the fact that there were a lot more bed and breakfasts and hostels than hotels in the area; they were ten a penny. It was only a matter of time before they hit the jackpot but it was time they didn't have.

The job looked to have been done by a professional, a hitman, and that would point to him being out of the area already and gone forever leaving no way of tracing him. Good for him, bad for them. The murder was a classic gangland execution, two shots to the head with a twenty-two from point blank range, no exit wound, and no clues. They would have to wait for the coroner to dig the bullets out of his head so they could do the ballistics on them. Find out what make of gun had fired the bullet, and then take it from there. So for now they had to make do with contacting every hotel and bed and breakfast in the area. Laborious work, painstakingly boring, but it had to be done. They were asking every hotel manager, owner, or clerk if they had anyone matching the description staying at the hotel. If they did have someone resembling the description at the hotel then a fax was sent containing the actual sketch. A lot of establishments had said yes they had someone fitting the description staying at their establishment. But to date not one of them had replied to the faxes, so one could conclude that they had compared the sketch with the guest to no avail. It was like looking for a needle in a haystack, literally. The same methods were applied; you sifted through everything until you found what you were looking for. Only you would have more chance of finding a needle in a haystack, than one face in five million.

Smit dialled the number and waited for the connection.

23

Less than a third of a mile from where Smit and Van de Berg were working, the hitman sat on his hotel bed. Fresh out of the shower and dripping perfect sphere-shaped droplets of water onto the thick plush carpet. He was naked from the waist up; his upper body was toned to perfection, with not an ounce of fat on him, anywhere. His six pack and lats stood out like coils of rope as he dried his hair. He had been out earlier taking in the sights, following on from yesterday's jaunt where he had met the cute little British girl. He hoped he might bump into her again today, but it hadn't happened yet, so here he was, alone.

The room had been cleaned, the bed sheets had been changed and remade so tight you could bounce a folded note off it never mind a coin. There was a towel folded origami-like into the shape of a swan and placed in the middle of his king size bed, which had made him laugh on returning to the room.

Life was rosy, all he had to do was meet the woman and collect his money and he would be out of here, tonight preferably, if not tomorrow morning at the latest. Destination, unknown. Which reminded him he needed to book a flight, he had seen an internet cafe on the walk back from Anne Frank's house earlier on. That would suffice. He could go before he met with the woman. Then he would be free to try and find the cute British girl, maybe have a wander down near where he walked her to yesterday, maybe bump into her, well that was the plan at least.

He was a man who liked the finer things in life, hence the hotel room with a view of the Royal palace. He considered himself as royalty and whoever had the fortune to hire him definitely regarded him as that, hitman royalty, they would shake his hand and tell him he was the best thing since sliced bread. Wherever he went he was welcomed into every old boy's club with open arms. While he was around he was everybody's best friend, because if you saw him it meant that you weren't his target, and you could breathe easy.

He was a lethal shadow, one that could strike out of the darkness at any time. He was the best at what he did, jack of no trades, master of only one—murder. He liked to be in, do the job and out, no fuss, no problems. He had honed his techniques to perfection, whatever the job required whether it was covert or overt, garrotte or knife, close quarters or long range. Whichever, whatever, he could adapt and compromise, which was his greatest talent. And because of his continuing workload he could afford to live extravagantly. When he ate, he ate the finest foods, Argentinean and Aberdeen Angus steaks, dauphinoise potatoes, Sicilian sun-dried tomatoes and so on. When he drank he drank the finest liquors, wines and beers from across the world. And when he travelled he travelled in style, which went without saying. He wasn't a dedicated follower of fashion; a trend-setter was what he was. He had his own style and it suited him, he wore what he liked when he liked and up to now it had served him well.

He was also a drifter, drifting wherever his work load took him. Of course he had a base; any man wanting to be taken seriously had to have one. If you didn't own a property of some sorts most people would regard you as a bum, and that was one thing he wasn't. You could call him most names and get away with it, like murderer, mercenary, bastard. They all hit the nail on the head, direct hits, but bum was so far off the mark it was out of the ballpark.

He had a modest two bedroom flat in Rotterdam, but he very rarely found himself there due to work commitments. After all it was just a base and nothing more. He liked to think of himself as a vengeful nomad, correcting the many wrongs that people do to each other every day. Business was booming, he had a lot to look forward to. A rendezvous with the cute British girl would be the icing on the cake. He would have to wait and see. There was still time for it to happen; yes he would take a walk near where he had left her yesterday. In the hope he might bump into her. And then take her back to the Grand Hotel Krasnapolsky so he could fuck her brains in, and then some.

He quickly towelled himself dry, and got dressed. He was suited and booted and now ready for the hunt.

He reached for his phone; it was on the bedside table where he'd tossed it before climbing in the shower. He scrolled down his list of contacts until he found the fixer's number. He pressed the green button once and waited for the connection.

24

*T*he fixer was sat in Jan's coffee shop when he felt his phone vibrate in his pocket. He quickly dug it out and answered it, taking a look at the screen to see whose number was flashing up before doing so. He instantly recognised the number. It was the hitman's. He hit the green button.

"Hello."

"You know who this is don't you?"

"Yes I do."

"I want you to put the wheels in motion. Make the call and set it up for as soon as possible, I have other business to attend to, I want to be out of here tonight."

The fixer said,

"Done."

And then cut the connection.

He turned round in his seat and gestured to Jan to bring him a refill over. He then turned back round and necked the dregs in the cup, the mud and the shit and brought the contact list up on his phone. This time he found the name he wanted and paused for a while, index finger pointing up to his temple and his thumb under his chin, for support. He was trying to figure a way of squeezing more money out of the deal. He wasn't happy with the agreed five per cent; he wanted more, much more. He pressed the green button once and waited while the connections were made. It started ringing. One ring, two rings, three rings, four rings. And then it was answered.

25

*T*he laughing barmaid was sat in her flat when her phone rang. She was scraping the kif from out of the bottom of her grinder to make a special joint. She was stressed out and needed calming down, and she knew a sprinkle of kif on a regular joint would do the trick. It had been tried and tested many times before. She quickly placed the grinder on the coffee table in front of her and reached over for her mobile, which was laid haphazardly on the sofa beside her. She looked at the screen before answering. It was her friend's number. The fixer. Sinister Carrott. She pressed the green button and then answered.

"Hello."

"It's me."

"Any news?"

"Yes he's just got in touch. He wants to meet as soon as possible; do you think you can arrange it?"

"Yes I think so providing she is back from being questioned, the police took her again. Leave it with me and I will get back to you as soon as I hear from her."

"Okay."

The line went dead, so she tossed the phone back on the sofa and went back to scraping the kif out from the bottom of the grinder. This way she could chill out with the kif spliff and play out the different scenarios in her head in order to iron out any kinks she found in her plan. Not that she expected there to be any. She was a cautious woman, and had been so from an early age. Life had taught her to be that way, to survive at all costs and fuck everybody else. She wanted out of this shithole, her flat, her job, her life, and it didn't matter whose lives she ruined in the process. It just had to be done.

Anna Timmerman was nearly twenty eight years old. She was an only child, born to alcoholic and drug addicted parents. Her mother died of a heroin overdose when she was just four years old, leaving her at her father's mercy until he too died. She was just fourteen years old when he died. But that day her father died and for the first time in her life that she could remember she actually felt happy, and alive. She had murdered her own father.

After her mother's untimely death her father would beat her constantly, until she sprouted tits that is, and that's when it all changed for the worse, for her. From the age of ten to fourteen she was systematically raped by her own father. Every night without fail he would force himself upon her, pin her down and do things what no father had the right to do to his one and only child. Anna would just close her eyes and bite her bottom lip and pray for it to be over quickly. Then one night while it was happening, weighed down by her father's bulk she just happened to look to her right and saw the remains of a meal on a plate with a knife and fork resting side by side. The next thing she knew her dad was slumped on top of her covered in blood with multiple stab wounds from both the fork and the knife all over his neck, body, and head. The fork itself was sticking out of his eyeball, and there was blood oozing out of the five holes it had created, slip-sliding down the old crusty wooden handle.

The one thing that brought her round was the sensation of his now limp dick slipping out of her. She remembers it now, all too vividly, she can recall the weight of his sagging body pushing down on her, restricting her breathing, and the stink of his last breath, and the smell of shit as his sphincter relaxed. In her mind it was as though it had happened yesterday, not nearly fourteen years ago. She was back on the bed, with him on top of her, stinking of beer, sweat and shit, panicking, gagging as she pushed the dead weight that was her father off of her and calmly washed and changed and packed the few items of clothes she could call her own, and then left to never return. On her way out she lit a rag and pitched it onto the living room floor. Walking through the kitchen in a daze, as she passed the cooker she turned the gas rings on and closed the door. Two blocks away she heard an almighty explosion as the gas and the naked flame acquainted.

That night she slept in a basement alcove entrance, sheltered only by the eight steps leading down to it, a dirty My Little Pony blanket, three sheets of newspaper, and a four by four red brick wall. She hardly slept a wink what with the strange noises of the street and the weirdos stalking it. Amsterdam is a dangerous place for a grown man, never mind a clueless naive fourteen year old girl. But still she felt alive.

After a week or so of struggling to find a safe place to sleep each night and eating out of bins she befriended a gang of young runaways. One of them was the friend whose mum hired a hitman to kill her husband, and another was the fixer, and another was Jan the coffee shop owner. They too were running away from one form of abuse or another. So there she stayed in the vicious circle of life on the street for over a decade until she finally decided enough was enough and it was time to sort herself out once and for all. She had tried a few times before, but her heart was never in it. Now she was determined to succeed at any cost.

She got herself a flat, a bar job and started night school. And tried to save enough money to relocate to London, where she hoped to realise her dream of one day becoming a fashion designer. But it was four years later and she was no nearer to the dream than she was on the day she started. She had eighteen hundred guilders put away in a high interest account, not a lot granted but it was hard earned and not hustled profits. On more than one occasion she had been tempted to draw the lot out and quadruple it in forty eight hours hustling powder on the streets, but up to now she had resisted the temptation of going back to her old life and ways. However scamming the hitman would provide her with the collateral needed to relocate, no question. She could be out of here tonight, and in the end that was all that mattered.

She sat on her sofa and took in her dingy flat and her meagre possessions and thought if this is what it means to be hard working and honest then I am doing the right thing. All she had to show for four years hard work was a few nice clothes and a bag of shit TV which you had to bang on the top to get a decent picture.

She had finished scraping out the grinder, and had now sprinkled the kif onto the regular joint she had spread out on the coffee table in front of her. After a couple of minutes of twisting and tucking she had the joint rolled and roached-up ready to smoke. She clicked the lighter and sucked hard on the kif spliff; she took the smoke in deep, intending to hold it in for a while but instead she coughed and spluttered and blew most of the smoke out straight away. She cursed herself under her breath—she had sprinkled too much kif along the joint, hence the bout of coughing. It was a fine balance when using kif and she had tipped the scales the wrong way. She would have to try and make do, taking short sharp hits instead of long pulls to help combat the cough reflex she felt every time she drew the smoke in.

Her mind slowly relaxed as the weed probed and stroked it into submission, the kif did its job, doing what it's supposed to do, easing the stress levels leaving the mind free to wander. Once you've let go of all the shit you carry around day to day then the mind can attempt to think laterally.

She reached for her mobile and propped the joint in the ashtray on the coffee table, it smouldered on for a while, little tendrils of smoke curling up in the air before disappearing forever adding to the years of nicotine and grease slime on the paintwork and ceiling.

She scrolled down her contact list until she found her friend's number, the dead gangster's daughter, the runaway. She pressed the green button once, stuck the phone to her ear and waited.

"I was just about to ring you." the voice said at the other end of the line.

"Was you." the laughing barmaid said reaching for the joint and then settling back down again. "Good news, bad news?"

The joint had gone out so she reached for the lighter and relit the joint while her friend spoke.

"Good news, I have just spoken to my mum; she is on her way home, no charges up to now. She seems to think that will be the last time they question her."

"That's good because he wants to meet as soon as possible for the money."

"As soon as she gets home I will get her to ring you."

"Okay, er, one more thing. Do you think we did the right thing, about your dad I mean?"

"For sure, one hundred per cent. In fact he got off lightly with two shots to the head, all the shit he put my mum through the years. He should have cut off his balls and let him bleed to death and even that would be too good for him. Why? You're not having second thoughts are you, not after what you did to your dad. Anyway it's a bit late for that, it's done and dusted, time to move on."

Yes, literally, the laughing barmaid thought to herself, but said,

"No, no I just wanted to make sure that's all."

White noise.

"Okay. Well believe me we did the right thing, he was a bastard. He had it coming for years."

"Just checking I didn't want it on my conscience that's all."

"Well we did the right thing. I will get my mum to ring you the minute she walks through the door and then we can put all this behind us."

"Okay see you."

The laughing barmaid tossed the phone onto the sofa beside her and then sprawled out with the remainder of the kif spliff and waited.

26

*T*he coffee shop was a small box room, maybe fourteen feet by fourteen with padded benches along the right hand side wall and window and a little bar nestled in the left hand corner. There were four tables spread out evenly in front of the padded bench, a few people had camped out on the bench and were half sat half sprawled out. That in itself I thought was a good enough indicator to stop here.

The bar was made of dark wood, and there was a pretty brunette propped on it, she was wearing an Ajax football shirt and a pair of faded figure-hugging denims. She had a shoulder length bob with a couple of fancy clips in it to keep it in place, and she had just squirted some moisturiser into the palms of her hands and was now gently massaging it in.

Fake cobwebs had been squirted into every recess to give the interior a creepy derelict look.

As always Sadie found a place to sit while I made for the bar. The brunette smiled when she saw me approach, one that started at her lips and ended at her eyes. Her whole face lit up like a Catherine wheel.

She was still wringing her hands as she spoke.

"What can I get you?" she asked me in a soft husky voice.

I thought it best to stick to coffee, I needed to stay alert. Pick the wrong weed and a hot chocolate on top and it would be good night Amsterdam.

"Can I have two coffees please, one with cream and one without and can I take a look at the weed menu as well?"

"Yes sure." she said and reached under the bar for a small tatty beige coloured exercise book which I guessed served as the weed menu. She tossed it onto the bar where it spun round and round until it finally stopped face up in front of me.

I picked up the menu and the pretty assistant turned round to make a fresh pot of coffee. She started off the coffee machine with a flick of a switch then spun back round to face me.

"See anything you like?" she said raising her eyebrows whilst giving me a cheeky smile.

"Still looking." I replied, looking up and tipping my head to the side before returning my attention back to the little beige book.

There was an array of different strains of cannabis on offer. All of them were scribbled in pen with the prices at the side, there were four different strains to every page, from Sativas to Indicas, resins and kiff. I was spoiled for choice like a kid at Haribo's warehouse. I just kept flicking through the five or six pages and back again, and just like the kid at Haribo's warehouse probably couldn't pick out any one single thing he wanted neither could I. After a couple of minutes careful deliberation I still couldn't for the life of me pick one out of the list in front of me so I said to the pretty assistant who was now leant forward on the bar giving me an eyeful of ample cleavage,

"What do you recommend? I could do with a mellow Indica, something not too strong if you know what I mean?"

She paused for a second placing an immaculately manicured fingernail to her lips.

"They're all pretty strong, but you could try a crossover." she said pausing for a beat, taking the exercise book out of my hands and spinning it round so it was the right way up for her to study.

She flicked back a couple of pages, running her fingernail down the list until it came to rest about three quarters of the way down the page.

"There." she said, tapping the page with her fingernail.

I looked down; underneath her fingernail was a doodle of a bee on a flower; underneath that was the words honey bee in a ball point scribble; and at the side of that was a price, twelve guilders a gram.

"Can I have two grams please?"

"Yes sure." she replied and spun round to retrieve the honey bee and the coffee which had just finished percolating; it smelled delicious, maybe a Nicaraguan strain, or possibly Colombian, definitely South American.

I took in my surroundings whilst the assistant fussed around the bar retrieving the cream from a small box fridge which was at the far end of the bar tucked to one side to utilise space. She rummaged around in a box and pulled out a couple of packets of complimentary biscuits, the type with only one or two in the pack. She placed the two cups of coffee on the bar in front of me, complete with two saucers, and laid the two packets of biscuits on each saucer respectively.

There were various pictures of long gone rock 'n' roll stars decorating the walls, Elvis, Jimi Hendrix, Jim Morrison, Janis Joplin, and Kurt Cobain to name a few. All were pictures of the stars caught in their prime. Elvis was pictured in a sparkling gold all-in-one jump suit, he had one hand on a mic stand and he was just about to sweep it off its feet so to speak. Jimi Hendrix was clad in denim and leather; he was on his knees playing the guitar with his teeth. The picture of Jim Morrison was just a head and torso shot, he had on a baggy white shirt unbuttoned all the way down and he was staring at some distant focal point, like he was in deep thought or something. Whereas the picture of Kurt Cobain was a stage shot, he was doubled up playing the guitar, hair flailing in all directions. Janis Joplin's was a stage shot too, she was dressed in a pair of faded tatty denims and a tight black vest, her left hand was clutching a silver topped mic and right hand was resting further down the mic stand for support.

The assistant had now used a key to unlock a filing cabinet of sorts, and she was flicking through a set of colour coded folders. She stopped at the yellow one and pulled it out. As soon as it was out of the filing cabinet I could smell it, it was a sweet smell similar to honey. She shook out a couple of buds onto the electronic scales, and then another. Satisfied she bagged it up and handed it over with a smile and a wink. I took the wink to mean she had put an extra bud in for luck.

"That's just twenty four guilders please."

I peeled off three notes from the bill fold in my pocket without looking and handed them over saying,

"Keep the change." I said

It was more than I normally leave for a tip but like I said before I like to have notes of the same denomination in my pocket so it was a case of either leaving a bigger tip than usual or having a pocket full of change that I didn't want, so . . .

She smiled and spun round to deposit the cash in the till, tucking her tip of a small note and change into her back pocket as she did so; it was a well rehearsed routine. Bump, tuck and spin.

I thanked her and stuffed the nip bag into the opposite pocket that my money was in. That way I wouldn't pull my money out by mistake when I eventually retrieved the nip bag. Always thinking, always alert, never attract attention to yourself, keep a low profile, always keep it in mind, don't just think it, do it.

I took hold of the two saucers and cups and headed for where Sadie had taken refuge, she had sat at the far end of the bench, the furthest from the door, leaving a space for me to sit at the very end of the bench. That part of the bench should be stamped with the words "Reserved, for Alpha Males only."

I plonked the two saucers on the table and scooted in next to Sadie. She smiled as I slid one of the cup and saucers over to her. Once sat down I slid my own saucer across the table so it was within easy reach. I ripped open the plastic packaging for the single serving biscuit with my teeth, spitting the piece of plastic I was left with into the ashtray; I tore the rest of the packaging away from the biscuit and dumped that into the ashtray too. I then swapped ashtrays with the nearest empty table, there's nothing worse than a lump of burning plastic in an ashtray when you're smoking. I took a little nibble from the biscuit and then dunked it. One bite and it was gone. It was nice but it was all over too quickly for my liking.

I stretched out so I could retrieve the nip bag from my pocket without too much discomfort and or trouble.

Sadie had started to put some Rizlas together so I relaxed, sprawling out like a tramp on a park bench. I dug the two phrases out from the safety deposit box in my mind and began to recite them over and over again. Just to make sure.

"Heb je het papierwerk?"

"Have you got the paperwork?"

Or in other words,

"Have you got the cash?"

Over and over again.

"Na vandaag niet proberen om mij te contacteren, dat aantal is verdwenen, ik besta niet."

"After today do not try to contact me, that number is gone, I do not exist."

Or in other words,

Fuck off.

27

The hitman never did anything lightly, from slicing someone's throat to booking a hotel. He liked to research, and he liked to do things properly. If a job was worth doing it was worth doing right. He was meticulous in his planning, checking and rechecking, then checking again, that's how it was; it was how it had to be. It was the secret to his success; it wasn't just an ingredient but the recipe itself, the very essence of it. It was the thing that made him stand out from the masses. It was the reason he was so sought after, his record of employment exemplary, he hadn't missed a target in all his ten years as a professional killer. If money changed hands you were as good as dead.

That's why he had picked The Grand Hotel Krasnapolski, he hadn't just come across it by chance he had spent hours and hours in front of a monitor sifting through page after page of reviews and write ups until he had narrowed down the possibilities to just one. The Grand Hotel Krasnapolski fitted the bill perfectly, it suited his every need. It was just a short walk from Amsterdam's Centraal Station which made the connection to Schipol easy. And that suited him just fine. Bang, bang, and gone. The only problem was he had to hang around for his wages, which could cause a problem in the long run. But as far as he knew the police had nothing to go on, no leads, and no clues. So he was prepared to relax his normally rigid procedure just this once. Plus he wouldn't mind fucking the woman, yes he could meet with the woman, bring her back to the hotel, give her some bull-shit excuse then bang, knock her out and tie her up, and then go looking for the cute little British bitch. Entice her back to the hotel where he would proceed to do whatever he wanted to each of them in turn, over and over again. Then when he was finished he could tie them both up and check out. He didn't care, he was booked in under a false name.

The hotel's history appealed to him as well; it stretched back through both wars, the second one, and the great one before it, all the way back to eighteen hundred and sixty six to be precise. The original proprietor whose name it still bore started it up way back when as a small bar. The owner's shrewd decision to create a few rooms on site blossomed into the majestic building it is today. And it is a commanding, magical site, especially at night, lit up by a multitude of carefully positioned sodium spot lights; it is enough to take your breath away, positioned where it is perched right on the edge of Dam Square, in the lively heart of the characteristic old centre of Amsterdam, it is without doubt the perfect location for such a beautiful building.

So he had booked it without hesitation, money being no object when a cloned credit card is being used, someone else was footing the bill. He liked to think that the original owner was a Jack the lad, a bit like himself. A man with the foresight to see the potential in something before a market was even established, just like me he thought to himself, a man who had come from nothing and made himself.

28

I t was now twenty minutes past one; the laughing barmaid was dozing on her sofa, she had drifted off after nailing the last of the kif spliff. She had the now threadbare My Little Pony blanket—which she had slept with every night since murdering her own father—tucked right up under her chin so only her face and arms were visible. Her lips were parted slightly, and her breathing was shallow. Rapid eye movement evident, her eyeballs jostled about under her eye lids causing them to flutter making it look like she was about to wake up at any second, when in fact she was slipping into a deep sleep.

Her phone started to chirp and vibrate and changed all that.

She woke up, disorientated at first. Then her faculties slowly returned and she realised it was her phone making the noise. At first she couldn't find it but after jumping up and a minute or so of frantic searching she located it; it had slipped underneath one of the bottom cushions. She turned the phone the right way up but in doing so she fumbled and dropped it; it bounced on the cushion and then onto the floor. As soon as it hit the floor it stopped ringing. She cursed under her breath as she retrieved it looking at the screen to identify the number. It was her friend's mum. She sat back down on the sofa with her phone held out in front of her and waited for it to ring again.

Her mind drifted. If everything goes to plan she thought to herself as she waited for the call that would change her life, she would be in London by the end of play tonight. She might even get tickets to see a show in the West End, which would be good, a fitting end to a first night in London. Yes that's what she would do; she would take a taxi from the airport. After all, everything she owned would be in the suitcase dragging behind her. She would find a decent B&B, dump her case then take the tube to the West End. She smiled to herself, she already sounded like a fashion designer.

There was a plane out of Schipol to Gatwick at eight o'clock pm every weekday. She knew because she had spent the last four years browsing different flight companies' websites, dreaming about the day when she would be ready to leave her past behind once and for all. No more sarky comments, no more untimely reminders, everything gone. The memories, the hurt—everything, gone. Dead and buried. She was even planning to dump her My Little Pony blanket in one of the bins at Schipol before departing. It would be symbolic, it would mean closure. It was a first birthday present from her mum and dad, when things were sort of okay. Well she couldn't remember that far back so she had replaced the memory with a fairytale image. It was how she coped. It was her defence mechanism. Without it she would have been long gone.

The phone chirped and then started to vibrate.

She looked at the screen.

It was her friend's mum again, the dead gangster's moll. The battered wife.

She pressed the button, but didn't answer straight away.

All she heard was white noise, and the odd crackle of static.

When no one was forthcoming she spoke.

"Hello."

"It's me, I'm back. They didn't charge me; I think I have convinced them, for now anyway. To tell you the truth I am sick of playing the bereaved widow, it's beginning to wear thin. Will you get in touch with your friend and see if he can set it up for as soon as possible please?"

Sick of playing the merry widow, the laughing barmaid thought to herself. He'd been dead less than forty-eight hours, what a joke. Now she knew she was doing the right thing, her friend's mum was a cold-hearted bitch and deserved everything she got.

"He's already been in touch; the man wants his money ASAP."

"Good. Do what you have to and let me know when and where."

"Okay."

The line went dead.

Instead of making the call, she started making a joint. A normal one to pep her up, she needed something to calm her nerves; it was make or break time. She either made it or she would be broken.

29

Smit, Van de Berg, Meijer, and Visser were all congregating in the squad room, they were all crumpled and downbeat, up to now they hadn't managed to turn up a single thing, and they all looked like they could use some sleep. They had been on the go now for over twenty four hours powered only by coffee and the odd hour's sleep grabbed here and there when the investigation permitted. They knew how the system worked, if you didn't find the killer with the metaphorical smoking gun in his hand standing over the victim then you were in for a long hard slog.

It was like the killer had disappeared into thin air, just like that. Smit and Van de Berg still had a few hotels and hostels to check in with, in the mean time The Grand Hotel Krasnapolsky had been in touch and Smit had spoke to the clerk on the front desk. She had listened to the verbal description and what Smit wanted but she had said that she would have to talk to her supervisor before divulging any information about a current guest and that she would be in touch as soon as possible. The Dam Hotel still hadn't been in touch. Smit made a mental note to ring them again after the meeting; he knew potential evidence could be deteriorating with every passing second.

There were four Styrofoam cups in front of each and every one of them, a fresh cup had been placed inside an old one, and they were all steaming slightly. Smit blew into the cup and took a sip of the steaming liquid. After swallowing it he said,

"So what we got?"

"Well." said Meijer, who happened to be the oldest of the bunch by a good ten years, at least. "We brought the woman in again and we leaned on her like we said we would, and guess what?"

Smit shrugged his shoulders.

"She kept her cool, I'll give her that, too cool for my liking. She had the air of someone who had something planned to perfection. She knows we have nothing on her and all we have is our suspicions; it was as though her answers were rehearsed like she knew what we were going to ask before we asked it, if you know what I mean?"

Smit nodded his hands steepled under his chin. He was in deep thought. After a couple of minutes silent deliberation he piped up,

"Maybe we should put her under surveillance, see what that turns up."

"Already on it boss." Meijer replied nodding. "When we didn't get anywhere with the questioning I had an unmarked car follow us when we dropped her off. They're in position now, last contact was ten minutes ago on the radio. She is still at home, no comings or goings up to now."

"Good." Smit said. "All we can do is carry on the road we're on and hope we come up with something."

They all nodded in unison.

He looked at Meijer. "You and Visser go back and canvas the neighbourhood again; you never know you might get lucky. And remember this guy—whoever he is—is a professional and is most probably armed so if you do bump into him don't be a hero, call for back up."

30

The fixer was still in Jan's coffee shop, playing with his thoughts. After all Jan was his best mate and had been since they were knee-high to grasshoppers, no pun intended. In any other city in Europe a kid might have had problems growing up with a camp best friend. Jan had been playing with Barbie dolls since he was two years old, the source of many a fight when they were kids. The bullying and taunts stopped when they made the leap into high school, Amsterdam was tolerant of the gay scene and always had been.

He was on his fourth coffee, and his fourth joint, and that was only since he'd been here. His weed of choice was the strain G13. There was a myth behind that particular strain, allegedly a cutting had been stolen from an American Government Growing Facility in Mississippi and somehow ended up on the streets. Another unsubstantiated rumour is that the University of Washington cannabis testing facility grew the strain for medical testing in the 1970s. Whatever, however he didn't care, it was potent and that was all he knew.

He was sat next to a pretty blonde, she had on a white roll neck top, a sheepskin body warmer, a short tartan skirt, not mini, but not far off either, white leggings and a pair of sheepskin ankle boots, the type where the tops are folded over. She was bent forward putting together some papers together and her skirt had hitched up slightly which had prompted the fixer's inquisitive mind into action. He had spent five minutes trying to guess what kind and colour of knickers she had on before acting on impulse. He had finally decided on either white lace, or commando. So now the fixer was trying to get to the right angle so he could see up her skirt without her cottoning on to what he was doing? It was a delicate operation, one which needed much cunning and attention but his mind was still on the deal and how he could squeeze more cash out of it. He had already come up a couple of ideas but after careful deliberation he'd cast them aside.

She turned to him, her eyes locked onto his like cross hairs. They were a piercing blue, like a clear Arctic sky. She pulled her skirt down as far as it would go, which wasn't very far for the effort she put into it, exaggerating every movement, like she was telling him she was disgusted with what he was trying to do. She kissed her teeth and then without another word spun round on the seat so that her back was facing him.

He shrugged his shoulders taking defeat gracefully and got back to more serious business at hand. The deal and how he could push up his stake in it, he wanted more, much more.

His phone vibrated in his pocket dragging him back to real time.

He fished it out and looked at the screen before answering. It was his friend the barmaid, Anna Timmerman. He pressed the green button and answered straight away.

"Anna, I hope you have got good news, the guy is getting impatient. He wants to be out of here as soon as possible."

"Calm down, she has just rung me they have let her go again without charge, so she's ready to meet. The only specification she has is that the location is Dam Square. She wants somewhere public, somewhere she feels safe."

Anna's voice somehow managed to sound sexy, even over the airwaves.

"Yes, I don't see a problem with that. What about the time?"

"Well, she said she wanted it done and out of the way ASAP. So let's say two hours from now Dam Square, it will give you time to organise things at your end."

"What time is it now?"

"It's half past one."

"Two hours, why the hold up?"

"She has to pick the cash up from the bank."

"Okay half past three Dam Square, make sure she's not late. We don't want to get on the wrong side of this guy believe me."

"Don't worry, I'll make sure she's on the money, she'll be there at half past three."

The line went dead.

The laughing barmaid waited for her phone to switch back to the default screen before accessing her last ten calls, she scrolled down until she found the cocky Brit's number. It was the one before the last call. She pressed the green button and waited for the connection, waited for whatever witchcraft was involved to weave its magic.

It started ringing.

31

The last ten years have gone by in a blur. If I wasn't cowering underneath drenched sheets, or working, then I tended to withdraw into myself. My head was and still is a place of refuge, a cave big enough to retreat to when times are bad. And I can provide my own entertainment, I can recall anything from my past and bring it to the forefront of my mind with such clarity that it's like I'm stood in front of the real thing for the very first time. It is a tool which has served me well, without it I would have given up a long time ago and cashed my chips in. But if anything I am resourceful, I can retreat into myself for days in a kind of meditative state. So this is what I found myself doing while Sadie was busy with a Sudoku. I was bored and I needed stimulation. I was re-running the last forty-eight hours in my head, from the skinhead's knock-out in the Irish bar, the interview with the police, and the proposition, to the conversation I had just had with the laughing barmaid. I could still picture the skinhead's razor burn in my mind, and the look of shock on his boss's face as his back up dropped to the floor, knocked out cold with one punch. I could even recall the laughing barmaid's creased nose clearly enough to count the wrinkles. I counted three; two on the left side and one on the right. I made a mental note to check it out when I next saw her to see if I was right or not.

Sadie looked up. She took a sip of her coffee and then gave me a smile.

I returned her smile and then she turned her attention back to the Sudoku.

I slipped back into my shell.

My phone started to vibrate in my pocket.

Sadie must have heard it too, because she looked up and raised her eyebrows as if to say, "Well are you going to answer it or not."

It must have been on the eighth or ninth ring when I eventually dug it out of my pocket.

I looked at the screen; it was the laughing barmaid's number.

I pressed the button to answer the call.

"Hello." I said.

"It's me; can you make Dam Square for half past two?"

I glanced at the screen; it was thirty two minutes past one. That gave us fifty eight minutes to make it there.

"Yeah, no worries." I replied.

"The real dude thinks he's meeting her at half past three. That gives us an hour to make ourselves scarce."

"That'll do me." I said. "I will ring you as soon as the exchange as taken place. I want to be outta here and gone, no fuckin' around."

"Okay."

The line went dead so I slipped my phone back into my pocket.

"What did she say?"

"She's just told me the meeting time is half past two, in Dam Square."

"That's good, gives us just less than an hour to prepare and get in position. Should be just about right."

"That's exactly what I thought." I replied finishing off what was left in the bottom of the cup. "Should we have another coffee here and then take a stroll up?"

Sadie nodded a reply.

I waggled my cup above my head to get the assistants attention, she looked up and I gave her Churchill's salute. She nodded to let me know she had understood the gesture. I wanted two refills.

"Should we have another joint with the coffee?" I asked Sadie.

"Yes I think we should." she replied. "Do you want me to do it?" she asked tucking the puzzle book away in her bag.

"Yeah you can do." I replied.

I saw the pretty assistant place our cups and saucers on the counter and then look in our direction. I lifted a finger up in the air to let her know I was on my way. I jacked myself off the chair and made for the counter. On the way I peeled a ten guilder note from my bill fold and handed it to her as I reached the counter.

"Keep the change." I said grabbing a hold of the two saucers with the tips of my two index fingers and thumbs.

"Thank you." The pretty assistant said spinning round and depositing the cash in the till retrieving the change and dropping it into her back pocket. Bump, tuck, and spin.

I slid in next to Sadie. She was half way through the rolling process; she was just sprinkling the buds onto the tobacco, green on brown. As she broke open the buds there was that sweet smell again, similar to honey.

I relaxed a little spreading my arms out across the bench and watched Sadie as she twisted and rolled the papers until it was ready for licking. She paused a beat, holding the joint in front of her face whilst she gained and maintained eye contact with me. Then she leant forward slightly and slid her tongue across the gum strip.

I shivered. It was too much for me to handle. I had to look away. I needed my mind on the job and that was a distraction I could do without, for now. All in good time I thought to myself.

*   *   *

The fixer rang the hitman and told him the meeting place and time; it was twenty to two when he passed on the information. The hitman thanked him and hung up. The fixer knew time was running out—he had an hour and forty nine minutes to come up with a plan. He set to work.

*   *   *

The hitman sat on the edge of his bed; things were falling into place nicely. He shrugged on his hoodie which was draped over a chair back and headed for the door via the bathroom and its mirror. He looked at himself and decided he needed a haircut, brushing the ragged strands of hair behind his ears. Yes he could definitely do with a haircut he thought to himself as he tilted his head this way and that, he wanted to look his best for the surprise three-way he had planned between the dead man's wife and the cute Brit. All he needed to do now was put his plan into action.

*   *   *

The laughing barmaid scrolled through her contact list until she found her friend's mum's number, she pressed the green button once and waited for the connection. It rang twice and then it was answered.

"Hello."

"Do you think you can make Dam Square for half past two?"

White noise.

Anna presumed she was checking the time.

"Yes, I have to go to the bank first but I should be able to."

"Good. I will phone you after the meet has taken place. I've got somewhere I need to be for a couple of hours so I won't be back until later. If that's okay with you, I mean you don't need me to stick around do you?"

"No I don't think so. Er, Anna."

"Yes."

"I just wanted to say thank you. He would have killed me eventually."

"Oh, okay. I'll ring you later bye."

Anna cut her off before she could say goodbye, she was racked with guilt and she didn't know how much longer she could keep up the pretence.

32

It was ten past two when we hit the Damrak. Twenty minutes to the rendezvous. My plan was to walk Sadie up to the internet cafe and then make my way to Dam Square to meet the woman. The Damrak is an arrow straight street which links Dam Square to Centraal Station, which also made it a thoroughfare for tourists. It was jam packed at this time of day and we had to jostle our way through the crowds—good for cover, shit for manoeuvrability. Maybe it was a bad idea to pick such a public place for the meet, but then again maybe not. The woman needed to feel safe—after all she was meeting with the man who had just put two bullets in her husband's head. Maybe I was just being over cautious, but it was better to be over cautious than to underestimate.

We passed the sex museum. The Grasshopper stood three stories tall to our left on the other side of the road. In the day it didn't look anything special. Without the neon light it was just another decrepit building. We walked another five hundred yards or so then took a right off the Damrak. A tram swept past us; the driver rang the bell—ding, ding. We took the next available right, and then the next left, we were now on the same street as the internet cafe. The crowds had thinned out a little but the streets were still busy.

Sadie hooked her arm round mine and she pulled me closer. I could smell her perfume, Marc Jacobs' Daisy, only for a second before the wind got up and swept it away. I was in a world of my own, mesmerised both by her aura and her fragrance. She was captivating, when you looked into her eyes you lost yourself. So for that reason I was avoiding eye contact, I needed to keep my mind on the job.

We stopped a couple of doors short of the internet cafe and huddled in an alcove. I pulled her close her head came to rest sideways on and I held her there for a couple of minutes with her listening to my heart beat.

It was time to go; I put my hands on each of her shoulders and held her at arm's length for a couple of seconds and then I leant in for a kiss. I pecked her twice on the lips and said,

"I'll be back before you know it, as soon as I have the cash I will ring you and let you know, that way you can be ready for when I get back here."

"Okay." she replied and made for the internet cafe's door. I followed close behind, like a shadow.

She pushed the door open and paused. Turning back to face me, her eyes found mine and she said,

"Be careful won't you."

"Course." I replied.

I leant in for another kiss and then she was gone, lost behind the glare of the door window. I turned and headed for Dam Square. It was twenty one minutes past two.

As I walked up to the meeting point I repeated the two phrases over and over again in my head, just to make sure.

＊　＊　＊

The hitman stepped out of the hairdressers and ruffled his hair with both hands. His hairline was crisp and straight, even after the fact there was not a hair out of place; it was still wet from the gel the hairdresser had applied whilst in the cutting process so it did as it was told, for the time being anyway. He wiped his hands on the ribbed hem of his hoodie and pointed upwards and flicked his wrist so that he could see his watch. It was nearly twenty past two; he got his bearings and then set off in the general direction of the internet cafe. He had a flight to book, and two women to fuck. He could hardly contain himself, this was going to be fun. He allowed himself a smile as he crossed the street. He was now on the Damrak. He knew a right and then a left would take him onto the street where the internet cafe was located. It was almost time.

33

*D*am Square has been in place since 1240, but its present form didn't take shape until the mid nineteenth century. I'd gathered little snippets of information from the many leaflets Sadie had randomly picked up, I'd gathered them up and then stored forever in the safety deposit box in my head.

It was twenty-eight minutes past two as I approached Dam Square from a side street. I was bang on time. I scanned the surrounding area looking for the mark, the woman who had paid to have her husband murdered. Straight ahead was the National Monument, an obelisk honouring the fallen from World War II. I paused for a beat as I drew level with it as a mark of respect, and then carried on my way.

The whole place was jam-packed solid with clustered groups all over watching street performers. All the street performers were stood on wooden boxes. Each one had a crowd of about thirty people huddled around them, who were all tossing coins into various vessels positioned in front of the performers. Some were hats, some were wooden or plastic boxes. One of the performers had just the lid from a plastic takeaway carton laid on the floor in front of his plinth. The lid was laden down by a mound of coins, there were even a few guilder notes stuffed in here and there.

As I approached one of the street performers, which just so happened to be the grim reaper, he stopped turning the way he was and spun full circle so that he was now facing me head on. Without eye contact I didn't know if he was looking at me or not. Even so I got the impression he was staring right through me, I shivered. As I drew level with him he held his hand out. I ignored him and he jokingly pretended to swipe me with his scythe. I carried on without looking back hoping it wasn't the sign of the things to come.

I clocked the woman. Even from the back I still recognised her from her clandestine meeting in Jan's coffee shop with the laughing barmaid and the fixer the day before. She had her back to me and was sat on one of the flat marble benches scattered on the outskirts of the Square. She was directly in front of me and she had her hand stuck to her ear, evidently she was on the phone.

I boxed round so I could come up to her from her left; that way I would still have the element of surprise on my side. I didn't want her to see me until I was right on top of her. I passed the Grand Hotel Krasnapolsky; I also passed the character from the Mask movie—he was stood stock still, only moving occasionally in a robotic way, his movements coincided with the tipping of a coin into his hat.

She saw me when I was about ten feet away. Her hand immediately dropped to her side and she slipped the phone into her pocket.

I nodded to her as I approached.

For an older woman she looked great. Her blonde hair was flopping slightly in the wind partly obscuring her delicate features, so she proceeded to tuck both sides behind her ears in order to see me clearly.

She was wearing a mauve satin dress which fell below the knees and was ruched at one side drawing it up a little, on her legs she had on a pair of skin coloured stockings and on her feet she had on a pair of nude high heels making her legs look longer than they actually were. To finish it off she had a mauve coloured Kashmir shawl wrapped around her shoulders. Her fingers were clamped onto a gold clutch bag which was dug into her knees; I guessed she was using it as a sort of comforter. At a quick glance she looked naked due to the fact that the dress hugged her curves and exaggerated them further.

I stopped a couple of feet short of her. There was no one else on the bench and she was perched on the edge of it, like a baby bird on a branch about to take its first flight.

I did a quick scan of the area. There was no one else in the immediate vicinity, no one within earshot so we were good to go.

I took another step forward and then hit her with the first phrase. That way she wouldn't have time to regain her composure. I kept the words short and sharp, like a dog barking.

"Heb je het papierwerk?"

"Have you got the paperwork?"

Or in other words,

"Have you got the cash?"

She nodded twice; they were only slight movements but they told me she was scared. She then looked down and reached into her bag and pulled out an A4-sized padded manila envelope; it was doubled over and it also hadn't been sealed so the top of it was flapping in the wind.

I took another two steps forward and then reached out and took the package from her. I didn't snatch it, I kept my cool. I then made a show of checking its contents, sticking my hand inside the envelope and flicking through the wads of hundred guilder notes. It all appeared to be there, none of the old tricks like only the top layer of notes being real money and the rest of it plain white paper cut to the specified size. I was an old hand at the scams. I can remember Craig, Ally and I had gone to the next village to ours scoring some weed and pulled the same trick on one unsuspecting dealer. Well it was money for nothing, and the chicks came by their own free will.

I looked up and caught her gaze, and then hit her with the second phrase. The one designed to make her want to back off.

"Na vandaag niet proberen om mij te contacteren, dat aantal is verdwenen, ik besta niet."

"After today do not try to contact me, that number is gone, I do not exist."

She nodded and then looked to the floor I took that to be my cue to make an exit. I spun on my heels and then started to make for the other side of Dam Square. If we were looking at a clock face the woman was seated at twelve o'clock, I had come from the right hand side of her, which was six o'clock. I was now heading to the other side, which in turn was three o'clock. My plan was to head that way, and then make the appropriate turns to set me in the general direction of the internet cafe. Piece of piss.

I turned around once and saw the mark get to her feet and walk forward, she stopped at the kerb for a beat and then crossed the road, turned a corner and out of sight.

I licked the gum strip on the envelope and then ran my thumb and forefinger across the top a couple of times to seal it properly. I then zipped my hoodie up tight and stuffed the envelope inside tucking it into the waistband of my jeans. I was on the home straight, just a couple of furlongs to go.

34

O nce I'd doubled back on myself and found my way I reached into my pocket and pulled my mobile out. I scrolled down until I found Sadie's number. I pressed the green button twice and waited for it to start ringing.

She answered it on the second ring; she must have had the phone in front of her waiting for my call.

"Hello." Sexy voice.

"It's me I've got it; I'll be with you in about ten minutes."

"Okay. Come into the cafe I will show you the hotel were staying at."

"Okay." I said reluctantly and then cut the line. I wanted to be away as quick as possible, not to be hanging around a geek joint.

I scrolled back on my contact list until I found the laughing barmaid's number and pressed the green button twice and waited for the connection.

35

The hitman was just minutes away from the internet cafe. He still had good time with just less than an hour to go until the meet. He was going to use the time wisely, to book a flight and to find the cute British woman. Mmmm, he thought to himself smiling. He could hardly contain himself, his manhood straining against his zip. He stuffed his hand down his jeans and readjusted down there so he could walk without hindrance.

He took the next left which he knew would take him onto the street where the internet cafe was located. As he walked the last couple of hundred yards or so various exotic destinations around the world kept on popping into his head, Florence, Rome, Bangkok, Beijing, St Tropez, Monte Carlo, Saigon, he could picture them all clearly. After a kill he had made it his custom to go on a vacation, it was how he coped with the taking of a life; it was his defence mechanism. Warm rays on a beach, or afternoon tea in a cultured restaurant were indeed good for the soul.

The hitman pushed the door open to the internet cafe and stepped over the threshold. He immediately caught sight of the cute British woman. She was huddled over a keyboard using one of the PCs furthest from the door. She had just pulled her hand away from her ear and as he got closer to her he saw her staring at the blank screen of her mobile, apparently lost in thought, miles away.

She looked up as he drew level and her face dropped a mile; it wasn't the welcome he was hoping for. This might be harder than he thought; he checked himself and then carried onto the geek behind the counter to pay for some air time.

The geek behind the counter was as generic as the decor, greasy hair and spotty, and even greasier clothes. He had on a grateful dead T-shirt that had seen better days, a pair of dirty denims, and his greasy hair was pulled back so tight his eyes were just slits on his head. His facial hair was trimmed into a goatee that could do with tidying up, and he didn't even want to think about his shoes. The hitman liked to think of himself as cultured, and a cultured man always always look after his footwear, so to see another man with battered shoes it was the ultimate insult.

The hitman blew out in disgust as he caught the geek's odour, he smelt like stew cooking.

"Can I pay for a half hour slot?" the hitman said.

"Yeah sure." the geek replied.

"How much?" the hitman asked.

"Ten guilders." the geek replied.

The hitman pulled an Italian leather wallet out from the back pocket of his Armani jeans, opened it up and separated a crisp single ten guilder note from his bill fold, pulled it out and handed it over with trepidation. He didn't want any skin contact whatsoever; he had to fight off a shudder of repulsion as the geek's fingers nearly touched his.

With the bill paid he spun on his heels and headed for an unmanned PC, preferably one behind the British woman so he could keep an eye on her without raising suspicion. He couldn't get behind her so he picked the station next but two to hers. There was no one in between them, there were only six people in the whole cafe and they were scattered here and there. It was a geek trait but one the hitman adhered to, he liked his privacy for obvious reasons.

He settled in behind the PC, moving the mouse to activate the screen.

He typed Schipol's web address into the box and pressed enter. The tower whined a little and then the screen went blank for a second before it projected the correct website. He moved the mouse and watched the cursor dance over the various segments, highlighting each one in turn. When the cursor hovered over 'International Departures' he pressed enter. One by one the international flights due out of Schipol popped up on the screen. He stopped on the New York flight due out at eleven o'clock tonight. The cursor quivered. He had never been to New York and he fancied it, so he typed in his cloned credit card number and waited for the transaction to go through.

36

Smit and Van de Berg were sat behind their desks. Both of them were hanging on by a thread, Smit had purple smudges under his eyes, and they both had oval damp spots appearing on their shirts. Smit had his top button undone, Van de Berg had his top two buttons undone, both men had their ties pulled down and hanging loose, like a hangman's noose.

Smit blew out a huge sigh and ran his hands through his hair as he dialled yet another hotel number taken from the list in front of him. Van de Berg was on the phone, nodding his head and trying to get a word in edgeways. It was all in vain, whoever he was on the phone to wouldn't let him. He looked over to Smit and shrugged his shoulders and said into the mouthpiece,

"Okay, thank you m'aam. You have a good day now, bye."

He cut her off looked over to Smit and shook his head solemnly.

"The guy seems to have disappeared of the face of the earth." he said, to nobody in particular.

Smit was on the phone for a couple of minutes before slamming the receiver down. It was the same old story, no sign of the killer; he had vanished into thin air.

"Thank you for nothing." Smit said under his breath.

Smit was an honest cop, a family man; he carried the weight and bore the brunt of any investigation he was involved in by himself, so when a killer went free on a technicality or they couldn't catch him in the first place he took it personally. It motivated him to the point of obsession, and he wouldn't have it any other way. It was what made him so good at his job, so for that reason he let it ride and learned to live with it. He sometimes found it hard to swallow. There had been a high profile case recently—months of groundwork and canvassing and the gathering of evidence to secure a conviction and thinking it was in the bag, only to then go to court and watch in amazement as a multiple child killer walked free on some crazy loophole. And adding insult to injury he had to then go back home to his wife and two kids and pretend everything was okay. Of course he had come across cases where normal rules don't apply and emotions get in the way but that was a hurdle every investigative cop would no doubt come across sooner or later and they all knew it was one they would have to clear, or they would fall, and if they fell that was it—career over.

No sooner had he put the receiver down then the phone started ringing. He pulled a face at Van de Berg and then picked the receiver up.

"Detective Smit."

"Hi I'm on the desk at the Grand Hotel Krasnapolsky; I'm returning your call. I got the manager's approval to co-operate with you so here I am. How can I help you?"

Smit jumped in his seat and waved to attract Van de Berg's attention. Van de Berg jumped up and came to rest by Smit's side.

"Yes, erm we're conducting a murder inquiry and we just want to know if you have a guest matching the description of someone who was seen fleeing the murder scene."

"Fire away."

Smit proceeded to pass on the description over the phone. He heard scribbling on the other end of the line together with the clerk um-ing and ah-ing.

White noise.

"We have a guest here now that fits your description, what do you want us to do?"

"Nothing. I will have a photo-kit sketch faxed over to you immediately. It is paramount you let us know if it's our guy or not. If it is I will have the hotel put under surveillance so when he shows up we will make or move and arrest him. If he shows up in the meantime you ring me, okay."

"Okay."

"When is he due to check out?"

Smit heard more rustling and tapping.

"Tonight, well that's what he said when he checked in, he told the night clerk he was only here for a couple of days on business and that he would be gone by tonight."

"Okay, I'll have that sketch faxed over to you as soon as I put the phone down. Don't forget to let me know straight away."

"No problem detective, I'm just glad we were able to assist you in your enquiry."

The line went dead and Smit jumped to his feet, nearly knocking Van de Berg over in the process.

"What's up boss?"

"We have a possible ID of our man. Get one of those sketches faxed to the Grand Hotel Krasnaposky now."

"What's the number?"

"I don't know, it's on my screen somewhere, you might have to scroll back a bit." Smit told his deputy, pointing to the screen where he'd spent all of the morning, and most of the afternoon.

Smit massaged his eyes with the knuckles of his index fingers, he was sure he was going blind slowly.

"I need a piss, wait by my phone and answer it if it rings. I don't want to miss their call, it could be touch and go if we catch up with him or not."

"Okay boss." Van de Berg said and then sat down in his boss's chair and waited for the phone call which could make or break their case.

37

Anna Timmerman was climbing the walls; she could hardly contain herself, picking her phone up every other minute just to see if she had any missed calls, when she knew there couldn't possibly be one. It was like waiting for Christmas, but she knew all good things come to those who wait. After all she had waited fourteen years for the opportunity to lay her past to rest so she was sure another couple of hours wouldn't be a problem. In her mind she already had one foot on the plane, and that was as good as gone. What could possibly go wrong?

She was just licking the Rizlas to make another soothing kif spliff when her phone started chirping and vibrating across the chipped coffee table in front of her. She reached out for it, squinting at the screen through piss-holes in snow. It was the cocky Brit's number; he must have the money, already. He was good she would give him that. The way he memorised the two phrases and was able to repeat them in a Dutch accent was phenomenal.

"Hello."

"It's me, we have a problem."

Anna's heart sank.

"What you mean problem? You didn't get the cash?"

"No I got the cash, the hitman's the problem. He has just gone into the cafe where Sadie is waiting for me."

"Why is that a problem? He doesn't even know you does he? I mean it might be a shock seeing the double of him but that's all it will be, you can handle that can't you?"

"He bumped into Sadie yesterday apparently. They had a coffee."

"I don't believe this, why didn't you say something before now?"

"'Cos I thought it was irrelevant that's why and it would have been if you hadn't decided to rob him."

"Okay, okay don't lecture me on morals, the question is what are you going to do about it?"

"I don't know, leave it with me."

The line went dead so Anna tossed the phone onto the coffee table and carried on with what she was doing, she needed inspiration.

38

I saw him first, the hitman, well I took it to be him, even from the back he looked like me, he had my walk, and my stance. It was uncanny, the likeness. He didn't see me; I made sure of that, I ducked into an alleyway and stayed out of sight until I thought it was safe to peer round the corner to see where he was going. I watched him saunter down the street and then duck into a doorway. I wasn't sure if he had gone into the internet cafe, not from current position anyway, but I knew it was close to it so I knew I had to do something and quick. I made a note that there was a waste bin directly across from the door way and headed for it. As I got to the waste bin I realised he had gone into the internet cafe after all. Fuck, fuck, fuck.

I carried on and crossed the road and doubled back on myself. Eventually I came up to the bench where I'd waited for Sadie the day before and sat down facing the internet cafe. I fished my phone out of my pocket, and pressed the green button twice, even without looking I knew it would be dialling the last known number which I also knew would be the laughing barmaid's.

After updating her I then texted Sadie warning her of the hitman's unexpected appearance. She texted me back straight away saying yes she had seen him and that he was definitely in the internet cafe, he was sat next but two to her. I texted her back and told her not to panic and to stay where she was until two o'clock precisely. I told her at two o'clock to just get up and leave, not to look at anyone or anything but to be blinkered, aiming straight for the door.

I told her I would wait outside for her, up the street, on the bench. She sent me an empty text which I took to mean message received and understood.

I smoked three cigarettes in that next ten minutes, chain-smoking, lighting the next one with the smouldering butt of the last one, and then stubbing it out on the floor and chucking it under the bench. Those ten minutes felt like ten days, there was a continuous throng of tourists passing by. It was like a conveyor belt of people, but my eyes never left the internet cafe's door, Sadie's life could depend on it.

She came out of the door right on time with the hitman following close behind. Instead of turning my way she went the other so I had a perfect view of them both. I watched in horror as the hitman moved in on Sadie. I saw him pull something from his hoodie pocket and stick it in Sadie's back; I watched as Sadie stiffened up, even from here I could see that her body language was awkward. I got to my feet and set off in pursuit.

I could hear my heartbeat in my ears as I crossed the road, it sounded like running water. I was now on the same side as they were about a hundred yards back. They turned left and I quickened my pace. I reached the corner ten seconds later and peered round. They were a quarter a way up the street, meaning I'd gained on them slightly. I stayed where I was for a couple of seconds and then set off after them. I used the crowded streets as a sort of urban camouflage, using groups of people as cover, moving from one to another always keeping Sadie and the hitman in full view.

I zig-zagged my way up the street after them, and I almost got caught out as the hitman glanced back, thank god I was covered by the American family in front of me. There were three of them, the mum was a big woman dressed in black leggings and a tent, the father was even bigger, he had on a pair of baggy denims and a marquee, and a stumpy, doughy child of about eight, he was wearing a full set of grey sweats. As I got closer I caught sight of the white tick embroidered onto the front of the left leg, just below the pocket. I thought to myself yeah, just does it, eat everything in sight.

"Hey look at that, these streets sure are small." I heard the father say as I passed them onto my next block of people.

The hitman and her stopped and waited at the kerb ready to cross the road. He glanced first left and then right checking if it was clear. By the time he glanced my way I had ducked into another shop doorway pretending to browse the merchandise on offer. It was a hearing aid shop, not the best shop doorway to hang around in granted, but it was more of a force put than a choice.

I looked into the shop and the assistant was nowhere to be seen, he/she was probably in the back, or in the toilet. Whatever it gave me a couple of minutes grace so I could keep tabs on the hitman and her without raising the assistant's suspicion. They were still at the side of the road waiting for a break in traffic. This wasn't how it was supposed to play out, what the fuck did he want with Sadie? And more to the point, why?

My head was full of shit as I loitered in the doorway waiting for them to cross the road. I couldn't understand how he had shown up at that place and at that precise time. I don't believe in coincidences, not in that context anyway. I came to the conclusion it was a double cross. But who could it be? Top of my suspect list was the laughing barmaid. I knew I couldn't trust her as far as I could throw her, and if I got a good run up I reckoned I could throw her pretty far, she must weigh all of seven stone wet through.

From my vantage point I could see very little, but whatever the hitman had stuck in Sadie's back was now nowhere to be seen, and whatever it was had the desired effect she was doing as she was told. He had his right hand clutching Sadie's arm and the other was resting on the small of her back, guiding her, like a rudder on a boat. They made their move to cross the road; I stayed where I was until they had got to the other side, and then I rejoined the endless stream of pedestrians, using them for cover. I walked about twenty yards and then I too crossed the road, making sure it was clear to cross, once bitten twice as shy. I crossed the road without hindrance; the hitman and her were half a block ahead of me.

As I walked suspects kept on popping into my head, for me the next in line was the fixer. He hadn't got to where he was, doing what he did, without being ahead of the game. He had to be smart and he had to be sly to survive in his world. So for that reason alone he came second.

Then there was the woman and her daughter, but I couldn't for the life of me come up with a good enough motive for them to be involved, added to the fact they had nothing to gain, plus they didn't have an angle to approach him, or a means for that matter, I quickly dismissed them as credible suspects but kept them on the list anyway. So in the end I came to the conclusion that it was a toss-up between the laughing barmaid and the fixer just as the hitman and her turned right. I again quickened my pace, another ten yards gained from here to the corner and I would have a textbook gap between us, far enough to keep me from being detected, and close enough to be able to monitor the situation.

Then the unthinkable popped into my head, what if it was Sadie? What if it was her who was behind the double cross? The thought of it stopped me in my tracks, only for a second because at the same time I saw her wrestle free from his grip and turn round. She was only free from him for a split second but it was enough for me to see that she wasn't there by choice, it was in her eyes and behind her facial expression, her fear was palpable even at this distance. I hugged the shop front in an effort to conceal myself; it did the trick, I remained undetected, Sadie saw me but the hitman didn't. I waited until the hitman had Sadie back in his grasp and under control again before moving, but I didn't walk towards them. I went the other way and ducked inside the next available shop doorway. I put my hand on the glass and peered inside; it was a slight improvement on the last one, it was a lingerie shop. I peered round the corner just in time to see the hitman and her crossing the road again. I rejoined the pedestrian traffic and kept them in sight. I had an idea where he was headed; we were en-route back to Dam Square. I dug my phone out of my pocket and pressed the green button twice, knowing it would be automatically dialling the laughing barmaid's number and I waited for the bitch to answer.

39

A
nna was still on her sofa but she had slipped into a horizontal position. Her left leg was draped over the back and the other was resting on the arm of it. Her jeans button was undone and her zip was half way down. One hand was buried in her knickers, and the other was seductively poised, resting on the top of her head. Her mouth was slightly parted and her right molar was raking across her bottom lip. She was past the point of no return, and her back arched as a powerful orgasm racked through her fragile body, and she gasped and let out one deep and throaty moan. She tensed up for a good ten seconds then her body fell limp, and she lay there panting like a thirsty dog, her hand still in place and her middle and index finger wiggling around and about her G-spot prolonging the feeling for as long as she could. She was a master at it.

She lay there for a while, maybe a minute or so, basking in her own delight, her face flushed and her eyes half closed with only the whites showing.

Her phone started chirping and vibrating dragging her back to real time. She left her left hand where it was, resting on the perfect spot and wiggled across the sofa so that she was within easy reach of her phone. She grabbed hold of it after a couple of fumbles and pressed the green button to answer without first checking the screen to see who was calling.

"Yes." she spat into the phone's mic; annoyance was clear in her tone.

"It's me. You better not have double crossed me, am tellin' you now I will fuckin' kill you."

"What are you talking about?" Timmerman said, jumping up off the sofa buttoning and zipping herself up as she did so.

"That fuckin' hitman has my girlfriend and if anything happens to her I'm holdin' you responsible."

"I swear to you I have nothing to do with it. Whereabouts are you?"

"I'm walkin' on that long road up to Dam Square; I can see the concrete knob in the distance."

"What?"

"The National Monument, the fuckin' memorial, you know the big concrete knob."

"How far are you down the street? Have you gone past a lingerie shop yet?"

"I'm about a third of the way, yes I've just past the lingerie shop. Why?"

"Coming up is an alleyway, it's a short cut to Dam Square, and there is a cheese shop on one side of the alleyway and a sports shop on the other. Can you see it?"

"Yes I can smell the cheese shop I'm coming up to it now, yeah, now I can see the alleyway."

"Right, make the turn into the alleyway."

"I am now."

PART 4

Win Some, Lose Some

40

I turned into the alleyway whilst still on the phone with the laughing barmaid, it was narrow; there was only enough space to fit one person comfortably, if another person came the other way we would have to turn sideways on and squeeze by.

Some of the bricks in the walls either side of me had started to crumble away and because it was so narrow there was very little natural light and I struggled to focus for a second. All of a sudden dusk was upon me as the trickle of sun light faded to nothing, little white worms and bacteria-like squiggles wriggled their way into my vision; I rubbed my eyes for a second and collided with the wall, not enough to knock me off balance but enough to ricochet me off both the walls like a pinball for ten yards or so until I regained the equilibrium and set off again, arrow straight. I put the phone to my ear and heard the laughing barmaid say,

"About fifty yards in on your right there's another alleyway, it leads onto Dam Square."

"Right." I said as I started off in a sprint. "Don't go anywhere, I'll ring you when am done."

I cut her off in mid sentence; I didn't give a fuck what she had to say, not at this moment in time anyway, but I still had a bone to pick with her. I stuffed my phone back in my pocket whilst in sprint mode. Once my hand was free I put everything into it, I had to reach Dam Square before they did, and I knew it would be a close run thing.

I didn't see the connecting alleyway until I was virtually on top of it; I took the corner like Scooby Doo and did a cartoon skid colliding with the left hand wall, but I regained my balance straight away and was soon at full pelt again. I could see a little pinprick of light at the end of the alleyway and as I got closer the pinprick turned into a mucky coin, and then again into a full moon, until it changed shape altogether, now the little pinprick of light was the size and shape of a single bed sheet.

I was about twenty yards off the entrance so I slowed down to a jog and then onto a complete stop ten yards further on. I reached the entrance hugging the right hand wall and I held my breath as I peered round the corner. They were nowhere to be seen. I looked left to make sure they hadn't passed by, they hadn't so I turned to my right again just in time to see them rounding the corner. The hitman still had Sadie in his grip, but I could tell she wasn't happy. They looked like a child and parent, with Sadie digging her heels in and the hitman pushing her every step of the way.

I ducked back behind the wall for cover and counted to twenty before peering again. They had covered half the distance between us; progress was slow due to Sadie's reluctance. I did the math in my head, it had taken them twenty seconds to cover half the distance therefore it would take them at least another twenty seconds to cover the rest. I reckoned it would take more on the lines of twenty five seconds due to the fact that Sadie was becoming more un-compliant with every step she took.

I started counting in my head. One one thousand, two one thousand, three one thousand, four one thousand, five one thousand . . .

41

S mit and Van de Berg were waiting patiently; they had faxed the sketch to the Grand Hotel Krasnapolsky and were waiting on a reply. Smit was using the time out to phone home; one of his kids had just come on the line and was uttering baby noises at him. Van de Berg had his chair tilted back and was gouching, eyes closed, and mouth open, he was snoring, only slightly but it was getting louder with every breath intake. Smit rummaged through his desk drawer until he found a blank piece of A4 paper which he proceeded to ball up and toss it at Van de Berg. It hit Van de Berg square on in the face, he didn't jump or even flinch in fact the only outwardly sign he showed was the opening of one eye.

He squinted in Smit's direction and threw him a one-eyed what-the-fuck look.

"You were snoring." Smit said in-between coochy coos.

Van de Berg nodded and then closed his eye again just as the phone on his desk started ringing; it was one long continuous ring. He sat up in his chair and picked the phone up with his left hand and rubbed out the tiny bit of sleep that had formed a layer of crust over his tear ducts with his right index finger and thumb. Then he flicked the two tiny rocks onto the floor under his desk, out of sight and out of his mind. It was the cleaner's problem now he thought to himself as he answered the call.

"Detective Van de Berg."

"This is the Grand Hotel Krasnapolsky, that fax you sent over, we have a guest here matching the description."

"You're kidding." Van de Berg said pitching the A4 ball back at Smit to get his attention.

Smit put his hand over the mic and said to Van de Berg,

"What's up?"

Van de Berg mouthed the words,

"It's our guy."

Smit jumped out of his seat still with his wife still on the line, he spoke quickly and quietly in order not to alarm her.

"Honey I've got to go, I'll be home as soon as I can."

He didn't wait for a reply, he just slammed the receiver into its cradle.

Van de Berg was still on the phone to the desk clerk; he was nodding and doing his level best to reassure him but he was falling short. How could he make assurances when nobody could foretell how things would pan out? It was what speeded the body's metabolism and got the adrenaline pumping they were walking into the great unknown. It was what all homicide detectives worked towards, the apprehension of a murder suspect, the closing of a case.

"No sir, we will do all we can to make sure there is no commotion, but at the end of the day we are trying to apprehend a killer—whatever will be will be." Van de Berg said into the mic while shaking his head and pulling a face at Smit.

He nodded twice more and then he gently placed the receiver into its cradle, like a mother putting her first born into a cot.

"We're good to go, we got a positive ID." Van de Berg said.

Now it was Smit's turn to nod.

"Get Meijer and Visser to meet us at the corner of Damrak where it meets the Square and we can take it from there. We will have to assess the area and find a decent observation points. I'm thinking Meijer can hang around the National Monument and use that for cover. Visser can get dressed up as a street performer and you and I will watch from somewhere in the car." Smit said after a short period of deliberation.

Van de Berg nodded and reached into his pocket for his mobile. He flicked his wrist and glanced at his ten guilder watch. It was now ten to two; he figured at a push they all could be in position within ten minutes. Both men made a dash for the door grabbing their bomber jackets and awkwardly shrugging into them whilst in full flight.

The phone started ringing, one ring, two rings, three rings . . .

42

Eighteen one thousand, nineteen one thousand, twenty one thousand.

I heard faint footsteps.

Twenty-one one thousand, twenty-two one thousand.

The footsteps were getting louder; they were less like scuffs and more like steps.

Twenty-three one thousand, twenty-four one thousand, twenty-five one thousand, any time now. Twenty-six one thousand, twenty-seven one thousand, twenty-eight one thousand.

Where the fuck were they? I didn't want to peer round again because it could give my position away, so I had to rely on audio and instinct.

I was poised ready to pounce, like a jaguar; every muscle was tensed and ready to launch an attack. I'd read somewhere that the reason dogs place their tails between their legs is in order to cut off the scent from the anal gland, so for that reason I clenched my arse cheeks together.

I heard Sadie's voice; they were about five feet away now.

"Let go of me, where are you taking me?"

I heard the hitman mumble something unintelligible.

They were real close; their footsteps closing the gap between us with every step, they had to be only a couple of feet away by now, and almost on top of me, just another couple of steps and then bam.

I had a plan, as soon as I saw Sadie's arm which would be the first thing I would see as the hitman was behind her, I would make a grab for her and pull her into the alleyway. If the hitman kept a hold of her, all well and good—we would be in a confined space and I was confident I could deal with him. And if he let go of her, well I would cross that bridge when I came to it, if not then at least I would be between the hitman and her which was my number one priority. Also I was pretty sure he was armed, he was right handed so the gun would be in his right hand pocket, if he kept a hold on Sadie and got dragged into the alleyway with her then I would go for his right hoodie pocket and unarm him, job done, mission accomplished.

I saw her arm; it was just a blur as it swung up and then down. I caught it on its way back down, clamped on and yanked and pulled with all my strength.

Sadie yelped.

The hitman held on. I saw the shock in his face as he was pulled into the alleyway. I let go as soon as Sadie flashed passed me and sidestepped left so I was directly opposite the hitman. It was like staring into a mirror, he was my spit double, except when I threw a punch the mirror image didn't. Instead his head shot back and smashed into the wall behind him, smack, crack, scrape, thud, game over. That was enough, he went down like the Titanic, quickly and quietly, only the muffled rustle of clothing scraping against brickwork and a dull thud marked his demise.

Some hitman I thought to myself as I rifled through his right hand hoodie pocket and pulled out a black semi-automatic pistol using my hoodie sleeve as a glove. I turned my back to the street while I worked the gun and ejected the cartridge into my free hoodie covered palm and then pitched it as far as I could. I watched as it skidded along the pitted surface, collided with the right hand wall and finally come to rest parallel with it. I dropped the gun by the side of the now defunct hitman and I turned to face Sadie. I could tell she wasn't a happy bunny; her eyes were on fire with rage.

"We've gotta get outta here now." I said and took her arm.

We made it onto the street. I took one look back at the fallen hitman. He didn't even stir, he was out for the count, and then the wall obscured my view so we carried on regardless. We took a couple of steps forward, we were now on Dam Square. I heard a women screaming behind me, I guessed she'd spotted the hitman and that was her reaction. We quickened our pace slightly, not enough to attract attention, just enough to put some space between us and him.

I noticed a man who was stood behind the National Monument break from cover and make for the screaming woman. As he got closer I recognised him; he was one of the detectives from the Irish bar. I looked to the floor and kept on going. In my eyes if there was no eye contact then there was nothing. I also noticed one of the street performers jump off their podium and run in the direction of the screaming woman. I just kept my head down and kept on going.

"Where was he taking me?" Sadie asked as we turned the corner on to the Damrak.

"I don't know." I replied. "I phoned Anna as soon as I saw him grab you. She swears it had nothing to do with her. That reminds me,"

"Reminds you what?"

"I need to ring her to organise a meet to give her her share."

Sadie rolled her eyes.

I dug my phone out and pressed the green button twice and waited for the connection. She answered on the second ring.

"What's happening?"

"Sadie's with me." I said short and sharp.

"What happened to the other guy?"

"He's out cold in the alleyway on the edge of Dam Square."

"You're kidding?"

"Nope, listen, I'll meet you at the bar in half an hour. Don't be late or I'm off with the cash."

I cut her off before she had chance to protest and then switched my phone off.

"Here." I said to Sadie, pulling the manila envelope out from my waistband and handing it to her. "I want you to wait at the hotel, you'll be safe there 'til I figure out what's happened."

"Where are you going to go?"

"To meet up with Anna and find out what the fuck is goin' on."

"You're going to walk me to the hotel aren't you?"

"Yeah course. I want you to wait in the hotel room 'til I get back, don't open the door for anybody but me okay."

"Okay."

43

nna came off the phone to the cocky Brit, not by choice, but because he had cut her off. She immediately rang her friend the fixer, Sinister Carrott. She checked herself in the mirror, and ruffled her hands through her hair and shook her head while she waited for the connection. She would show the fucking cocky bastard, she would bring the fixer in on the deal and cut the Brit out. See how he liked that.

It started to ring in her ear. One ring, two rings, three, and then he answered.

Anna had hooked up with the fixer the week after she had murdered her father, with the other runaways. Jan the coffee shop owner, Vincenia the dead racketeer's daughter and a couple of others who had since fell by the wayside. The foursome had remained good friends and would do anything to help each other, but the fixer's loyalties were with Anna and not Vincenia. They had been an item for four years and bonds were made during that time which would never break or falter. So when Anna had come to him and asked him about the probability of him hiring a hitman he could hardly say no. He hadn't even batted an eyelid when he'd made the call. Business was business, and he needed to eat, smoke, drink, and fuck.

"Hello." the fixer answered.

"It's me." Anna said back.

"I know."

Anna proceeded to bring the fixer up to speed. She told him everything, every last detail, from the night at the bar with the Brit and the knockout, to the scam they had cooked up to fleece the hitman, to the Brit now having the hitman's cash and calling the shots.

"So what do you want me to do?" the fixer asked, his voice reduced to just a series of tinny grunts due to the reception and the shit quality of Anna's phone. "If he's disposed of the hitman he is someone I don't wanna be messing with."

"He is on his way to the bar where I work; he will be there around quarter to three."

"And." The fixer's impatience was evident, even over the airwaves.

"We take him into the back, crack open a bottle of champagne to celebrate, slip something in his drink and we take the money. You can drag him into the alleyway; there is a skip directly outside the door to the left. Prop him up at the back of it by the time he comes round we can be long gone."

"Long gone, where?"

"London, I have a ticket for tonight's flight, all we have to do is book you on the same flight. We could be out of here forever. You know it's what I've always wanted."

"What worries me is the fact you were going to your new life on your own without saying a word, it was a done deal and the only reason you came to me now is because now you have a problem you need fixing."

"I didn't think you would want to come, in fact you don't have to. Just help me and you can have the Brit's share, half. I would rather you did, but in the end it's up to you."

White noise.

"Okay." the fixer said after thirty seconds. "I'll help you, but I want a sixty/forty cut and I am not coming with you, you're on your own. How much are we talking about by the way? And don't fucking lie to me or I'll have you dumped in a skip."

Anna did the math in her head, she would end up with forty thousand pounds sterling, and it would be more than enough to relocate. In the end that was all she cared about, her dream. It was a lot better than her original share of five percent, and only slightly less than the straight fifty fifty split with the Brit.

"Three hundred thousand guilders." Anna said.

"Sounds good to me, I will head straight for the bar. How long before you're there?"

"I can be there in fifteen minutes tops."

"Me too, I'll see you there." the fixer said and cut the connection.

"Okay see . . ."

Anna pulled a face and glanced at the screen; it was back to the default setting. The bastard had hung up on her, this was becoming a bit of a habit. Maybe I'm losing my touch she thought to herself as she took one last look at in the mirror on the way out. It was time to go.

*   *   *

The fixer stuffed his phone into his baggy sweat pants pocket and gestured over to Jan that he should join him. Jan gave him the two minute salute with his index finger and middle finger. The fixer nodded and spun back round on his chair, so that he was facing the door again. He had little over three minutes before he had to set off, it should be ample enough. The fixer sat with his thoughts while Jan served his customer. After a minute or so Jan joined him at the table, he scraped a chair out and sat opposite the fixer.

"What's up Matt?" Jan said to the top of his head.

"I've got some work on, do you fancy going out tonight when I've finished?"

"Where? I was going to stay in tonight and wash my hair." Jan replied.

"I don't know, your call, wherever you want to go mate, my treat."

The door opened and a regular tourist walked in and started to shuffle towards the counter/bar.

"Anywhere?" Jan said eyeing the newcomer, leaning over slightly so he could ogle some more.

"No gay bars." the fixer said, looking up and locking eyes with Jan for the first time since he'd sat down. "Other than that, wherever. I'm not fussed."

"What about a show?" Jan said, meaning a sex show.

The fixer tipped his head and pulled a face and said,

"Yes, and then we'll go and get slaughtered."

"Providing neither of us pulls."

The fixer got up to go, Jan followed suit.

"I'll see you later." the fixer said, giving Jan a playful bump on his shoulder and then he made for the door.

"I'll pick you up at eight at your place." Jan said.

The fixer waved without looking back, and then he was out of the door and out of sight, gone.

Jan made his way over to the counter/bar, pausing for a beat just before it to have one last lingering look at the male customer's butt.

44

I walked Sadie to the hotel entrance; we gave each other a hug and a peck on the lips. I promised her I would be as quick as I could and reminded her not to open the door for anyone but me. She nodded and we parted company reluctantly. I watched her as she made her way solemnly through the foyer and towards the lift. Our eyes locked for a split second and then her head dropped. Only when I saw the lift door slide shut in front of her did I do an about turn and start the short walk to the Irish bar which was two blocks away. It was twenty to three, I was bang on time. Not early, not late, just right on the money, ha.

I made the turn onto some Rak I couldn't pronounce in my head or out loud at two forty three; the Irish bar was just up the street, about thirty yards away. I reached the last twenty yards and time slowed down and switched into slow-motion mode. At ten yards out, I took one last look up and down the street; nothing to see, just your regular mish-mash of tourists and natives alike, mingling, mixing, and going about their business. I started off at a brisk pace and headed for the door, keeping my eyes focused on it and nothing else. I used my foot to open the door, pushing it open as opposed to kicking it, that way my hands were free to deal with any immediate threat. I needn't have bothered, the scene before me was a chilled out one. There was a new barmaid serving today, she was a little older than the previous two. I'd put her in her mid twenties if I was trying to fuck her, otherwise it was mid to late thirties.

I scoped the area, perched on two out of the three bar stools were a couple of native barflies. Both men were in their late twenties, both were cradling the froth and the dregs in a glass on the bar in front of them. They were both half leant, half sat at the bar, facing each other in a crooked sort of way. Both men looked bedraggled and the worse for wear, like they had started at noon, and then some. Neither of them looked up when I entered the room so I discarded them as a credible threat. Maybe if I spilt one or the other's drink I would have a problem on my hands, otherwise I was okay.

Beyond the two barflies at the far end of the bar stood the laughing barmaid, and beyond her nestled in the corner and perfectly camouflaged was the fixer. Beyond them the smoking area was empty as were the tables leading up to it. Through the open door I could see the chef hard at work, chopping and shuffling the contents of a pan.

I took a step forward and let the door close behind me.

The fixer and the laughing barmaid both turned at the same time; it was as though it was choreographed. The barmaid behind the bar turned round and jabbed a finger towards a midi hi-fi and all went silent. It was a classic Wild West saloon entrance, where the music stops and everybody turns to look. Even the barflies stopped talking amongst themselves and with over exaggerated movements turned to look my way.

I made for the bar. When I drew level with the last barfly I stopped and sidestepped him positioning myself in-between him and the laughing barmaid. If we were stood on a clock face the two barflies were at ten o'clock and eleven o'clock, the older barmaid was at twelve o'clock, the laughing barmaid and the fixer were at one and two o'clock, and the entrance at nine o'clock. I was stood on the pinhole in the middle where the hands come out, neutral.

I nodded to the barmaid.

She nodded back.

"Can I have a small lager please?" I said to her, completely ignoring the laughing barmaid and the fixer to my right. Instead I nodded to one of the barflies. "Y'alright mate."

He nodded back and nearly fell off the chair, having to steady himself with a hand on the bar. He soon turned back to his inebriated buddy and carried on with the shit talk, oblivious to everything around them.

The barmaid had spun back round and now she had the glass tilted under the pump; the glass was half full and filling, she looked up and forced a smile.

I gave her a wink and turned to the laughing barmaid and said,

"So what's the story?"

"With what?"

"The fuckin' hitman, you know what."

"I've already told you, I had nothing to do with that."

"The fuck you did, so who was it then, you?" I said, turning towards the fixer.

"Let's just calm down." the fixer said, pushing himself up off the bar. "We should be celebrating the job is done, the hitman is out of the picture. We can split it three ways."

"Fuck that, I want my agreed half and you and her can do what the fuck you want with the rest." I hissed.

"Can't we talk about this?" the fixer pleaded.

"There's nothin' to talk about." I said, turning back towards the other barmaid who had pulled the drink and was now waiting dutifully for my attention.

I gave her a cheeky smile.

"That will be three guilders please." she said shyly. Her hands were behind her back, like a naughty schoolgirl.

I stepped back one pace and peeled one note from my pocket billfold and handed it to her.

"Keep the change." I said and turned back to face the laughing barmaid and the fixer, taking the top of the lager off in one noisy slurp as I did so. "Aren't you going to introduce us?" I jerked my head in the fixer's general direction, which was slightly to my right.

"I don't even know your name."

"Need to know." I said. "You can call me Brit."

The laughing barmaid smiled and nodded and turned to the fixer and said,

"Mister Fox meet the Brit, Brit meet the illustrious Mister Fox."

He nodded once.

I nodded back, no need for handshakes; this wasn't a business meeting or even a business deal. It was just a bunch of scallywags up to no good trying to squeeze what they could out of someone else's misery.

"Do you want to go through there?" I said nodding in the general direction of the smoke room.

Whatever the game was, I was holding all the cards, plus I had an ace up my sleeve, a sucker punch.

I followed the laughing barmaid and the fixer into the smoke room kicking the door shut behind me. It wouldn't make it sound proof, but it would do. The two of them stopped half-way in and went to sit down, I carried on walking to the table furthest from the door and sat down. Instinct and common sense ruled here, from my position we were less likely to be heard from anyone outside. They looked at each other and then resigned themselves to the fact that I was right. The fixer shrugged his shoulders and looked towards the bar, leaving the laughing barmaid to make the decision by herself, she made a move towards me.

They both followed me deeper into the room and settled in at the table across from me.

They were both nervous, edgy. She was biting her bottom lip and he was nervously wringing his hands on the table.

I switched to DEFCON 2.

"So who cut you in on the deal?" I asked the fixer, staring him out.

"I've been in on it from the start, who do you think arranged all this?" he replied with equal venom.

"I'll give you that." I said, keeping eye contact. "But I'm not interested in the original deal, I'm on about ours." As I said it I drew an imaginary line between the laughing barmaid and myself and back again still keeping my eyes firmly fixed on the fixer. As far as I was concerned the only credible threat came from him, I was completely ignoring the laughing barmaid and her capabilities. She was about as threatening as a fish out of water, and weighed just as much.

It was his turn to tip his head in a silent salute.

"There's no way you're going to leave here without giving me my agreed cut."

"Which was?" I asked

"Five per cent." he replied.

"Okay." I said and looked to the laughing barmaid who up to now had hardly said a word. "We'll split his cut between us." While I spoke I jerked a thumb towards the fixer.

The laughing barmaid nodded and said,

"Maybe we should celebrate the deal with a glass of champagne."

"Whatever." I said.

The laughing barmaid got to her feet, squeezed past the fixer and made her way to the sliding door. We both watched her waddle her way to the sliding door; I had to admit her arse cheeks were somewhat hypnotic as they swayed sexily from side to side.

After she had slid it shut behind her I turned my attention to the fixer who was fumbling around in his pockets. He already had some rolling papers, a cheap refillable lighter and a carton of Marlboro scattered on the table in front of him.

"So what did she offer you to get rid of me then?" I asked him.

He looked at me puzzled like he couldn't understand a word; and then he shrugged his shoulders after a couple of beats and looked away.

"How much of the pot did she promise you?" I re-phrased.

"She wanted to split it fifty/fifty, but I told her sixty/forty."

"I suppose the cash was for services rendered?" I said, meaning the disposing of me.

The fixer nodded.

"What did she want you to do?" I said glancing at the two barmaids, the laughing one and the other.

I saw the laughing barmaid fumble in her pocket for something and then pull it out in front of her to examine. Whatever it was, it was smaller than her hand, a piece of paper, maybe a phone number or something. Whatever I was curious enough to keep one eye on her while I listened to what the fixer had to say.

"She wanted me to take you out but that's not what I do, I never get my hands dirty, I'm a middle man and nothing else. In the end I convinced her that I would be able to talk you round and come to some sort of arrangement."

He was lying. I could tell. There are two types of liars, co-operative and non-co-operative. Co-operative liars are the ones that tell you everything apart from what you want to know. The non-co-operative liars just don't tell you anything.

This revelation turned my full attention to the two barmaids, completely ignoring the fixer and his feeble attempts at intimidation; his whole facade was crumbling before him.

The laughing barmaid had now leant forward slightly, she looked left and then right. The other barmaid was peering over her dipped shoulder. She caught me looking and said something to the laughing barmaid who proceeded to stop what she was doing and rock on her heels while she slid whatever it was back in her pocket.

I didn't trust her an inch, she was definitely doing something dodgy, but what? I made a conscious decision not to take any of the drink just in case. I wouldn't put it past her to slip something in it; in fact the more I thought about it the more I became convinced it was something she would do, the type of low-down thing she would stoop to, to get her way. And if that was the case the fixer was sat beside me filling me with a load of shit.

"Is that so?" I said half distracted by the laughing barmaid's movements, or lack of them.

She had not moved an inch since the other barmaid had spotted me; it was as though her feet were rooted in concrete, but now she bent down to pick up the three flutes of champagne and turned round, exchanging looks with the other barmaid on the way.

The laughing barmaid headed our way; she had two flutes clutched in one hand, and one in the other. The fixer saw her approach and went and slid the door open for her, they exchanged words at the door, but I couldn't hear what was being said from where I was; it was all hushed voices and low tones, inaudible. He waited until she was inside the smoke room before he slid the door shut behind her.

I watched them both as they walked towards me; the laughing barmaid was wearing a smirk and she had an evil glint in her eye, like the cat that just got the cream, or the second mouse that got the cheese. The fixer's expression was deadpan; in that respect he was unreadable, like a blank piece of paper or an empty screen. They both dillied and dallied their way up the gangway. He was still busy watching her arse, and as they homed in I could see she was just plain nervous. Her eyes were darting all over the place like a sprayed fly.

I didn't know what to do, but I knew one thing. It had to be clean and it had to be quick. Just like the other night in the bar. One punch. Done.

They both settled in across from me, the laughing barmaid slid in first, her brow was furrowed, and her nose creased a little in concentration as she made sure I got the right glass. I was right with the crease count, two on her left hand side and one on the right. That's when I knew for sure there was something in my drink, that and the fact that it was written all over her face. As she plonked a carefully selected flute down on my table I noticed a thin film settling over the top of the bubbly surface, settling and then breaking up amidst the bubbles, like urine in a public pool.

I picked up the flute by its stem and brought it up to eye level, twirling it from side to side as I pretended to study it.

"Here's to . . ." I said.

I cut off mid sentence and squinted at the flute.

"I'll just change this glass, it's filthy." I lied. "I'm sure you can entertain yourselves while I go to the bar."

I watched them both for tell-tale signs as I got to my feet.

They exchanged puzzled, worried looks, I saw the fixer's eyes shoot to the left as if to say to her quick you change it and then the laughing barmaid jumped to her feet and said,

"It's okay I'll do it."

"No worries." I said as I made for the door without looking back.

If I wasn't a hundred per cent sure before I was now, the drink was spiked.

I kicked the door open and left it where it was while I walked to the bar, no need to sound-proof the smoke room if I could—I wanted to be able to hear what was being said.

The other barmaid was busy serving the barflies, she had one glass tilted under the pump, and the other was stood on the bar next to it. The froth inside it slowly slip sliding down. She lifted her head up when she heard me approaching with the soiled flute and forced a smile. I guess I was the last person she expected to see, I could see it in her eyes, the way they contracted until it was almost a total eclipse of the iris.

I waited until she had served the barflies and then slid the flute along the bar towards her. It only slid a couple of inches but it was enough. Some of his contents splashed over the sides and ran a crazy line down to the rim forming a miniscule puddle all around the base of it on the bar.

"Can you pour me a fresh drink please, that glass has lipstick round the rim." I said and winked at her. "I believe Anna is pickin' up the bill." I said as an afterthought.

I leant on the bar and turned round so I could see what the laughing barmaid and the fixer were up to; they had their heads together and they looked to be in deep conversation, and they both kept on looking up in my direction, simultaneously. One would look up whilst the other spoke and vice versa. I figured they were busy cooking up a plan B, due to the fact that I'd pissed on their bonfire good and proper.

The other barmaid came as close to me as she needed to, scooping up the flute at arm's length and then retreating back to the safety zone, which in her mind was anywhere out of my reach. I had them all in the palm of my hand and I was enjoying my new found infamy, I could get used to it I thought to myself as I watched the two lowlifes conferring, heads stuck together like Siamese twins. Satisfied I'd seen enough I turned back to the other barmaid and watched her as she poured me a fresh drink and brought it over to me. She was warming to me, I could tell. She plonked it on the bar in front of me and gave me a smile, this time it reached her eyes; maybe she was ready to change sides.

I scooped the flute up and downed it in one, nodding to her to fill it up again.

"Just bring the bottle." I said.

She spun on her heels and retrieved the bottle.

As she poured another drink I said,

"Lock the door; I don't want any other customers to come in while I'm here. You got that?"

She nodded frantically.

"Don't panic, I'm not goin' to do anythin' rash. Just make yourself scarce, take your break early. By the time you come back I'll be gone. Okay?"

She nodded, slightly less frantically than the last time, an indicator she was calming down and she would be more likely to do as she was told.

I made for the smoke room, as I reached the open door I glanced back at her and nearly turned back round, she was frown-pouting like a sixties sex kitten. Brigitte Bardot sprang to the forefront of my mind, like a rabbit out of a magician's hat; it came out of nowhere then disappeared back into the darkest recesses, accompanied only by shadows and ghosts.

The other barmaid's expression was a mixture of hurt, confusion, and lust, but it was lost on me, I had business to attend to.

Once inside the smoke room I kicked the door shut behind me, the laughing barmaid and the fixer greeted me with worried looks, they had nothing left in their locker, it was over for them and they knew it. They didn't even have a bargaining point to barter from.

I sat down and plonked the flute down on the table in front of me all cocky like, before sprawling out on the bench. I wanted them to think I didn't give a fuck, and it seemed to be working, for now. It was one of the few weapons in my armoury I could call upon if needed.

I noticed the other barmaid locking the door in the other room, I watched her as she made her way through the bar passed the smoke room and into the kitchen area beyond and out of sight.

I broke the ice. With a jigga pig.

"So, say I don't wanna pay you your share, theoretically like, what happens. You get on the phone to somebody they come and sort me out and you end up with a bigger share."

The fixer didn't say anything he just nodded, he seemed to be shrinking by the second, like a recently ejaculated dick.

"Who? I already took out one of your so-called hitmen." As I said so-called hitmen, I lazily scratched a pair of quotation marks into the air. There was a layer of blue-white smoke like marsh mist hovering at shoulder height waiting on the aircon to whip it away.

I was feeling very confident and why shouldn't I; I had it wrapped up like a mummy, and they were going to be hard pressed to come out of this with anything at all. It was time to relax a little, take my foot off the gas and see what unfurled.

"I could call on a few people; they would be here in five minutes." the fixer protested.

"Cut the bullshit pal, to do that you would have to ring them, and you won't be able to do that for some time." I said and got to my feet.

Adrenaline hurtled round my body at light speed, geeing me up to the task in hand.

"What do you m . . . ?"

As his mouth formed the shape to say the word mean, I hit him with a perfect right upper cut, ka-boom. I knew all the hours I spent on the punch bag would come in handy one day, and that day was today. Good for me, bad for him. My fist caught him bang on the most vulnerable part of the jaw, the socket, underneath it not full on, and his head shot up like he'd just suffered an aneurysm, and then his body sagged on the chair, like a fat suit with no one in it. He was out of the picture for the forseeable future; the credits were rolling in his head.

In my head movie he only had a cameo role, in and out. Literally, in and then out cold.

Anna tried backing away from me whilst still sat in the chair which was backed up fully against the makeshift wooden wall. She had nowhere to go; her feet were scrambling on the floor in vain, like a crab caught in a net.

"Calm down, I'm not goin' to hurt you." I said and sat back down so as to appear less threatening to her.

She scrambled on for a couple of seconds and then she stopped dead still, shock and fear looked to have moved in as her eyes and face were full of them, they had both teamed up changed the locks, nailed scaffold boards to the inside of her eye sockets and were claiming squatter's rights.

The fixer rolled off the chair and landed on the floor with a dull thud. He groaned once and rolled over so he was face down under the table. He wasn't going anywhere for the next couple of hours, guaranteed.

I looked at him as though he was a piece of shit and then turned to the laughing barmaid and said whilst nodding in the general direction of her crumpled friend the fixer,

"See what happens when you rope people in on your daft scams? They get hurt like your man down there. So if you wanna be conscious when I leave in two minutes I suggest you let me go without a fuss."

The laughing barmaid's face dropped a mile; like she was having a stroke. It had just dawned on her she was getting nothing; she obviously thought she could still scrape something from the deal. Not a chance, it was dead in the water, I was in no mood for charity.

"Please, I need my share to relocate; I have to get away from here." she pleaded, giving me the puppy dog routine; her eyes had a sorrowful glaze.

Her pleas were falling on deaf ears; it wasn't working, I wasn't interested in anything she had to say.

I just shook my head and stared her out.

"You've gotta be kiddin' me." I said finally.

I stood up.

"You blew your chance of a share when you brought him in on the deal and tried cuttin' me out."

I reiterated what I was saying by giving the fixer a sickening kidney kick with each word starting at cuttin', three kicks, and three squeals. He straightened up in agony before returning to the foetal position. He groaned once more and then all went silent.

"You don't understand."

"Or I do, you think you can do what you want. Well not this time, not with me sugar."

"No I mean you don't understand why I have to get away from here."

"Tell it to someone who gives a fuck. Do I look like Trisha?"

"Huh?"

"Nevermind. Give me one good reason why I should give you anythin' other than what you deserve? Which is fuck all by the way."

I turned to leave, but she stood up and grabbed a hold of my sleeve, tugging on it, begging and pleading with me to give her what we had originally agreed. I shrugged off her feeble attempt to stop me and turned back pretending to go for her so she would back off. She backed off, her face was a picture all crumpled up with grief. I almost felt sorry for her until common sense retained the driving seat and got the better of me. What was I thinking? To even contemplate it was an indiscretion on my part and one that I would rectify at once.

"Na vandaag niet proberen on mij te contacteren, dat aantal is verdwenen, ik besta niet." I said. That and another phrase was the only bit of Dutch I knew, but it worked.

"After today do not try to contact me, that number is gone, I do not exist."

It seemed fitting that a phrase she had taught me to use as a back off to earn her some money was being used as a phrase to back her off and scam her out of it.

I gave her one last look; her head dropped as I turned and made for the sliding door without looking back and not bothering to kick it shut behind me.

I was home free, well almost. All I had to do was meet up with Sadie at the hotel and then hole up somewhere until the flight.

I unlocked the door and turned left and waited on my hippocampus to kick into gear and steer me back to the hotel, hippocampus being the name for the part of the brain that deals with your particular environment, the routes you take, and your spatial memory and so on. The anatomist Julius Caesar Aranzi likened it to a sea horse in the sixteenth century using the Latin word hippocampus to describe it. To my ignorant untrained eye it just looks like a rotting ear, but there you go, what do I know?

I took two steps and then it hit me, well something did, bang.

One red flash, and one white simultaneously, and then blackness, like someone had thrown a thick blanket over me.

I welcomed it like an old friend.

Emptiness.

Nothingness.

Blackness.

The only way I can describe it is to compare it to the empty TV screen of old when all the programmes had finished and the visual had shrunk to a white dot leaving no picture and just a high pitch whine. Well that's where I was at this moment in time, in that room, on that screen.

Beep, beep, beeeeeeeeeeeeeeeeeeeeeeeeeeeeeeeeeeep.

Flatline.

45

I must have been out for a while because when I eventually came round there was hardly any light. I couldn't focus properly at first; it was just shapes and shadows. I tried to swallow but couldn't possibly manage it, which was worrying. Slowly but surely I started to comprehend my surroundings. I was in some kind of out house or barn; it had just one room and one storey, an oblong shaped twenty by twelve. It was freezing cold, my initial reaction was to scream but I fought the urge and as the wind bit through my layers I started to shiver; my teeth chattering like a set of wind-up joke gnashers. I bit down to stop it and to be able to hear myself think. Shit, shit, shit. Fuck, fuck, fuck. This can't be happening, plus I could kill a smoke, yeah kill a smoke and then pulverise the bastard that blindsided me. Karma, swings and roundabouts, what goes around comes around, dress it as you will it's coming to the party.

First things first, where the fuck am I?

That was irrelevant; I just needed to get out of here and fast. Only I couldn't, I was bound tight to the solid four legged wooden chair I was sat on, bound and gagged, with a foul smelling rag stuffed down my throat, so even if I wanted to scream I couldn't. Even my thighs had been secured to the base of the seat with half a roll of duct tape. It was tight but not tight enough to stop the circulation and for me that was a base to work from. I started to wriggle my hands which were bound separately to different slats on the back of the chair. I had to stop every twenty seconds or so, the pain was unbearable, it felt like the devil was inside me tearing me up. My head was throbbing from where I'd been sucker punched, beaten at my own game. What a let down, I should have been more aware. Instead of cocky I should have been focused. You win some, you lose some. I was down but not out, I was on the ropes and ready to bounce back. I wasn't done yet. I had to adopt that mindset otherwise it would be over for me.

I timed every bout of wiggling in my head, one one-thousand, two one-thousand, three one-thousand . . . Pain, flashes of light, the works, I battled through it all.

In-between bouts I scoped the area. I quickly came to the conclusion that this was somewhere condemned, somewhere left to rot, like me.

Every new bout I willed myself to beat the last time set. I was now on seventeen. But the pain had taken its toll on me, so I was having a breather. I was trying not to panic, calm down I told myself, you've been in a similar situation and lived to tell the tale. It's a matter of keeping your head when everyone else around you is losing theirs. So instead of screaming at the top of my voice, which is what I wanted to do, I was trying to commit the memory of the room into my internal navigation system, my hippocampus, the decomposing ear in my brain. My saviour.

Cobwebs hung limply from every possible ambush site, from the rafters, around the both window frames, and from the ceiling. They were the colour of an old man's beard, wispy, and gently swaying from side to side, like a hypnotist's pendant. There was nothing on the walls, just bare brick, cracked plaster and crumbling mortar. In some places where the plaster had begun to fall away in chunks but was still attached to the wall it had been carpeted by the resident arachnid; in a mucky white film like Rumpelstiltskin's yarn.

The wind howled in the eaves, all I needed now was for a thunder storm to start.

There were two windows that I could see either side of the door. Each window had three half scaffold boards nailed horizontally across it and two vertically. In my eyes it looked like a macabre noughts and crosses board, something to resort to if I needed to keep my mind occupied.

Underfoot was just muck and dust.

The light that had made it through the cracks and gaps in the scaffold boards nailed to the inside of the rotting frames was dirty, almost black. There were two piles of sawn-in half scaffold boards stacked up Jenga-style to the left of the old thick wooden door which was directly in front of me. When I tried to move my head to have a look around, pain exploded in me like a flash bang grenade. It was too much for me and I passed out again into the comfy abyss.

Ahh, bliss. I could've stayed there forever . . .

When I finally came back round I thought I was dying, I could smell shit. Until I opened my eyes and was greeted by a pitch black room and two long thin wiry things crawling over my face. Their bodies covered my whole face and their tales stretched onto my chest, their claws were scraping against my five o clock shadow, and it was their collective breath that I could smell. It didn't take me long to realise they were rats looking for food, and that I was a source for it.

I was taped to the chair so I couldn't bounce them off; I had to wait it out shaking them off my head then remaining dead still until they lost interest and fucked off. Now I was back to the default sounds, the creaks in the structure, the wind in the eaves, and my own heartbeat in my ears.

On the inside every nerve ending was frayed, almost shredded, and there was a voice screaming in my head, but on the outside I was the epitome of calm. Something within me, something hidden, was spurring me on. It was my courage rearing its ugly head, thank fuck for that I thought I was on my own.

Instead of going with the panic I concentrated on my breathing, on the cold sensation at the tip of my nostrils as I breathed in and the warm sensation at the same place as I breathed out. It took me less than two minutes to steady myself until I was almost a part of the process, in, out, in, out, in, out, cold, warm, cold, warm, in cold, out warm.

I was making way with the duct tape, but nowhere near where I wanted to be. It was still tight, and there was no way I'd wriggle my out of it not in a million years. So I decided to save my energy, save it for when I might need it.

I must have drifted off again, because the next thing I knew I was coming round. All was quiet, nothing moved, nothing stirred, it was still pitch black, I couldn't even see my knees now it was that dark. It was like I'd woken up to a post apocalyptic world, everyone gone and just me left taped to this chair.

I was dying for a piss; it came on all of a sudden, it came from nowhere straight to bursting point. This was not good, to my knowledge I hadn't pissed myself since I was a kid, well apart from a couple of damp downs while out of my head, but they don't count. I didn't know what to do. Should I just let it go now, or hang on as long as I could in the hope that someone would come? I decided to let it go now because the longer I held it in the more liquid there would be, not to mention the energy I'd waste in the meantime. So I pissed myself; it was a nice feeling, warm for about thirty seconds before the chill set to work. Within a minute I was shivering again, fucking bastard and it stunk worse than normal due to my dehydrated state. What a way to go, drenched in piss and stinking. This was going to be fun.

* * *

Approximately ten miles away, as the crow flies, Sadie sat on the edge of the hotel bed flicking through the channels one after another, staring blankly at the screen. There was nothing on, she finally settled on the BBC World News. She'd showered, changed, packed and was ready to go, and had been for the last three hours. She was growing more restless with every passing minute. Where was he? And why has it taken him so long? He should have been here ages ago.

While she watched the news she rolled up the last of the blueberry. She needed it to calm her nerves. She cracked the window a couple of inches and lit the joint whilst holding it between thumb and forefinger, slowly twiddling it round and round so it lit evenly. She knew it was decriminalised and legal to smoke it, but it was just good manners not to stink the place out, besides this particular hotel might not look favourably towards the smoking of it in the rooms, so it was polite not to, or if you were going to indulge then at least try and mask it as best you can.

When it was finished and flicked she checked her phone for the time; it was now six pm. It was dark outside, pitch black. What could have kept him? She thought as she tried to think of something else other than her missing boyfriend. Well she'd been doing a good job for the last four hours but sooner or later it would come back round, and that time was now.

46

I didn't know how much more of this I could take, it was mental cruelty, and I needed a piss again, plus to top it off I could feel a shit coming on, it was on its way, in the post, bang on, just what I needed. I was just about to piss my pants again when I heard footsteps outside, a few of them; I reckoned there were at least three sets, possibly five.

The door opened with a creak, and in walked five shadows. I could tell who the front two were by their respective shapes, and the way they walked. The first man in was the skinhead from the Irish bar, and the second man in was Jan the coffee shop owner. The other three were a mystery to me. The two at the back split up from the front three and both groups flanked me. The two on the right were holding objects of some sort, the one next to the back looked like he was carrying a suitcase, and the one at the back looked to have a mic stand in his right hand.

I was at their mercy.

They fanned out around me; from left to right it went Jan, mystery man 1, the skinhead, suitcase and then mic stand. Suitcase dropped his object at his feet; the noise it made was a tinny scrape as opposed to a dull thud which set me thinking, mic stand placed his object on the uneven ground just in front of me.

The skinhead broke the semi-circle first, he took two steps forward and then hit me with a crunching hook right on the jaw-line; he gave me a taste of my own medicine. The chair toppled over backwards and then rolled onto its side leaving me with my left cheek on the floor staring at his boots, little puffs of dust erupted from the ground with every snort of breath as it forced its way out.

Ouch, that fucking hurt.

The skinhead came up close. I thought he was going to kick me, if the boot was on the other foot I know I would have. He looked left and then right for encouragement, when there was none forthcoming he turned back left to where suitcase and mic stand were stood and said,

"Set that generator up and let's get some light in here."

So it wasn't a mic stand and a suitcase, it was a generator and a portable light.

Suitcase obeyed, he hunkered down by the generator and pulled on the rip cord. It almost caught on, but it died down after coughing and spluttering like an old smoker. Now I know where the word kaput came from. It did eventually catch on after the third pull breaking the silence with its monotonous chug, chug, chug, and chug.

Mic stand unravelled a cable stretching from the portable light to the generator and then hooked it up to it. Instantaneously I was blinded by a bright white light. I closed my eyes but I could still see the imprint on my retina; it looked like the image of Jesus, but slowly it diminished until it was just a pin-prick, and then nothing, just darkness, and the chug, chug, chug, and the five sets of eyes burning ten-penny shaped holes in me, that's what it felt like to me anyway.

"Open your eyes."

It was the skinhead who broke the silence.

As I opened my eyes mic stand twisted the pole so the light wasn't directly on me; it helped. I squinted at the five desperadoes in front of me. Their collective breath pluming above each and every one of them, this told me they were nervous, they were panting and twitching as though they were daring each other to throw the first punch even though it had already been thrown. They were here to make up the numbers and that was it.

From left to right Jan had on a pair of beige Farah's, a pair of white pumps, the kind you used to wear in gym classes, and a gaudy Hawaiian shirt; the shirt looked like someone had thrown up on it. Mystery man 1 had on a pair of faded denims, a dark hoodie and a pair of black low tops. The skinhead was dressed similarly in a pair of blue/black denims and a non-descript white vest under a black leather jacket. Suitcase was wearing a matching tracksuit; it looked to be in the colours of Ajax, and a pristine pair of white Air Max. Mic stand was draped in shadows; I couldn't tell what he had on, it could have been a boiler suit for all I knew.

I rolled my jaw a couple of times to try and get some feeling back into the area; it was numb like I had just smeared my gums with grade A coke.

Skinhead took two steps forward and reached out, pulling the duct tape off which was securing the rag in my throat in one quick jerk. He then proceeded to pull the rag that was blocking the entrance to my windpipe.

Ow, ow, ow, that hurt more than the punch, but I was glad the rag was out, swings and roundabouts.

He turned back round taking off his leather jacket and dropping it on the floor as he did so, it crumpled at his feet.

I bet he wishes that was me, not a chance.

Underneath he wore a white vest. As he turned back round I noticed he had one tattoo on his right shoulder; it was a bulldog side on, stood to, proud as punch. Underneath the bulldog was a scroll encrypted with the words Ajax and Amsterdam, in-between the two words was the Star of David. The skinhead was huffing and puffing, flexing his pecs, acting the hard man—only it wasn't working. He might well look the part but he had the heart of a jellyfish. I was tougher than him in both respects, mentally and physically.

He took two steps forward and slapped me, his right hand catching me full on the cheek. That hurt more than the punch and the duct tape put together and I told him so. This prompted another two slaps, one right and one left. That'll teach me to keep my big mouth shut, not.

"You can either have it the easy way or the hard way, it's up to you."

If I could have shrugged I would have.

"What do you want from me? An apology."

The skinhead shook his head.

"So what do you want?"

"Money."

"I haven't got any."

No sooner had I spoke then someone's mobile phone chirped up; it came from the left so it was either Jan, or mystery man 1. I turned to look, evidently it was Jan. He reached into his Farah side pocket and pulled out a Nokia brick. He turned away to take the call. With his back to me, phone stuck to his ear and his arm hung limply at his side his silhouette took on the shape of a little teapot short and spout.

Two minutes later Jan turned back round and stuffed his Nokia back into his pocket. He looked to the skinhead and beckoned him over. The skinhead walked over to Jan, the others looked like extras on a movie set.

Another minute later both the skinhead and Jan turned round to face me; the skinhead's face was like thunder. He took a step forward and then stopped, such was the psychological grip I had over him; he was still scared of me, even though I was tied up. He nodded to mystery man 1 and then jerked his head towards me, as if to say your turn.

"Hold his head." the skinhead said.

I watched helplessly as mic stand detoured around me and then felt his hands clamp on either side of my head. Once in place the skinhead took another step forward and landed an uppercut under my chin, my head and neck snapped upwards like fifty thousand volts had just surged through me. It was a good punch, I'll give him that; even loosened a wisdom tooth. I pushed my tongue against it and a bolt of pain shot from it ricocheting around my skull before slamming into my brain at warp speed. I quickly decided not to do that again.

The situation had become desperate fast; I started to weigh up whether or not I would see daylight again. The only good thing I had going for me was the cash, in fact it was the only thing I had going for me. As far as I knew they knew nothing about it and I wasn't going to tell them, I would only use it as a last resort.

"Jan's just had a phone call from Matt Fox. Apparently this piece of shit knocked him out and took his share of a deal, fifteen thousand guilders."

Mic stand whistled.

"He did a runner with the pot; three hundred thousand guilders."

Mic stand and mystery man 1 blew out huge sighs and started rubbing their hands together

"Matt's in the hospital by the way, having his jaw wired up."

The skinhead had turned his back on me again. He was tensing his back muscles for show and massaging his right fist into the palm of his other hand. It was all bravado though I had to admit I wouldn't be able to take much more, four punches tops and I would be a goner. It would be a toss-up which gave in first, his fist or my jaw. If there was a book running on it, it would be evens.

"Listen." I said with a bit of a lisp due to the loose wisdom tooth and the numbness it created.

My mind was working overtime.

The skinhead turned round to face me.

"You want the money. I don't have it on me, my girlfriend has it. But there's no way she's coming here with me like this."

"So." the skinhead said gesturing with his hands for me to come up with a solution to the problem.

I didn't want to give the money up, but I wanted to live more, so there was only one way to go. Bastards. If I had come up against the same scenario three weeks ago I wouldn't have given two fucks, but now I had something to live for . . . I had Sadie.

"Where's my phone?"

"In my pocket." the skinhead said.

"Bring the contact list up, find Sadie, press the green button, and bring it over here so I can speak to her."

"No way."

Up to now none of the others had spoken a word, but it was now Jan's turn to pipe up.

"We call the shots, not you." he said from a safe distance.

"It's the only way you're gonna get the money. I gave her strict instructions not to leave the hotel and if I didn't show up before it was time to go to the airport for our flight then she was to go without me. And before you ask, I'd rather die than give up the name of the hotel."

Mystery man 1 and suitcase were scratching their heads; skinhead was rubbing his chin, they didn't know what to do for the best, they were in over their heads. Skinhead was the muscle and they were the numbers. I had them right where I wanted them, in the palm of my hand.

"The only way to do it is my way." I said and left them with their thoughts.

The semi-circle shrunk into a huddle as they got together to decide what to do. They were still none the wiser, so I threw my two penny's in.

"I think I have a way that works for us all."

"Go on." the skinhead said. "We're listening."

"Let me make the call and I will her arrange for her to come here with the money."

"And." It was the skinhead again, anxious. His scalp was glistening even though it was freezing cold, another sure sign.

"Is there a train station nearby?"

"Yes round the corner en-route from Centraal to Schipol. Why?" It was Jan who answered my question with an answer and then a question.

"How many stops is it after Centraal?"

"Two. Why?"

Two stops. Perfect, I remember from the train journey from Schipol to Centraal it was three stops and a twenty minute ride. That meant Schipol was the next stop on, about five minutes away.

A plan was materialising.

I couldn't pause to think or they might get suspicious so I blurted straight out with it, if it worked it worked and if it didn't, well, I would die here and Sadie would be rich.

"Here's what I propose, like I said I make the phone call, arrange for the money to be brought here."

They were all nodding like they had Parkinson's disease. That was the easy part, now came the hard part.

"One condition." I said.

They all looked at me like I'd just pissed up their respective partners, which wasn't a good sign.

It must have started raining outside because the roof sprang a thousand leaks. As each droplet hit the ground it sent a puff ball of dust into the air a couple of inches before floating back down again like tiny parachutes.

"You untie me before she gets here."

"No way." Jan said.

"Hang on, let me finish. Like I said I will arrange for the money to come here, but what's stopping you killin' us both once she's handed the money over? At least with me untied we stand a fighting chance."

"What's to say we won't kill you when we untie you?" Suitcase said.

I just shrugged.

"I say no." It was Jan who wasn't convinced. "Once we untie him who knows what could happen, he could go berserk and attack us."

It wasn't working. I had to make it sound more appealing to them. Think, think, think.

"How about this." I said. "To make it easier for you, don't untie me until she's on the train. When the train pulls up at the stop before, if she doesn't hear from me she stays on and gets on a plane with the cash 'cos there's no way she's comin' here wi' me like this. Me I'll tek ma chances."

"What do you think?" the skinhead said to Jan.

"I don't know, it's your call. Do you think you can handle him?"

The skinhead nodded in reply and said,

"Yeah sure, besides it's only a couple of minutes walk from the station to here, there's five of us and only one of him. I think we can cope don't you?"

Jan didn't answer he just pulled a weird face and then turned away.

I took that to mean the deal was on.

The skinhead walked over to where his jacket was in a crumpled heap directly in front of me at twelve o'clock and reached into a pocket. He rummaged around for a couple of seconds. Eventually he pulled out a mobile phone, my mobile phone. As he powered it up the glare from the screen made his face scary; almost demented. It reminded me of those Hallowe'en nights as a kid telling ghost stories with a torch under my chin trying to scare my mates, ha ha.

He must have found Sadie's number because he walked over to me and stuck the phone to my ear, hunkering down by my side so he could hear both sides of the conversation. All he said was "It's ringing."

So he wasn't completely daft, just a bit. It was enough.

It rang twice in my ear and then she answered.

"Kev, where've you been, I've been worried sick. Fancy not c . . ."

I cut her off in mid sentence, she sounded worried, tired, strained but I didn't have time for niceties.

"Sadie we an't got time for that, I need you to do something for me."

White noise.

"Sadie?"

"I'm still here."

"Don't be pissed off with me I'll explain later I just need you to do one thing, well a couple of things really but it all amounts to the same."

"Are you okay? You sound funny."

I didn't want to panic her so I played down my injuries.

"Am okay 'av just had an accident, nothin' that won't heal."

"Where are you?"

"Not far, I want you to pack both bags into one. Whatever won't fit in of mine throw it, but make sure you pack mine at the top I need to change. Then check out and go to Centraal station and buy three tickets to Schipol and get the first available train, except I want you to get off at the stop before Schipol. Prank me when you get on the train. If you don't hear from me, go straight to Schipol and get the first available flight, anywhere."

White noise.

"You got that?"

"Yes, pack both cases into one, yours on top, throw whatever of yours that doesn't fit, go to Centraal, buy three tickets to Schipol, catch the first available train, prank you, and if I don't hear back from you catch a plane, if I do hear from you I get off at the stop before Schipol."

"Can you do it now?"

"I can be on a train in twenty minutes depending when there is one. It could be earlier if that's any good."

"Yeah perfect, and Sadie . . ."

"Yes."

"I love y . . ."

The skinhead snatched the phone away before I had chance to finish what I was saying but I hoped she got the gist, just in case I never got to see her again I wanted her to know how I felt about her.

"I need a piss." I said to the skinhead's back.

He just ignored me so I shouted louder.

"Hey I said I need a piss and I could use a drink."

The skinhead walked over to his coat and pulled a bottle out from one of the pockets. He then walked back over to me where he stood hovering like a cloud whilst he cracked the seal on the bottle.

"What about a piss? I'm bustin'."

He just shook his head and started pouring the drink over my face. It was some kind of orange juice, weak and piss coloured. Fitting I thought to myself as I pissed myself for the second time in two hours. I only managed to lap a few drops up but it was enough; it wet the palate and stopped the burning. The skinhead tipped the last few drops into my hair and then threw the bottle over my head. His face screwed up as he caught a whiff of the fresh urine. I was okay, I was warm again, swings and roundabouts.

Mic stand and suitcase were stood facing each other; suitcase had his hands out Oliver Twist style holding a single large Rizla and tobacco while mic stand sprinkled the good stuff on top. They were both talking non-stop in their native tongue.

Jan had his back to me, he was on the phone. As he cut the line he turned to me and gave me a dirty look, ouch. It might work in your world sonny but not in mine. I just stared him out and after ten seconds or so I said,

"You're just mad 'cos I banged him first."

"You what?" Jan said making a move towards me, arms flailing like a windmill.

The skinhead intervened, pushing Jan away. He looked at me and said,

"Any more wise-cracks like that and I will take your fucking head clean off."

I had to do something. I was trying to amuse myself as well as counting off the seconds in my head. Sadie reckoned she would be on the train in twenty minutes or less, I was looking at twenty, so I was counting up to twelve thousand. I was up to two hundred and eighty six, nearly five minutes which in turn was nearly a quarter of the way through. All good things come to those who wait, and in my case that good thing was Sadie.

47

At one thousand and twenty one seconds precisely my phone rang once and then rang off. I looked to the skinhead, it was the signal. If they didn't untie me in the next five minutes the money would be lost and one of these would be digging a shallow grave somewhere because I sure as hell wasn't.

Skinhead beckoned mic stand and mystery man 1 over to him; they all huddled together whilst they went over their plan. When they were done mystery man 1 walked over to my left, bent down and picked something up. As he walked back over I could see he had a lump of wood in his hands. The goon was stooped and because of the poor light he resembled a Neanderthal armed with a club. Suitcase handed skinhead something and they crowded round me. Skinhead approached me, he had a knife in his right hand, here we go again, and memories of Ally's front room came flooding back. The skinhead didn't fuck around making out he was going to stab me, he just started to cut me free. If he'd have cut my hands free first I might have been tempted to have a go at them, because I was convinced if I took him out the others would fall into line. But he didn't, he started by cutting my legs free from the side while mystery man 1 stood guard over me with his club.

Once free I stood up and brushed myself down. They stepped back giving me some room, puffing and panting, each one of them was looking nervously left and then right, trying to get reassurances from their compadres. Skinhead tossed me my phone but I fumbled it and it fell to the floor. It didn't break so I bent down, picked it up, pressed the green button twice and brought it up to eye level; it said Sadie calling. I slowly put it my ear. It rang twice and then she answered.

"Kev?"

That one word was like a gospel choir in my ear, heaven sent.

"It's me, everythin' go, okay."

"Yes."

"You haven't passed the stop before Schipol yet have you?"

"No, it's coming up now, another minute or so and I would have been gone. Should I get off?"

"Yeah. Stay on the line though and I will direct you to me."

I nodded to the skinhead.

He nodded back.

I took that to mean he knew I would be requiring directions soon.

I moved the phone away from my ear and put my hand over the mic and said to the skinhead,

"Which way?"

"Turn left out of the train station and head straight on for about five hundred yards first left is an industrial estate, make the turn and follow the road—it's a dead end, we're the last building on the left."

"Sadie?"

"Yes."

"Find the exit and turn left and go about five hundred yards, take the first left and you will see an industrial estate, 'am at the last building on the left on the industrial estate. I'll see you when you get here okay."

"Okay."

I cut the line and turned to the skinhead and said,

"She'll be here in about five minutes."

He nodded once in reply. That was all I expected, no need for small talk. I wanted to be on a plane within the hour and out of here, vamoosh.

48

As the second count hit fifteen hundred the door opened up with a creak. A figure stood in the half light; the silhouette looked liked catwoman. As she came closer and the light brought her to life the catsuit metamorphised into an all in one blue tracksuit. Her hair was tied up in buns explaining the ears away. She was dragging the little suitcase behind her, handle out to the max; the wheels were having a tough time over the uneven ground, rather than rolling they were bumping and scraping. She looked pissed off, proper.

I walked towards her, gesturing to the others to wait where they was.

"Kev, oh my God, what happened to you?" she said reaching a hand out to inspect my injuries.

I turned away from her and said,

"Have you got the money?"

"It's in the suitcase. Why?"

"I'll explain in a bit, I need it."

She laid the suitcase on its back and proceeded to unzip it, struggling because it was almost full to bursting point. She had to run the zip up and down to get by the more stubborn bits, but soon she had the flap open fully and was rummaging through the few clothes of mine that had made the cull. I hunkered down by her side and put an arm round her and whispered in her ear,

"Don't make it obvious but see the skinhead."

She nodded slightly as she pulled out a hoodie and reached into the all in one pocket at the front.

"He cold-cocked me at the Irish bar earlier, it's the one from the other night. They want the cash and then we can go, we will be out of here in five minutes just follow my lead."

She nodded again and pulled out the padded envelope that contained the cash. I took the envelope from her and jacked myself up. I covered half the distance between us and them and then stopped.

"The cash is here." I said, holding it out as though it was an offering, and it was, it was a sacrifice, either that or me.

The skinhead nodded once.

"No hard feelings." I said and then tossed the envelope onto the floor; it spun a couple of revolutions before stopping, and if it was a game of spin the bottle I would have won. It was a small consolation, but I took it anyway.

I turned back towards Sadie who was now bent down stuffing the clothes back into the suitcase. When she had finished I took the suitcase from her and we walked out of the door into the cold night.

"You okay?" I asked as we turned right and made our way to the train station.

"Yes, what about you though? You look a mess."

"I'll be okay once I've changed on the train and had a wash, it's only superficial."

She smiled.

I looked behind once and the coast was clear, phew, that was a close call.

We made it to the train station in one piece and lo and behold no sooner had we sat down then a train came trudging up the tracks. We boarded and found seats quickly, drawing peculiar looks from the passengers we did pass; we were like beauty and the beast. I slung the suitcase on the seats opposite and unzipped it. Pulling out whatever came to hand first, it wasn't a fashion show.

"'Am just gonna get changed. Have you got the other tickets in case the conductor comes while I'm gone?"

"Yes." Sadie replied.

I made my way down to the toilet, closing the door behind me. Once inside I took a look at myself in the mirror; it wasn't as bad as I thought. I had a bruise the size of a tennis ball under my chin and a similar sized one on my jaw-line, like I said superficial damage. I took whatever they'd left in my pockets, a nip bag with a little bud in it, and stuffed it into my clean pair. Then I quickly stripped off, rolling my discarded clothes into a long sausage and dumping them in the waste bin at the side of the toilet. I washed and changed, five minutes later I reappeared looking almost as good as new.

I sat down next to Sadie and said,

"New York, here we come."

"I'm not sure about it; I think I just want to go home."

"If that's what you want."

She nodded. As long as she was happy so was I.

No sooner had I sat down then the conductor informed us the next stop was Schipol. We got to our feet and I grabbed hold of the suitcase and we made our way to the exit.

After replenishing my cash supply at the airport's ATM we found a pub two blocks shy of Schipol; one that would let us smoke the good stuff, so that was good, it meant I didn't have to throw what was left of my stash, there was only a couple of joints but I still begrudged losing it. Sadie went and found some seats while I waited at the bar, she sat at the table furthest from the door, good she was learning. I ordered a double Southern Comfort lime and soda for Sadie and a double Jack Daniels and Coke for me. I necked mine in one fiery gulp and slammed the tumbler down on the bar, nodding to the barkeep to fill it up again, which he did dutifully.

"How much do I owe you?"

"Er let's see." the barkeep said. "One double Southern Comfort lime and soda, and two double Jack Daniels and Cokes. That will be nine guilders please." While he said this he jabbed each figure into the ancient till.

I peeled off two notes and handed them over to him saying,

"Keep the change."

I scooped up the two tumblers and made my way over to where Sadie was sat. She was fumbling around in her handbag for something. A couple of minutes later she resurfaced with a carton of Marlboro Lights and a lighter and a smile.

"That was close." I said.

"Too close." Sadie replied. "I just want go home and go to bed for three days." she said and smiled. She had an amazing smile, like a sunrise in the respect that it lit her whole face up.

I dug in my pocket and pulled out the nip bag; there was one bud in it. By my reckoning it would do two joints.

"You got any Rizlas?"

"Should have somewhere." she replied and started digging her way through her handbag again. Almost immediately—miracles will never cease—she pulled out a large packet of silver Rizlas.

"Here you go." she said and handed them over to me.

I took them from her and started the procedure off. It was ingrained now, buried deep into my subconscious. I didn't even have to think; it just came naturally, fold the skin in half, break off three quarters off the cigarette, and sprinkle it in and the good stuff on top, nip and tuck, and lick and roll. It was the worst joint I'd ever rolled; it was so baggy it resembled a sausage roll, so much so that when I'd lit it I went to take a big hit off it and the roach stayed between my lips. I looked at Sadie who had now doubled over, creased up in laughter at the state of the joint and I said,

"That dun't bode well does it?"

After the words I blew out a huge sigh.

She doubled up in stitches and nearly fell off the chair she was laughing so much, we both were, until it hurt and even when we had stopped laughing my face still felt like it was. Despite us giving away the cash we were in high spirits and nothing was going to spoil it. We would fall into bed within two and a half hours max and that was reward enough for me. You win some, you lose some.

49

S mit and Van de Berg were back in the squadroom, they both stank of stale sweat and coffee and both men had gone way past the five o'clock shadow mark. They were both flagging after spending the last six hours at the hospital waiting on their suspect to regain consciousness. All they needed now was a drink but there was still a lot of work to do, so one quick one would have to suffice. The hitman had finally opened his eyes at seven forty-eight pm. A full five and a half hours after they had found him unconscious in an alleyway just off Dam Square. The gun he'd used to kill Vincent de Vries was found beside him and after a thorough search, a magazine with just the right number of bullets left in it to secure a conviction was found in the alley. The hitman wasn't happy, but then again what criminal would be in his position, locked up and looking at life imprisonment. It was the end of an illustrious career, and an era. He had nothing to lose and he wasn't going down on his own. He folded and flipped on Cornelia de Vries who in turn flipped on her daughter Vincenia de Vries who in keeping with the trend flipped on Anna Timmerman and Matt Fox. It was the end of the road for them, in more ways than one.

*　*　*

We sailed through passport control and Dutch customs. Once beyond all the commotion we found ourselves three seats, one for the suitcase. We had fifteen minutes to wait; it was a time to reflect on how lucky we had been me in particular, and we did, I almost fell to sleep. Just before we boarded I went to the toilet, I needed a piss, plus I wanted to make a call before shutting off the phone for the flight. I shut the cubicle door behind me and scrolled through my contact list; it wasn't long before I found the number I wanted. It was under D for Dim; it rang six times and then went to voicemail.

"The number you have called is not available please leave your message after the tone."

Beep.

"Dim it's Kev. There's been a change of plan, 'am coming back to England tonight, just wondered if there was any work for me? Gimme a call yeah, cheers."

I cut the connection and stuffed the phone into my pocket and rejoined Sadie in the departure lounge, we were good to go.

Little did I know we would be walking straight into a trap.

Kev and Sadie will return in

OUTLAWED—
LOOKING FOR TROUBLE

Acknowledgments

The author would like to thank the following people, my family and friends for their ongoing faith in me, Jim Gregory & Grosvenor Media for their guidance and support, my Facebook friends, Louise Coe, Sheila North, Slogger, Adam T, Tench, BUB and his missus and all the usual suspects—without them I would be nothing.

P.S. Keep letting me steal off you and I will keep on writing.

Mark has his own website *www.authormarkhowell.com.*

28852289R00160

Printed in Great Britain
by Amazon